LATIN SUBMISSION

by

LEO BARTON

CHIMERA

Latin Submission first published in 1998 by
Chimera Publishing Ltd
PO Box 152
Waterlooville
Hants
PO8 9FS

Printed and bound in Great Britain by
Caledonian International Book Manufacturing Ltd
Glasgow

LATIN SUBMISSION

Leo Barton

This novel is fiction – in real life practice safe sex

Chapter One

'Welcome to Buenos Aires.'

I had been expecting David to meet me, my old friend from the days when we were novice journalists in London, not the beautiful full-figured blonde who stood in front of me, a cardboard sign held chest-high with my name scrawled on it in black felt-tip.

After thirteen hours on a plane and several more gin and tonics than were good for me, I was a little bewildered to be offered the black-gloved hand of this gorgeously sexy woman, and not one of those casual little back-slaps that David would habitually give me when we met on one of his increasingly infrequent visits home. My first reaction was that it was some kind of joke, a little set-up, like that time in Convent Garden when he had... Well, later, maybe.

'I am David's wife, Andrea. I am sorry, he is not here. He is on business in Santiago.'

It took a little time to take her all in: the bouncy shoulder-length hair, the almond-shaped eyes, the full rosy jut of her mouth. She wore a black leather skirt cut two clear inches above the knee and dark vampish tights showing her full thighs and the delicate curve of her calves. It took a little time to take it all in but, like most good things in life, it was – she was – well worth it.

Through my jet-lagged haze, my first inklings of arousal were counterblasted by the realisation that she had just told me she was David's wife.

So okay, this wasn't a moral issue. I had dumped sexual morality on the aeroplane. The fact that she was David's wife or anybody else's wife would not have stood in my way. After five years of fidelity, of nobly and loyally refusing to let my cock stray from the conjugal bed, and then discovering that my lover and partner of those drearily monogamous years had been putting it about with anybody and everybody who wanted it; then any sense of those devotional requisites – like not betraying your husband by giving a blow-job to the next door neighbour in your very own garden shed – were out. But that was me: commitment, a thing of the past; honesty in relationships, kicked into touch; faithfulness, never to be tampered with again.

This had all been decided whilst perusing my manhood in the aeroplane toilet, after the first of my complementary gins. From now on I wanted sex – wild sex, hard sex. I wanted to exorcise all those long years of pain and bitterness by doing anything I desired, however fantastic or perverse – and to do it with as many willing women as I could find. That was all. Simplifyingly, glorifyingly, I would seek carnal enjoyment as merely a pleasure in itself, not some kind of adjunct to a mutually rosy-coloured concept of connubial bliss.

But that, as I said, was me. I might as recently as six hours ago have dedicated my life to pleasuring my cock. I might have been, as David had indicated in a call only forty-eight hours previously, fresh. But I was not Andrea. Andrea, even if there was the faintest possibility that she could be attracted to me, may not have discarded all the antediluvian marital myths that I had done. She might be – and God, what a waste of those glorious breasts and those wonderful thighs – still in love, and still faithful.

As she walked me to her car, I observed the pleasant plumpness of her bottom and the highly seductive way she moved on three-inch heels. Now, so close to her as we headed to the centre of the city, I could see what a delectable

6

smile she had, especially when her eyes strayed from the road to meet mine. And how delightfully arousing she was when the tip of her tongue jutted from her lips in an overly conscious demonstration of concentration, as she focused her attention back to the maniacal drivers in front of her, the taxi-drivers maddeningly lane-hopping.

'So why is David in Santiago?'

She shrugged dismissively, alluringly. 'David is always away. Is a contract with cable television.'

My God: after all those days living with an English girl with precise Home Counties diction, it was such a turn-on to be stuck in traffic with a beautiful Latin woman who forgot the necessity of using impersonal pronouns at the beginning of her sentences.

'Is a contract.'

Fantastic! Andrea's English was good, very good, but this little mannerism, this little linguistic tic, was enticing; as was her sensual Argentinian intonation which seemed to add syllables to English where they should not exist.

'What do you do, Andrea?' I asked as I glanced at her long slender fingers, then up to her nails coated with deep scarlet.

'I am a dance teacher.'

'Classic?'

'Classic and modern.'

'Maybe you can teach me to tango, while I'm here,' I said jokingly.

'You must come to visit my studio,' she said, turning her eyes once more away from the road to look at me, momentarily displaying a dazzle of perfectly formed teeth. I imagined her leotard-clad, the rounded hips, the bare expanse of flesh between throat and breast.

'Love to.' I would have loved doing just about anything with Andrea, but the prospect of a rendezvous in the privacy of her dance studio was certainly high on my list of potential shared activities.

She smiled again. The smile was at first open and warm, until her lips slightly twisted to the most tantalising of smirks; I hoped that perhaps she was thinking about the carnal possibilities that might occur if I took up her vague invitation.

As I tried to make conversation with her, I was frequently distracted from my genial line of interrogation by the delightful bulging of her breasts, or the occasional swaying of her hair as she would answer a question in the negative, or by the sheen of her black tights – did I dare dream stockings? Yes, I did.

'How was your flight?' she asked after a brief lull in the conversation.

'Long, very long.'

'And how was England?'

'Cold, very cold. Have you been?'

'Never. I never been,' she said sadly.

'You must go.'

'I will. I went to Paris and to Rome, but not to London.'

'Why doesn't David take you?'

'David – huh!'

I was beginning to be encouraged, especially by the dismissive, almost parenthetic expellation of air that had followed her retort. It did not strike me that their relationship was going so well, as Andrea shrugged and further sighed her seeming disillusionment with her absent husband. 'David is always too busy.'

From the air, Buenos Aires had impressed me, at least in its regularity; the tidy rows of streets that formed the grid pattern of the city had sprawled way beyond into the distance. There seemed little of the ramshackle about the place, none of the higgledy-piggledy growth of London streets. Buenos Aires looked planned, orderly, precise: a city that knew what it was about. A city that knew where it was going.

I was wrong.

As we sped through the broad avenues of the centre, the assumed horizontal precision of urban planning gave way to vertical chaos. A mess of architectural styles bludgeoned my sight; traces of Paris and London and Madrid competed in the grandeur stakes, while modernistic skyscrapers dwarfed quaint colonial-style buildings.

Needless to say, any profound consideration of architectural style or the niceties of urban planning were totally subsumed by my interest in the sexy blonde beside me, although they did offer subject matter for our increasingly amiable chat.

'Yes, Buenos Aires is a mess, a big mess. No planning, *nada*. This is not Europe, *señor*. We have the rules, but nobody pay attention. Money is the language and the law here.'

I liked the passion of her little diatribes; they added another element to the appeal of this ravishing woman. During the first twenty minutes of our journey to town, I was favoured with robust criticisms of the police, the army, the judiciary and, of course, the government.

By the time we had been driving for half an hour, Andrea was joking with me like a long-lost friend, interspersing a light-hearted history of the city with lengthy anecdotes from her domestic life, telling me how she often found David's business colleagues dreary and boring. 'What do you English say, so stick in the mud? Especially, maybe I shouldn't say this,' but she did, 'some Englishmen. *Dio mio*. They need to relax, I think.'

I laughed. 'I know.'

'Not all, eh, only some. Not you, I think.' I was graced

by another glancing smile. 'Maybe, Jonathan, we can have a good time together. I like laughing. You make me laugh already.'

The morning streets were virtually deserted of pedestrians, but cars thundered down the broad six-lane highways that dissected the centre of town. I had thought it was only the cavalier taxi-drivers at the airport who drove like madmen, but everybody drove like crazy here, even Andrea – especially Andrea. I was torn between the delicious looks she would throw me, and my desire that she concentrate her attention on driving. I was relieved when she haphazardly parked the car in a narrow, deserted side street.

'I take you for coffee, yes?'

We walked along the street, my eyes taking everything in around me; the pompous grandeur of the wealthy tenements, the slick brightly lit cafés, all called *confiterias* here, the multitude of banks and offices, the tiny *kioskos*, shuttered and locked.

The street opened onto a broad tree-lined avenue, the recently risen sun already making the asphalt shimmer, even though it couldn't have been much later than ten in the morning.

'This is the Avenida de Mayo. To the north is Congress. To the south, Plazo de Mayo,' Andrea said, gesticulating with her arms. 'That is where the pink house is, where the President lives. You are in the very heart of Buenos Aires.'

'You should have been a tourist guide,' I joked.

'Oh, you think so? Maybe, but I prefer to be a dancer.' She made an elegant little semicircle with her left foot. 'Maybe for you, Jonathan.' A little impish smile passed across her lips.

'You can take me anywhere,' I said, flirting.

She took my arm in hers. 'And now I take you to the

most famous café in the whole of Buenos Aires – maybe in the whole of South America – the Tortoni. Famous for the tango, for literature and lovers and, like many people and things here, famous for being famous.'

The café was huge and sparsely populated, a few *porteños* – the name used to describe the people of Buenos Aires – were spread out among the round marble-topped tables. The atmosphere of the place was sombre, the maroon waist-coated waiters serious and, to me, a little foreboding. Huge thick pillars pompously lined the centre of the café and the dark wood panelled walls did not brighten the ambience. It seemed a café consciously aware of its own importance and its reputation, more church or library than drinking establishment. I didn't like it much, but I didn't care. I was more interested in my companion.

We took a seat near the main door.

'This is the Tortoni,' Andrea said, glancing at me. 'What would you like?'

That was obvious. What I would have liked was Andrea, naked and writhing above me, slapping down on my stiff prick. I settled for a coffee. '*Un cortado*,' I responded, attempting my best Spanish pronunciation.

'*Bien*.' She perused the glossy menu, her tongue brushing her upper lip as she deliberated on what she would have.

'So tell me about the tango,' I said, after a portly moustachioed waiter had taken our order.

'Ah, the tango! You ask the right question, because the tango is Buenos Aires. The tango, how to explain the tango,' she mused to herself. 'Well, is showy, obsessive, passionate and a little perverse.' Here her eyebrows raised slightly. 'The tango is about suffering and joy, and many *porteños* don't seem to know the difference between pain and pleasure. The tango wants to be seen, wants to be watched. Is about loving and not being loved, about loving and hurting. Is about nostalgia, about not having what you want, and losing what you once had.'

'There doesn't seem to be much joy in it.'

'The joy comes, I think, from being miserable. *Porteños* like to be unhappy, can only be happy being unhappy, especially when they have somebody to speak with about it.'

'You don't seem particularly unhappy.'

'I'm not,' she said, laughing heartily, 'but I am not a *porteño*, not really. I come from Cordoba, a city in the north. We are different. We prefer to be happy getting what we want. I always try to get what I want. Don't you?'

'Yes, I do.'

Her eyes looked piercingly into mine, and then she glanced away. 'We are not so, so self-obsessed in Cordoba. Buenos Aires is a city of *egoistas*. Listen, I have a joke for you, yes?' Her hand leant over the circular marble table, her fingers lightly resting on my knuckles. 'Well, in English, maybe it's hard. Okay, I try: how can you get a *porteño* to kill himself?'

'I don't know. How do you get a *porteño* to kill himself?' I repeated with mock pantomime intonation.

'Get him to jump off his own ego.' She burst into laughter. I laughed too, as much at the infectiousness of Andrea's laugh as at the actual joke.

'Unlike most women here,' Andrea continued, 'I am not an *egoista*. I'm not self-obsessed. For example, I do not go to the psychoanalyst.'

'Why should you?' I asked, bemused that Andrea would even mention herself going for therapy. She seemed an advertisement for mental health.

'Everybody else does. Psychotherapy is the *porteño's* biggest indulgence. The English collect stamps, we go to the – what was the word that David told me? – yes, we go

12

to the shrink and tell him all our problems and how unhappy we are.'

'You're not a believer, then?'

'I believe in different kind of therapy, *señor. Cosas mas natural.*'

'Your therapy?'

'No, I joke. My therapy is getting what I want, so I am not dissatisfied. Not always, but then perhaps it is not always good to get everything that you want. But I get enough, that's all.'

Her eyes looked into mine again, then she broke into laughter. 'Oh yes, and fact number two. Did you know that the women of Buenos Aires spend more money on their underwear than in any other part of the world? I told you, we are a little perverse, the women of Buenos Aires.'

I imagined Andrea in a basque, in a chemise, in silk and satin and cotton, in decorative panties, in lacy bras. I imagined rolling my tongue along her stockinged legs, tugging her breasts free from the lacy cups of her bra, of pulling aside the gusset of her panties and nibbling on her quim.

It was all happening so quickly. Sex seemed to hover over us, our every word imbued with its scent, every sentence loaded with innuendo, potential... I wasn't totally sure. I was never totally sure, but I began to think that I was going to have this woman before the day was over; especially when she said, after we had finished drinking our coffee and she was driving me north from the centre of the city, 'Your hotel is here, but first I take you home.'

Her apartment was in what I was later to learn was the district of Belgrano. It was a lavish four-bedroomed affair with all mod cons, the essentially slimline and discreet, a blend of modernistic minimalism and classical chic: vertical

13

blinds, red leather sofa, antique chest of drawers, glass-topped coffe-table.

She poured me a large whisky and sat on a chair to the right of me. 'So why did you come here?' It sounded like a genuine question, as if it puzzled her as to why anybody would uproot themselves and travel across the world to Argentina.

'I deserved a long holiday. I wanted to see David; he's always inviting me, and I wanted to meet you.'

Again our eyes met.

'What did David tell you about me?'

'Only good things.'

She looked quizzical.

'Not much.'

'Good.'

She sipped on her whisky. I couldn't take my eyes off that fabulous chest, the slight heaving of her breasts as she drank, the gratifying pinpoints of her nipples visible beneath the thin stretched wool of her black polo-neck sweater.

'You separate from your girlfriend?' Andrea was resting her whisky glass on the arm of the sofa with her right hand, while her left hand hugged her legs below the knee.

'My wife, yes.' I looked at her eyes. Again the silence, but no discomfort. How could there be with that radiant face beaming across at me? Nor did the question sound intrusive – more conspiratorial.

'Are you sad?' She sat up straight on the sofa and took a long gulp of her whisky.

'No. I'm very happy, relieved. I like the idea of being a free man again.'

'Sorry, I ask too much. I'm too curious. It is the Argentinian way. We are too honest sometimes, too – what do you say, frank? And then sometimes we lie too easily.'

14

She laughed to herself a little, then looked at me almost disappointedly before taking another sip of her drink.

'No, I don't mind, really. Ask what you want.'

'Have another whisky. Take yourself,' she said motioning to the whisky bottle that lay behind me. She pulled out a packet of cigarettes and lit one. I watched as she tossed her head back slightly and inhaled the smoke deeply, all the time keeping her eyes fixed on me.

I could feel my dick bulging in my pants, my balls a granite weight between my legs. She was brushing her knee with the tips of her fingers. It was enticing, but maybe it was done innocently, almost subconsciously. She had told me in the lift how easy she found it to talk to me, but what if I were misreading all the signs, if I were mistaking mere friendliness for something else, something wholly more interesting?

I sat down and self-consciously crossed my legs. I placed the whisky glass on the coffee-table before me.

'How's David?' I wanted to test the water a little, before trying a more direct approach.

'Oh, David is okay, when I see him. He travels so much. So... so busy all the time. He speaks of you often.' She took another drag from her cigarette and languorously exhaled.

'We go back a long way.'

'I know. He told me. Everything!' Her eyes dilated as she emphasised the 'everything'. As far as David and I were concerned, everything used to mean a lot.

'Has he changed, David?'

'No, not really. He's a little more serious now. *Demasiado*! Too much stress. He talks already of retirement, but work is like a drug with him. He can't stop.' She shook her head disapprovingly as she spoke.

'I wouldn't spend so much time away from you, if you

15

were my wife.' The words seemed to spring from my mouth with no intercession from my mental processes.

'Really?' She laughed, tossing her head back again, splaying her arms out, before bringing them together in a bright clap. I noticed the undulation of her breasts as she chuckled at my remark. 'Oh, English gentlemen.'

'Don't believe Englishmen are gentlemen.'

'You know there is a belief in Argentina that all Englishmen are gentlemen: gentlemen and homosexuals. Is it true?' she said, laughing again, before taking a deep drag on her cigarette.

'That we are all gentlemen – or that we are all homosexuals?'

'Both.'

'Well, you're married to one.'

'Exactly, and I am still not sure,' she said, before she started to laugh again without any hint of bitterness.

I must have raised my eyebrows and looked quizzical.

'No, *señor*, I am joking. I am only joking. David is not always a gentleman, although he can be, and I don't think he is a homosexual.'

'You don't think?'

'No, I am sure he isn't.'

I was laughing, too. It is difficult to convey the sheer vivacious charm of the woman, of Andrea then as she sat before me, the conviviality of her personality, the sheer openness, the sense of joy and playfulness which seemed to suffuse her words, the fruity naturalness of her manner.

Her free hand was still toying with the hem of her leather skirt.

'But sometimes, he leaves me alone, the bastard.' Said jokingly, almost lovingly. 'And it is no good to leave a woman like me alone. I do not like to dance solo.' Her face flushed, momentarily tinged red, and then she laughed again delightfully, coquettishly – and then the laughter suddenly halted. 'I like you, Jonathan. I like you much, very much.' She stubbed out her cigarette on the ashtray that lay on the side of her armchair.

'I like you too, Andrea.' I did not dare dream where this might be leading. I feared to make an ass of myself so quickly, and with David's wife. I had been out of the game too long, which is why I was so hesitant, unconfident.

'It is strange, no, to like someone so quickly, without knowing them so well? Strange – and for me, is a little exciting.'

'Very exciting!' I could barely believe what was happening. It was becoming clear that I wasn't misreading the signs: her seduction was too obvious. Her next question dismissed any remaining doubts.

'Are Englishmen always this slow?'

'Sorry?'

'I mean, here I am giving you – what does David call it? – the come-on, and you not say anything.' Her eyes sparkled as she looked at me.

'But...'

'But what? David? Forget David. I told you, he leaves me alone. I don't ask about him. He doesn't ask about me. I said, I like you. Is there a problem? I mean, you are an Englishman. Maybe you don't like me?'

'Of course I like you.'

'I mean, you don't want to make love with me?'

'Yes. You're beautiful.' My heart was thumping, pounding with lust and I could feel my prick pulsing as she spoke.

A brief hiatus and then she said, her voice softening, 'Why don't you come here, Jonathan? Come to me... come!'

My head was spinning. A beautiful woman was inviting

17

me to make love to her, one hour after I had arrived on the other side of the world. Not that this seemed like the other side of the world: this seemed like a parallel universe where your deepest, darkest wishes are fulfilled, where what you had only sadly dreamt of or fantasised about becomes real, wonderfully real. Only some fifteen hours before, I had been standing freezing in London: cold, lonely, feeling trepidation at the outset of my new, single life. And now, here I was in the bright city summer heat, with one of the most attractive women I had ever seen in the whole of my life beckoning me to her.

I slugged back a mouthful of whisky and walked over to her chair, went to take her, to lean over and wrap my arms around that fabulous body.

'Stop!' she commanded before I could reach down. 'I want to look at you.' She reached her manicured fingers to my crotch and began to unzip my flies. She glanced up to my astonished eyes, flashing a smile at me before returning to the zip, her tongue excitedly snaking out of her mouth.

She pulled out my cock, teased it from my boxers. It stood to attention before her eyes. A glistening rivulet of semen trickled down my shaft and onto the blood-red nail of her finger as she pulled down my foreskin. She gasped, 'Is fantastic!' She stared at my prick and then up to my eyes as I inched my member closer to her face. 'What a cock!'

Suddenly, she poured the dregs of her whisky into the palm of her hand and began massaging the alcohol into my pulsating cock, all along my throbbing shaft, down to my heavy balls, sighing her pleasure, anticipating her delight. I felt the sting of the alcohol, making my already hot flesh burn like fire.

She rolled the head of my cock against her cheek, drawing a thin trail of semen across her soft flesh, and then she rolled it across her parted lips, nipping it painfully between her fingers before plumping her lascivious mouth over my helmet, soothing the burning sensation where the whisky had stung.

With her free hand she lifted my cock and, pulling her lovely mouth away, she began to lick along the shaft, the movement of her tongue growing more furious and more frantic. My hand stroked and tousled the stream of her blonde hair.

How long did this last? I can't say. It seemed like an infinity, an infinity of joy, a rekindling of a sexual pleasure that had lain dormant in me for too long. A woman was spreading her long tongue all over, all round and along my cock, intermittently squeezing my testicles as she did so, looking up to me, smiling with her eyes, treating my rod in a way it hadn't been treated in a long time. I had almost forgotten how good it could feel.

Spreading her hand through the apex of my thighs, now unencumbered of trousers and pants, she grabbed my buttocks and ran a finger down the ridge between my anus and my balls before thrusting my cock further and further into her mouth, past her full red lips, until I saw it bulge in the side of her cheek.

I grabbed her hair, her beautiful silky hair, blanched in the summer sun. I held her head as she propelled her mouth forward onto me, as she took me deeper and deeper inside her mouth and her dextrous tongue worked on me.

I could feel myself coming, exploding inside her. I could imagine my come spurting down her throat. I felt my legs tense, my whole body go into spasm. A wave of orgiastic pleasure was shooting up from the base of my bursting shaft.

She must have sensed it, too, for suddenly she slipped her mouth from me.

'Not yet… not yet,' she murmured sweetly.

I was pleased. I didn't want to come before I had explored the jewel of her body. I grabbed her swelling breasts through her black woollen sweater and felt the hardness of her nipples, pinching each one between my finger and thumb. She moaned with pleasure through the momentary tang of pain.

I lifted the polo-neck over her head, exposing a black lacy bra. I stooped and sucked on her hard nipples through the lace, taking each one briefly between my teeth. And then, reaching behind her, I undid the strap at the back, so that her lavish breasts were freed against my face. She pulled on my hair as I sucked her breasts, tenderly nibbling each rosy peak, moving from one to the other, and between, licking the deep valley and then the tender underside, sweeping my tongue from the base of each soft breast to the nipple, and then back.

And while I licked and sucked her breasts, my hands crept slowly and steadily up her stockinged legs. Yes, stockinged legs, as I jubilantly discovered the bare flesh of her thighs. She was moaning now, moaning hard. My fingers reached her lacy panties and grasped her moist sex. She was already wet, her knickers damp with lust.

I pushed my index finger inside her panties, found the opening to her vagina and inserted my finger. One finger, then two. She groaned with pleasure.

I removed my fingers and traced the delicious outline of her sex-folds before slicking her juice over her skin, tracking, as she had done with me, from her sex to her anus, tickling its puckered entrance, before sliding my finger back into her quim.

I left her glorious breasts and knelt down before her, unzipped and then pulled down the leather skirt that had ridden up her hips to her waist, and whipped her panties down, sniffing their delicious musky aroma before throwing them behind me. I spread her legs wide until both her calves rested on the leather arms of her chair and finally dipped my head to her pussy.

My tongue sought her labia, lightly brushing against her moist flesh, before I descended onto her clitoris. I did it slowly, licking her, listening to her wail with pleasure. I flicked her clit this way and that way, felt it swell under the tip of my tongue. Her head was tossing from side to side, following the rhythm of my licking.

I felt her legs tense, felt her thighs arch around my ears, clasping my head in her tightening grip, squeezing me hard.

Then, as she had done with me, I pulled back. I did not want her to come yet. I teased and tantalised her with my tongue, with my mouth, lapped her viscous love juice, spread her sex wide and tongued her.

She was grunting now as the pink coral of her sex-lips glistened before me. My hands gripped the plump cheeks of her bottom, my nails digging into flesh as I feasted on the perfect wet centre of her sex. She pulled my head up by the chin, opened my mouth with her tongue and French-kissed me, clearly exhilarated by the taste of her own cunt on my tongue and lips.

I could sense how delightful she had found the pain I caused her as my nails dug deeper and deeper into her flesh. A pressure had been mounting inside me, a tension in my chest, in my mind, and then suddenly something clicked. I was like a caged animal that had been freed, invigorated by my liberty. I wanted to do everything to her, to release all the strain that had built up in me over the slow years.

I tugged her up from the armchair and, sitting down on the sofa, roughly pulled her over me so her fleshy buttocks rested over my lap. She looked up over her shoulder, seemingly astonished at the feverish change that had overcome me.

'Please, please,' she murmured, begging me to hurt her, although her eyes betrayed fear: I was still a stranger to her, so she could not know how far I would go. It added a dangerous fire to my already feverish mind.

I pushed her face into the leather of the sofa, as I felt my erection press against her pubis, raised my free hand and brought it down onto the soft flesh of her buttocks in a thunderous smack. Her yelp was muffled in the thickness of the leather. I could feel my palm tingle as I whacked her bare bottom again, much harder than the first time, the loud clap ringing in my ears. And again and again, until her delightful buttocks flushed red. She gripped the arm of the sofa as she wriggled and writhed on my lap. Another smack; I was almost out of control.

Again and again I hit the quivering flesh, my head spinning, a deep anger surging within me with each mighty slap, and receding as my hand beat her silken skin, only to build up again instantly as I watched her bare bottom jerk under the weight of my blows.

Her head wriggled free from my hold. 'More, *por favor*, more!'

I needed no encouragement as I slapped her tingling flesh again, my hand rising higher and higher with each stroke, my dazzled eyes fixed on her blushed bottom.

'Fuck me, now. Fuck me! Please fuck me!'

I let her clamber up from the sofa and move dreamily to the oblong coffee-table where my forgotten glass of whisky still awaited me. With one sweep of her hand she recklessly cleared all obstacles: a vase, my glass, and a few books toppled and fell to the floor. The task complete, she lay prone on the table, her breasts squashed against the glass and her hands gripping the sturdy cylindrical legs. Her reddened buttocks were invitingly perched in front of me, as if waiting, excitedly anticipating the immense pleasure I would bring to them.

For a moment, as I knelt behind her, I studied her immense beauty. My stiff rod twitched at the sight.

'Take me, please. *Duro, duro* – hard. Take me hard. *Jodeme.*' She was insistent, demanding.

I grasped her hips and slipped my aching cock into her tight pussy. She sighed with pleasure. Her whole body shuddered as I entered her. I slid deeper and deeper, pulling her further onto me.

'Hard, hard – *duro, duro*,' she coaxed, her voice pleading. I took her hard, so hard: riding her, riding in and out of her tight pussy as she screamed and screamed for more, each stroke pushing further into her.

'Harder, deeper – *mas profundo*!'

She reached back, grabbed my hand, and guided it to her hair.

'Pull hard!'

I pulled her hair as my thrusts grew more frantic. My sweat mingled with hers, coating her buttocks. I could hear the noise her breasts made as she slithered on the glass.

'Harder, harder!'

I pulled on her hair. I watched her head arch back as she tried to resist the pain she most ardently desired.

And then, almost as if I wasn't there, she entered a kind of ecstatic reverie, as my rod pushed deeper inside her. I felt the muscles of her quim grow taut, squeezing me, the slicked walls of her sex milking my throbbing helmet, leading me to the greatest orgasm I could ever remember.

She came again, as I erupted deep within her. It seemed like it would never end, my seed exploding like lava, soaking her quim. Her wondrous muscles squeezed all the more, gripping like a vice. Her mouth gaped. She gave another guttural groan, and then she sighed, sagged, and relaxed in her orgasmic release.

Slowly I pulled out of her, and nestled my softening cock in the cleft of her bottom. I wanted to savour every luscious moment. My heart was still pounding. Sweat trickled down my back. A gorgeous sheen of our mingled perspiration covered the small of her back and her fleshy rear. Reluctantly, as Andrea breathed deeply, drifting back to some semblance of normality, I sank exhausted to the floor.

She turned to me and sank elegantly from the table to her knees. She bent and took me affectionately into her mouth, sucking the last remnants of pleasure from me. Her eyes smiled up at my reddened face.

I lay back, sated, and watched her gentle actions. She reached up and kissed me on the lips, and then said:

'Welcome to Buenos Aires.'

Chapter Two

After we made love, we took a shower together. What an experience: lathering her sweet-smelling skin; cleaning every inch of her flesh; seeing her breasts quivering as I washed her lithe and clinging body. Andrea loved being looked at; loved being appreciated for the wonderful – and wonderfully imaginative – woman that she was. She sucked me off as the water lashed down on us, her mouth taking me in completely, her throat greedily swallowing every drop of my seed.

I have an eidetic recall of my first encounter with Andrea: the musky aroma of her; the touch of her skin; her pubic hair; the perfect rotundity of her bottom, of her breasts; the laughing eyes that said to me *all things are possible*.

I hadn't fallen in love with her. I was still too bruised, too raw for that. I had fallen in lust with her, in love with the idea of screwing her – of touching her sensual flesh, having that ready and willing body. She was too perfect to love: to encumber with all the burdensome paraphernalia of domesticity, petty disagreements, drab deceits, and constant and intrusive intimacy. But Andrea dwelled in my mind, took up residence in my thoughts; my waking and sleeping hours were inhabited with the indelible memory of her body.

After our shower, she cooked some pasta and over a glass of wine and, remembering the excited look she had given me when I spanked her, I asked where she had developed her taste for corporal punishment.

'Is a long story, Jonathan. For me is not only punishment,

is pleasure and punishment. Do you know the Chinese fruit, the kumquat?'

'Yes.'

'For me the kumquat is strange. I can never know whether is the outside that is sweet or the inside. Do you understand? If you eat the kumquat whole, there is a wonderful mixture of the bitter and the sweet. Is a confusion, a marvellous confusion. Like love, Jonathan. I never quite know where the pain ends and the pleasure begins. But I do know that when they are united, they are irresistible. In the same way I am not always submissive. I like to be dominant, too. You will see.' She smiled at me as she spoke, slightly parting her lips, giving me another fantastic glimpse of her delectable tongue.

'But you said to me you weren't a *porteña*.'

'Ah, the pleasure and the pain. Maybe I'm more *porteña* than I told you. Maybe, Jonathan, like most of the city's inhabitants, I have a taste for the hypocrisy.'

We both laughed easily.

Andrea began to tell me about her childhood, speaking mainly in English, but occasionally she would slip back into her native language, making sure I had fully understood every detail that she related.

'I told you I came from Cordoba: that is where my parents lived and where I grew up. But when I was fifteen I was sent away to a boarding school in the countryside, a very religious school run by nuns and priests. It was in the middle of nowhere, surrounded by miles and miles of pampas.

'At first I was terrified. The place was run like a prison. It was hundreds of years old, founded by some Christian brothers, although our teachers no longer knew what the meaning of Christianity was. They were cruel and heartless. Most of the girls there were orphans or they were abandoned. The priests and nuns could do whatever they wanted to them.

'Every morning I had to get up at daybreak for matins, and after I would have to scrub and clean the cloisters before our school day began properly. We could be punished for anything: if our shoes were not polished, if a button was missing on our tunic, if our dormitory was untidy in the slightest way.'

'Why did your parents send you there?' I asked, curious that Andrea, who had spoken kindly about her family, should have endured such a draconian adolescence.

'It was a terrible time in Argentina. My parents had to flee the country for their lives. They left me in the charge of my uncle. They had no choice. He sent me to that horrible place. Being such a pious man, he thought I needed a religious education. He also thought it a way of hiding me away. Coward that he was, he did not want to be associated in any way with his sister or her husband while the military were still in power. He even changed my name, my papers, everything. Once I was there, and feeling he had done his Christian duty by his sister, he could completely ignore me. He never even wrote me. So, thanks to him, I was in exactly the same position as most of the other girls.

'At first I hated that place. I rebelled, of course, but it was futile. They locked me in a dark room for a day; they beat me with a cane across my hand. So I behaved better. I could only tolerate my suffering because I knew that one day my parents would come back and take me away and I would leave the treacherous school forever.'

Looking at her, I would never have imagined that the beautiful woman had suffered so much.

'In the afternoon they would bring the bad girls into the school assembly to cane them before our eyes, as an example, to make us behave in the way that they wanted. We would all sit in rows: two hundred girls in neat navy blue uniforms, our eyes transfixed on the small raised stage where our teachers sat waiting for the girls to be called for their punishment.

'Some girls could not stand to watch; they would shut their eyes tight and wait until the ordeal was over. But this could be worse, because inattentiveness was a crime, too, and any girl that did not watch could be summoned to the stage for a thrashing. I would glance around when the caning started and watch the terrified girls flinch with every cruel stroke of the cane, their mouths twisting in fear and disgust.

'And then one day there was a new head teacher, a middle-aged priest, a cold distant man that nobody liked, not even the other teachers. He was cruel, very cruel. He was also handsome. Very virile-looking, very strong, with thick grey hair and beautiful blue eyes. You would never think that a man who looked like that could be so merciless.

'The headmaster was responsible for disciplining us. I am sure that the other priests enjoyed caning the older girls too, but this priest, Father Stefano, loved it. You could see how he watched them; his eyes would widen and brighten when he brought the rod down hard, much harder than the others.

'The girls tried not to scream but the pain was always too much. They could not help it, but the more they cried, the more he hit them. By the time he was finished, his face would be red and his breathing heavy. I could see from his eyes that he would like to hurt these girls more; he always seemed disappointed when there was nobody left for him to thrash.

'I must have been about seventeen when he came to the school. Seeing such pleasure in his eyes made me very curious. There was a dramatic change in my attitude: I realised that it excited me to watch the girls being caned on the stage, to watch the priest lift the long stick above his head, to hear the swish through the air. I started to look forward to it. I felt my heart beat with each stroke; my skin would prickle as I listened to the muffled sobs of the supposed guilty, their hands raised straight to shoulder level, trembling in fear.

'He began to obsess me. I would do bad things just to be one of the girls to be caned by him, but it was never enough. However hard I was caned, I craved more. I couldn't sleep at nights for thinking about Father Stefano, dreaming of his strong firm hands on my tender body, imagining the subtle and unsubtle ways he could punish me. Eventually I could bear it no longer: I devised a plan.

'On Thursday evenings he heard confessions until eight o' clock. I made sure I was the last girl to go into him. I remember how my heart throbbed in my chest as I waited to see him. My palms were slicked with sweat and there was a terrible mingling of excitement and fear as I entered the confessional.

'I said, "Father, I cannot fight my lust. I masturbate, Father. Every night when the others are asleep in the dormitory, I masturbate and masturbate. I have terrible dreams. I dream of men touching me. I dream of touching men. What can I do? I crave their flesh, their touch, their love!" I couldn't make out his face through the metal grill, but I could imagine his lascivious eyes boring into me.

'"And how do you touch these men in your sinful dreams, Andrea?" he asked.

'"I touch them between the legs, on their *penna*. I go down on my knees and lick them with my tongue. I kiss them, Father." I don't know why I said this, exactly. I suppose, because I had a good imagination and it was the most sinful thing that I could think of.

'"And who are these men?" he asked.

29

"'I don't know how to say this, Father – but it is you, Father, that I dream about. I cannot stop it. I dream of kissing you, there, Father."

'I don't think the priest knew exactly what to do. He was not used to girls talking to him like this; confessions in the school were compulsory, but confessionals were rarely repositories of honesty. For a seventeen-year-old girl to confess that she masturbated about him must have excited the priest very much. I continued, "I think I must be punished, Father. I want to be punished, to make my soul pure for God."

'There was a painfully long silence. He perfunctorily went through the process of advising me to think only pure thoughts; then, in mumbled Latin, he said the prayer of absolution.

'When he was finished, I asked him: "And my penance, Father? What should my penance be?"

'"Andrea, you must wait by my door," he said.

'He took me to his little room. There was nothing much inside: a metal bed, a small desk, an oak wardrobe and two wooden chairs. A sacred heart picture hung on the wall above the headboard. It was a matter of pride that even the headmaster lived humbly.

'At seventeen I was already very beautiful. My legs were long and slender, my breasts were big and firm. He examined me under the fading dusk light, his eyes roamed my body as I had seen him do a hundred times before when he was up on the stage, gently tapping a cane in his hand, anticipating his sadistic pleasure.

'He placed the two chairs in the centre of the room, back to back, so they were half a metre apart. "You were right, girl, to come to me. We must drive the devil from your soul. I am going to punish you very hard to purge your evil mind of its sins. Now kneel on the chair."

'I knelt as he instructed, resting my hands on the seat of the other chair. My back was now perfectly horizontal. I was facing the small latticed window looking out onto the empty darkness of the sky. I turned my head to see him fetch the long wooden cane from behind the wardrobe.

'He stood behind me, tapping the cane to his palm, taking in the view of my teenage body. What a wonderful sight I must have been for him! I wear a navy blue blouse over a white vest and a matching navy blue school skirt, my bottom pushing out the flimsy fabric.

'He walk up to me and roughly lifted my skirt until it hung from around my waist. I was wearing little cotton panties. I hear his heavy breathing beside me, and smell a faint trace of communion wine on his lips. He was shaking a little. My panties were already wet. My heart was beating. I wanted him to start. The anticipation was good.

'Suddenly he tugged my panties down my thighs. I felt his callused hands clasping my bottom as he crouched down, pulling the cheeks of my buttocks apart so he could look at the tiny hole of my anus.

'He stood up. I hear the noise of the cane as he bent it between his strong hands, then swished it through the air. I was so wet. I was dying for my punishment. I hear another swish as he raised the cane behind him and brought it down onto my bare bottom with all the force he could muster.

'It was such a beautiful feeling, that first sharp sting of pain sending my flesh tingling, the pain receding, then the swish of the cane in the air again and the hard clear sting as he tanned me again. It was so exhilarating to feel this cruel man's power, to submit to his iron will, to know that he could do anything he want with my body.

'I did not make a sound, my teeth gritting, savouring every stroke on my naked flesh. Stroke followed stroke until the pain was so unbearable I thought that I was going to faint.

'"Now, my wicked girl, we must cleanse your evil mouth. You must suffer for your sins," he said, his breathing heavy with his exertions.

'"Yes, Father," I humbly replied as he stood in front of me, his crotch half a metre from my eyes. He unbuttoned his trousers to expose a huge erection, and took the thick rod in his hand.

'"Do you know what to do, girl? You must take it in your mouth." He pulled down the foreskin to reveal his smooth dome and, holding my nape of the neck, he pushed his whole penis into my mouth. He was big – very big – and I was frightened that I would not be able to take it all, but he pushed into me, rocking my head back and forward. He did it harder and harder until I felt his creamy seed shoot inside my mouth, hitting the back of my throat. He held my head there until I had swallowed every drop.

'"If you feel sinful again, you must come to me without delay," he said as he buttoned up his trousers.

'"Father," I said, "there are others who need to be punished in the same way. I see them looking at you with lust. They should be thrashed, too." I could see his eyes light up as I spoke.

'"You must bring them to me, then," he answered, "but remember, do not speak of your special punishment to anyone else, because then you are in danger of committing the sin of pride. Now go, Andrea."

'The next assembly, my eyes scanned the hall, looking for girls as excited by what they saw as I had been. Lucila was the first. I recognised in her eyes the same intense passion, the same burning curiosity.

'Lucila was a raven-haired beauty with a wonderful figure. She was my age, although she looked a little younger. To her friends she was kindness personified. Her teachers had never known such an obedient girl; but I could see that behind her innocent smile there was something darker, more complicated. I had seen how the bud of her mouth opened as she watched every stroke of the cane, how her trance-like eyes stared at the cruel priest.

'After assembly finished I found her in her room and told her that Father Stefano wanted to see her after Sunday benediction, although I did not say why. She looked very worried but, behind her anxiety, I thought I could detect a certain raw excitement. I, myself, was elated to have my first victim.

'The priest was waiting for us when we arrive the following Sunday, only this time there were three chairs in centre of the room. Father Stefano command us to sit down. He sat facing us.

'"Lucila, I have heard stories about you," the priest began. Lucila looked shocked. Her eyes momentarily glanced into mine, sensing that I had in some way betrayed her. How lovely to meet those gorgeous brown eyes so startled by my trickery!

'"What stories, Father Stefano?" Lucila ask in a wonderful imitation of innocence.

'"Stories of sinfulness, of impure thoughts, of lust."

'"I don't know what you mean, Father. I don't know who has told you..." She look at me again, this time imploringly. I could see she was starting to panic. In all the time that I had been in school, I had never known her get into trouble for anything.

'"Never mind who has spoken to me. I want to know if you have impure thoughts," the priest continued, his voice hard, developing a cruel edge. I watched Lucila's ample chest trembling in fear.

'"I never have any impure thoughts, Father," the girl said, her eyes pleading with the cleric.

"'Don't lie to me, girl. It will be worse for you if you lie." The voice was so masterful, so callous. Father Stefano would have made a wonderful inquisitor. I could see Lucila's enormous brown eyes moistening. "Now, do you have any impure thoughts, thoughts about your body, about the sins of the flesh, about men or boys? Tell me the truth!" he continued, confusing her further by gently taking her perspiring hand in his own.

'Lucila was weakening. She knew she have to say something. "Sometimes I think it would be nice to have a husband when I am older."

"'Why?" the priest asked.

"'To have children, to share my life with."

"'To touch you?"

"'To share..."

"'To touch you?" he almost shouted at her. Lucila's voice were as moist as her eyes. Father Stefano was so intimidating, Lucila was so desperately frightened of him.

"'Yes, Father..." The girl was on the verge of breaking down.

"'To touch you where?" Lucila sat in front of the priest, her eyes looking downward. The priest lifted up her chin so she had to look into his face. "To touch you here?" Father Stefano asked, placing his firm hand on her tender breast, squeezing hard through the cotton of her blouse. "Or here?" He moved his hand lower down onto the seat of her chair, his palm disappearing under her skirt, making her jolt upright. Her hands were shaking with fear. "Tell me," he bellowed at her. "Tell me!"

"'Yes, Father; yes," she said. She would have said anything to appease Father Stefano, so terrified was she of his cruel power. Lucila had no family. Her whole childhood had been spent in the school; the place was her life, her family, and it had formed in her an unquestioning obedience.

She began to sob pitifully, burying her tears in her trembling hands.

"'So you lie to me. You do have impure thoughts – and for that, Lucila, you must be punished. Stand up!" he order.

'She stood up, pitifully whimpering, her whole body shaking in fear.

"'Kneel on the chair!" he order again.

'She stumbled onto the chair. Knowing what was going to happen, I also stood and placed the two chairs in the same position as before, as the priest cast his lusting eyes over Lucila's lovely body. Father Stefano let me organise Lucila so her bottom perched up on one chair and her hands rested on the seat of the other.

'Lucila was so submissive, completely unresisting, her sad eyes brimming with tears. How delicious it was going to be watching Lucila not only try to withstand her fear and the pain that she was undoubtedly going to feel, but to resist the unwanted pleasure that her pain was going to bring her.

'I stood behind the girl and witnessed the same ritual as I had experienced only a few days before. I see Father Stefano pull up the navy skirt, pull down the little cotton panties and then separate the cheeks of her bottom and stare at Lucila's anus. Only, this time, I could see his leering eyes as they feast on the tiny aperture in the centre of her wonderful bottom. I could watch Father Stefano as he retrieved the cane from behind the wardrobe, swish it in the air, roughly move me aside and then bring it down across her rear. I see Lucila flinching with the exquisite pain, the flesh of her buttocks rippling with the stroke.

'After several lashes he passed the cane to me, and told me to continue. Then he stood in front of the poor girl.

"'Now, Lucila, your mouth must be purified." He undid his trousers and placed his huge penis between the girl's reluctant lips, at the same time pulling her navy blue blouse out from the waistband of her skirt and grabbing her nipples in both hands. He pinched them so hard that Lucila shrieked.

'He looked at me, annoyed that I had not continued his ministrations. I brought the cane back as far as my outstretched arm could reach, before lashing the girl as hard as I can, her bottom already lined with the red marks of the priest's thrashing. As the cane landed on her bottom, the priest cruelly nipped the pinpoints of her breast, so the pain caused must have been very intense. I cannot tell you how excited I was at that moment, watching Lucila's reddened bottom, the jerking and twisting of her body, the rhythmic bobbing of her head.

'I hit her again and again as the priest came to his climax, now pressing the submissive girl's head further onto his pole until, with a violent jerk, he ejaculated, his seed gushing into her mouth. I continued to whack her with the cane, as I hear Lucila gurgling on the stiff tool.

'Slowly, Father Stefano withdrew his rod from her mouth and, as her face turned sideways as she gasped for air, I could see his seed dribbling down from her lip. Lucila was beyond tears. The cleric commanded the meek girl to stay exactly in the same position while he came to stand behind her, pushing me aside again as he did.

'He parted her legs further, and tilted her bottom up so he could see her sex. It was obvious by the thick redness of her sex-lips and the gleam of juice around her quim that, for all of her sobbing, Lucila had been aroused by her thrashing. I had been correct that Lucila would take great pleasure in being disciplined.

'"So, you have enjoyed your pain, Lucila," Father Stefano said, snaking a finger around the folds of her quim. "This means that you are a more sinful girl than I had thought. We must beat that out of you!" Lucila looked up to him with her doe eyes, but said nothing. He turned to me, and grabbed the cane from my hand. "Remove your clothes!" he demanded, as he lashed the swollen cheeks of Lucila's buttocks.

'I pulled the cotton blouse over my head, and then removed my T-shirt in the same manner, my erect nipples meeting the priest's eyes. I pulled down my panties and my skirt also, then stood obediently, wearing only my white ankle socks and my plimsolls.

'Father Stefano was sweating. I stood before him naked and trembling, fearful but more excited than I had ever been in my life. This time, the cane descended on the top of my thighs, hard and fast. I thought that I would die with the pain that he was causing me. Again, his aim accurate, he thrashed me one more time in exactly the same place, an incipient red mark from thigh to thigh, stretching across the thin wisps of my pubic hair. The pain was so acute, my whole body seemed to ache. My nipples throbbed excitedly and the taut skin of my upper thighs stung with an intensity I had never known before. He thrash me across my breasts so forcefully it cause me to stumble backward.

'Then he turn his attention to Lucila. "Stand up! Remove your clothes!" Lucila's eyes were puffy with tears. Tentatively, she removed her top to reveal the fullness of her beautiful breasts, two hard brown nipples riding on the crest of her porcelain-white flesh.

'Father Stefano lashed her every bit as hard as he had lashed me. Lucila jerked backward with the force of the blow, her delicate skin reddening immediately, her nipples extending under the stroke of the cane. She gasped in her agony, unable to prevent a shriek emitting from behind her pursed lips. Another thwack, the hard clear sound reverberating around the small room. I looked at her face:

37

her mouth was contorted in pain, her eyes shut tight. This time she manage to stay silent.

'While her eyes were still tight closed, the priest walked up to her and tugged down the panties that Lucila, protecting her modesty, had pulled up once she was allowed to stand. "You are an evil girl," Father Stefano said, crouching down so his eyes were at the same level as her pubis, his forefinger feeling the moistness between her legs before he trail it up to her bottom. He press the surrounding flesh of her anus before inserting his finger in the tight opening.

'Lucila look at me through the mist of her tears, incredulous at the multiple indignities that had befallen her, as the priest push his finger further inside her, then slowly slip it out. He grab the girl firmly by the wrist and toss her violently onto the white sheet of his bed.

'He stood behind me, threading his arms under mine so that his hands could clasp my breasts, his forefinger and thumb grasping my nipples tightly and then squeezing hard. It felt like electricity was coursing through my body. There could be no pretence that this had anything to do with Christian admonition or school discipline. He was giving free rein to his own sadistic perversions.

'He flung me onto the bed beside Lucila, then squatted between our two naked bodies, his manic eyes staring at our flesh.

'He alter my position so I face Lucila's black pubic hair, then forced my head between her legs, pressing my mouth against her clitoris. I licked it. He move to the other side of the bed, forcing Lucila's mouth onto me. I felt her moist tongue lick me. Father Stefano went from me to Lucila, giving instructions to suck hard, to use all our tongue, to take the clitoris between our teeth and bite.

'As my body still smarted with pain, my breasts burning

red, the top of my thighs tingling, I concentrate on the delightful sensation that Lucila's tongue was bringing me. At first it was gentle and soothing but soon I feel an intense sensual itch spreading from my clitoris. It make me lick Lucila harder. I could feel the bud of her lust growing under my attention.

'Father Stefano watch us avidly, clearly pleased by our act. Suddenly he leap up and retrieved his cane. "Whores of Babylon!" he wailed at us, as he viciously lowered the cane onto my sore hip. The pain seared through my skin. Lucila sucked my clit hard. I could feel the sweet pleasure of her tongue and the burn of the lash at same time.

'Roughly, the priest rotated our bodies, so Lucila lie under me, her hands gently clasping my bottom, her neck craning up so she can continue sucking on me.

'I never been so aroused before, the exquisite mingle of pain with the sensation of pleasure.

'Father Stefano continued to cane me, as Lucila licked and sucked. My whole body began tensing, seeking orgasmic release, each thwack of the cane intensifying my need. The sting of the rod, the heat between my legs, stiffened my body. I start to jerk my hips down onto Lucila's mouth, to feel the pressure of her tongue and teeth on me, as the priest lash me and lash me.

'I was coming, and the fear of what would happen if Father Stefano saw me only intensify my pleasure. There was white heat burning inside me. I could no longer feel either pleasure or pain, but something else, something more, a burning and suffocating need that surpassed all sensations. I could not resist. My body spasmed in my orgasm. I was no longer in the room, removed onto some transcendental plane beyond either my present circumstance or my previous knowledge.

'This sensation went on and on, as Lucila was not allowed

to stop sucking on me, and as the priest continue to lash me. One orgasm follow another, until there was an unbearable surfeit of pleasure, until my body was racked with it. I want it to stop. I begged Lucila, but she could not, too fearful was she of what Father Stefano would do to her.

'Then something click in my head, something protective. Unable to stand either the pleasure of my pain or the pain of my pleasure any longer, I lost consciousness.

'When I awoke, he let us both get dressed, telling us that we must tell no one, but that both of us must bring other sinners to him for purification. We knew that what he meant was that he wanted us to procure fresh virgins – young women, the same age as us – to satiate his sadistic desires. He let us go back to our dormitories separately.

'I did not speak to Lucila after that. She look hurt and frightened every time that our eyes meet but, one week later, as I was waiting outside his room, having escorted another girl for Father Stefano, I see Lucila exit, a serene look about her.'

'You mean she went back for more punishment?' I asked, having been riveted by the story.

'Most certainly, Jonathan. I told you, I could tell from that first time I notice her staring at Father Stefano. Is my special talent. I can always tell those who like to be disciplined, who seek satisfaction in pain and punishment.'

'How?' I swigged back the last of my wine.

'Oh, I am not sure. But you, for example, I know straight away even in the airport, the way you look at my body, even the tone of your voice. I know what your pleasure is. You don't believe that I have this gift of knowing? I will show you the next time we meet. I promise you.'

40

Chapter Three

Andrea dropped me off at my *hospedaje* in Palermo. She pecked me on the cheek as we said goodbye and promised me I would be seeing a lot of her, as much as I wanted to, while I stayed in Buenos Aires. She would ring me soon.

After she had driven away and I had checked in, I clambered up to my rooms with my suitcases. My residence was a humble enough affair, just on the right side of spartan: a tiny kitchenette, a spacious living room, and a small bedroom with a largish double bed. The rooms were not expensive and they were more than adequate for me. They were clean and luminous, the big window of the living room looking out onto a sycamore-lined cobbled street.

I put my suitcases down, climbed onto the bed and fell into the most satisfying of slumbers.

When I woke up, dragging my mind to consciousness from a sensual dream about Andrea's luscious body, a question haunted me: why had I come to Buenos Aires?

To escape.

Isn't that why most people cross continents? I was not a political or an economic refugee, but maybe an emotional one. In truth, after splitting up with Marie, I found the idea of putting a continent between us extremely desirable. I felt that she had cheated me out of five years of my life, especially my sexual life, which had withered to non-existence while I was still being faithful and soft. Any feelings of love or even magnanimity that I had once had for her had drowned in the acrimony of our separation and in my own bitter sense of betrayal.

She hadn't made love to me for months before we parted, but she had been screwing others at every given opportunity. It had all come out that night after the garden shed affair, culminating in her malicious confession: our swan-song, a crossfire of barbed digs, of slanders, of vicious lampoons that laid bare once and for all the sheer antipathy we felt for one another and the grim predictable sham our marriage had become.

These things leave scars that aren't so easy to forget; that explains why, behind the surge of liberation I had felt once untethered from my wife, there were still remnants of anger and disillusionment.

Andrea had already gone some way to dispelling them, to making my sense of freedom a palpable resource, a necessary prerequisite of my new life. I believed that sexual liberation could be my saviour, the core of my regeneration, and every encounter I would have would take me further away from the still painful memory of the separation, of my wasted years with Marie.

But there were other reasons to take a sabbatical in Buenos Aires. For one, my career was up shit creek. In the heady days when I had worked with David in London, I had dreamt of being an investigative reporter, of writing a column in a Sunday supplement, of orchestrating ground-breaking docudramas. There seemed to be so many paths to take.

David had a high-powered job working for a monthly glossy. As his career had progressed in leaps and bounds, mine had stagnated. My last job in London was researching for a middle-brow encyclopaedia, and occasionally freelancing for the local press, which largely entailed mind-numbing trips to flower shows and garden fêtes, and reviewing a couple of books here and there for the likes of the Hammersmith Gazette or the Walthamstow Echo.

And yet somewhere inside me I still had this crazy idea that I could write something worthwhile, something personal, something publishable. Argentina might provide some necessary stimuli. I believe – I needed to believe – that a new place could change my life.

Another reason: David was here. I did want to see him again. We had been best friends. Had, past tense, because it had been two years since we had met, although he was good for an Email every other month, usually imploring me to visit him. The last time I had seen him in London I had sensed, though, that he had changed. Not only had he physically aged, paunchy and balding, but he seemed to have lost any interest in what he had left behind or who he had left behind – including me.

Our meeting, nostalgically arranged in one of our old haunts, on nostalgic hunting ground, had been constantly interrupted by the electronic bleep of his mobile. With frequent apologies he would growl or bellow into the streamlined plastic, conversing in a rapid Spanish that was far too advanced for me to understand, and then he would drift back to our shared memories, distracted and seemingly uninterested.

This seemed a far cry from those old days when we were still apprentice journalists working in London for an international news agency. David, though we weren't to know that then, was springboarding his career, racing up the greasy pole where I was to slip and slide.

A seminal memory was one that I often recalled when I thought of him. And now I'd met Andrea, it made me realise why she was – in theory, at least – such a compatible partner for David.

It must have been the mid-eighties. Both of us worked very hard then, but we also spent hours on the town together. It was almost a matter of principle for us to burn the candle constantly at both ends.

It was early summer; the light night still stretched before us. We left our city office accompanied by Victoria, our new office temp. We had both spent the whole week trying to chat her up. She had seemed reluctant to go out with either David or myself alone, but comfortable at the prospect of going out with both of us together. Or that's what we had thought at the time, as we bantered together by the coffee machine. A light bit of joshing, a little bit of a competition, we had decided that we would both try our luck with her and may the best man win.

Victoria was posh – alarmingly posh. Too good for me, David had joked. He saw himself as a more cultivated Lothario than I. Victoria spoke of her country home, called her parents 'mummy' and 'daddy', said 'gosh' a lot, without irony, and dressed rather primly in white blouses and knee-length patterned skirts. Even in the heat of summer, she always wore some kind of chiffon neck-scarf that – to me, at least – seemed the height of aristocratic chic. In the nomenclature of the day, Victoria was a Sloane.

She was certainly not without her attractions. She had bobbed hair which left the pale nape of her neck exposed; her breasts were small but firm, as was her bottom; and her legs were marvellously long and shapely. She laughed easily, too, often repressing a natural tendency to giggle by reaching a hand up to her mouth as if to smother her mirth.

For an hour she had kept us entertained with tales of the horsey set, her twenty-three or so years hidden behind a more knowing self-deprecation and the cheerful cynicism that peppered her comments. We were sitting either side of her, both of us trying to impress by employing our wit, embroidering our experience, bluffing our knowledge and exaggerating our education.

Our competitiveness might have been light-hearted, but I wanted to win. I wanted to grasp those tight buttocks with my hands, wanted to see her naked, pull off that white silk blouse, pull up her mid-length skirt and stick my cock in her wet, aristocratic pussy.

'Oh, boys, you're such a larf,' Victoria said, chortling, after David had told us a racy tale involving Victoria's present boss and his last PA.

'We like you too, Victoria,' David said, leaning over her, ten inches from her face.

'Some of those men in that office are so ghastly, so – so fuddy-duddy. But you two really brighten up my day, although sometimes you're a little too rude for me.' Victoria giggled into her white wine, her clear blue eyes resting first on David and then on me.

'You find us a bit coarse, not Hooray Henry enough, Victoria,' I said, teasing her a little.

'No, a breath of fresh air – but you can get a bit too near the knuckle sometimes. Remember, I've led such a sheltered life.' She was mocking herself, joining in the fun at her own gentle expense.

'Oh, I'm sure you country girls aren't so naïve,' David said.

'Oh, David, yes we are,' she insisted, laughing.

'Would you like another, Victoria?' I asked, pointing at her empty wine glass.

She hesitated and then looked at her watch. 'My goodness, is that the time? I really must dash.'

'Oh, what a shame! I was going to suggest we all go up town for a meal. I went to a very good French restaurant last week in Soho, Le Marseille. Do you have some special plans, Victoria?' It was David again. I knew he hadn't eaten in any French restaurant at all last week. The closest he had got to Gallic cuisine was picking up a local from Mile

End where he lived and successfully enticing her back to his flat with the promise of a Chinese takeaway.

'Well, I haven't got anything so special, but you know I have to work tomorrow.'

'All expenses paid. On the company, Victoria. We'll have you home by eleven.' I added a nod in support of David's suggestion. This was going to cost; neither David nor I had an expense account.

'Well, it might be a whiz, I suppose. My flatmate has gone out tonight so I don't have company, and I suppose it would make a change, and it is Thursday and nobody seems to do any work on Fridays, anyway.'

'That's the spirit, Victoria,' I said, lightly stroking her hand, close enough to smell her expensive French perfume.

'But I have one condition.'

'Yes?' David and I blurted, almost in unison.

'I couldn't possibly go out in these clothes. This is office wear, not fit for French cuisine. Would you mind escorting me back to my flat and waiting for me while I change? My flat is just round the corner. Or if you prefer, you could wait for me here. I won't be more than twenty minutes.'

'No, we wouldn't dream of that – would we, Jonathan?' David flashed a lascivious smile across at me.

'We certainly wouldn't. We're firm believers in chivalry.'

We walked back to Victoria's flat, both of us taking her by the arm. My spirit of competition grew more fierce, fuelled by the several glasses of wine I had consumed. Victoria chuckled away as we lightly bantered and mocked our drab office colleagues, inventing ludicrous gossip about them to amuse her. David and I were both trying to outdo the other.

'I'm afraid the flat is a little poky, not exactly bijou,' Victoria said as we climbed the two flights of stairs and entered her apartment, more spacious and lavish than the

46

cramped bedsits that we both rented.

The flat was decorated with the tastes of the time: brightly coloured patterned carpets, Monet prints on the wall, primary Habitat colours, wicker chairs.

Victoria invited us both to take off our jackets and tidily placed them on a coat stand in the corner of the room. Beside the wicker chairs and a couple of enormous bean bags there was a large sofa big enough to seat three people. David and I plumped down on each end. Victoria went to the kitchen and returned a moment later with a bottle of the finest Scotch malt whisky.

'I suppose we could have a little drink before I get ready.'

'There's plenty of time,' I said, taking the bottle and doing the honours.

As she hung her own coat in the bedroom, David winked at me. I wasn't sure what exactly he had in mind, but I was already beginning to wonder whether we were still in competition, whether he hadn't already thought himself the clear winner. He had been the more loquacious, the wittier and, judging by eye contact he was certainly ahead on points, or so I had thought – and that I should do the decent thing and admit defeat, leaving him free to enjoy the spoils of victory.

'That's better,' Victoria said as she sat down between us. 'Five minutes' rest and then I'll change.'

We chatted amiably for twenty minutes or so, Victoria showing no intention of changing her clothes, preferring to merrily down a couple of glasses of whisky. David and I both became a little more tactile with her, stroking her arms. David stealthily slipped his hand around her shoulder, lightly caressing the nape of her neck. Victoria occasionally rested her slim hands on our upper legs. We joked about who she might fancy in the office, offering her preposterous potential boyfriends, some of which made her shriek with laughter.

'Geoff Harris?'

'No, couldn't possibly. I'd never get in the bathroom.'

'Rod Staines?'

'Far too macho.'

'Jeremy St. John.'

'Too upper-class.'

'What, there's somebody who's too upper-class for you?'

'Of course there is. Who do you think I am? Anyway, I think Jeremy would be more interested in you two.'

'How do you know these things?'

'Sometimes a girl can tell.'

'Who else is there...? Of course, what about me and Jonathan? Do you like us?'

'Oh, you're both handsome boys, but I...'

'Couldn't choose?'

'Couldn't possibly.'

'Well, Victoria, I have a suggestion.'

'Yes?'

'The truth is, Victoria, we both have a confession.' David sounded in earnest. I wasn't sure what exactly I had to confess, or where exactly David was leading, but I suspected some kind of foul play on his part – a huge cock-and-bull story which would further impede my chances with Victoria, a game, set and match strategy that might even mean that I had to eject myself from the room as hastily as I could. Something along the lines of my having to go home to look after some ageing relative, or defend the virtue of some damsel in distress.

I was about to be proved very wrong.

'Oh, really, a confession? I love confessions.' She smiled at both of us but I detected a slight uneasiness in her manner. David was stroking the side of her face, brushing her skin lightly with the back of his hand.

'The truth is, Victoria, that Jonathan and I are both very attracted to you...'

'Yes?'

'Well, I mean, we would both like to go to bed with you.'

'Gosh!'

'He's my best friend. I really don't want to fight with him over you.' By this stage, he had taken her hand and was caressing her palm. I was latching on to the idea. I took her other hand in mine. Victoria looked shocked: a little shocked, that's all.

'So maybe the best thing...'

David was stroking her arm now. I moved my hand onto her beige skirt and felt her thigh underneath the material. Victoria immediately flinched, but then relaxed.

'...the best thing would be if we...' David reached to her blouse, slid his hand inside and grasped her breast, as I moved my hand up and squeezed her quim over the fabric of her skirt.

'Oh, I don't know,' Victoria said in a tremulous whisper, anticipating what David was about to say.

My hand rubbed over her skirt and panties, while David pinched her breasts. She glanced at me and then David, her eyes slightly red with alcohol.

'...if we both made love with you.'

Victoria moaned as I squeezed her. 'I've never done anything like this before,' she whispered.

'There always has to be a first time.'

David began to unbutton her shirt. I looked on, still squeezing her as I stared at the little white bra and her nipples visible beneath it. The pale skin of her neck reddened with anticipation. Victoria looked at me and smiled as I stared at her chest, before reaching out and pressing on her covered breast. I could feel her nipple harden under my palm.

We pulled her shirt over her shoulders. She arched her body forward to make it easier for us. Then we turned down one cup each of her bra. Her nipples poked out.

'We want to suck your tits, Victoria.'

Victoria didn't say anything as we both suited action to word. Her firm ruby nipples grew under the attention of our tongues.

'Do you like it when we suck your tits, Victoria? Do you like it when we make your nipples hard?' David asked, before taking her nipple between his teeth and pulling at it.

'Oh yes, David, I do.' Obviously, she still wasn't sure where all this was leading. The intonation of her voice was jokey, exaggerated as it had been in the wine bar when she had teased us about being rude.

'Say it, Victoria. Say you like us to suck your tits and make your nipples hard.'

'I like it when you suck my breasts, David, when you make my nipples hard. Yes, I like it very much, really.' She was laughing again, but there was a greater sense of urgency growing in her voice, a little less of the mock and more of the genuine.

I flicked her nipple with my tongue and then tweaked it slightly between my teeth, feeling her body tremble as I did so. I could hear and feel the rapid beating of her heart. David worked on her other breast, his left hand reaching behind her and expertly unfastening the bra strap; something I always found difficult to negotiate without fumbling like an over-excited schoolboy.

'Would you like us to look at your cunt now? Would you like that? Would you like us to look at your cunt, Victoria?'

Victoria nodded, despite his crude terminology. Any remaining mirth in her voice had gone. She seemed to becoming mesmerised by her own desire, her face flushing red, her chest heaving as she panted with lust, her hands holding us both by the neck as we toyed and sucked on her fabulously erect nipples.

'Stand up, Victoria.'

Victoria did what she was told. She looked at us both, clearly not quite believing what she was doing, what she had let herself do.

'Lift up your skirt so we can look at you.'

Victoria lifted the hem of her skirt. Inch by slow inch, more and more of her shapely legs were revealed, encased in beautiful white silk stockings. As the hem tantalisingly reached her thighs she seemed to hesitate a moment, aware perhaps that if she went any further there would be no turning back.

'Come on, Victoria,' David urged.

The skirt went higher and higher, above the whiteness of her thighs, until she revealed her lemon cotton panties, a damp patch at the centre of the crotch.

'You're wet, Victoria.'

'Yes.'

We were both staring at her panties. I was helping her to hold her skirt around her middle so that nothing obscured our view.

'Show us, Victoria,' I said hoarsely. 'We want to see your cunt.'

Victoria smiled at us, as she pulled aside the thin cotton strip of her panties and revealed her pink pussy-lips.

'Use your fingers, Victoria.'

She elegantly slid an index finger into her juicy pussy, maintaining her classy aura all the while.

'Deeper, Victoria, deeper.'

The finger disappeared further, all the way to the knuckle of her slender hand.

'Let me lick your finger.' David took her hand and sucked the glistening digit into his mouth, while I held her skirt, hungrily eyeing the succulent labia framed by her cotton panties.

He released her finger. 'Put it back.'

She did so.

'We want to see you push it in and out.'

Again, without a murmur of complaint, she did so.

David smiled. 'Would you like us to remove your panties now, Victoria?'

She nodded, seemingly distracted by her own pleasure as she continued to push her finger in and out of her delicious sex.

David slightly adjusted her position until her quim faced him. As I held up her skirt he slid down her panties, revealing the unblemished porcelain globes of her bottom to my grateful eyes.

'Now, Victoria, we are going to punish you,' David stated matter-of-factly. 'Do you like being punished?'

The atmosphere in the room changed completely. Victoria seemed alarmed at the proposition. I always knew that David had a predatory nature, but I had never known about his particular sexual penchant for discipline. The revelation excited me immensely: even more so as I looked up at the trepidation written on our victim's face as she slowly shook her head from side to side.

'You will do as we say, Victoria,' David insisted confidently. 'Do you understand?'

'I don't think...'

'You *will*, Victoria.' His voice was firm and strident. 'You will learn tonight to enjoy pain as much as you enjoy pleasure.'

Her face changed colour, blanching under David's stern injunctions.

David suddenly stood up, took her nipples between his fingers and pinched them hard, much harder than I had done. I watched her brow furrow prettily at the pain.

'You want to be punished, don't you, Victoria?'

She said nothing.

'You need to be punished, don't you?'

To my astonishment, she nodded.

'Tell me you want it. Tell me you want to be punished.'

Victoria remained quiet.

'I knew from the first moment I saw you, Victoria. I can always tell about these things. You're a submissive. You dream about it, don't you, Victoria? You dream about being punished. Tell me want to be punished now, Victoria… Now!' The incantatory repetition of her own name had an almost hypnotic affect on the girl as it laid bare the true nature of her sexual desires.

'I want to be punished,' she whispered, her voice faltering, a dreamy sadness spreading across her lovely features.

David began to undo the thick black leather belt of his trousers. Victoria's eyes widened as he did so.

'Kneel on the sofa, Victoria. Yes, that's right.' I was amazed to watch her doing exactly as she was told, kneeling in the middle of the sofa, her arms outstretched along its back, her white bottom raised proudly.

David ran the tips of his fingers between her buttocks, making her inhale deeply as he gently tickled her, before suddenly pulling back and spanking her firmly with his tensed hand. She shuddered and groaned, clearly savouring the crisp strike.

'Did you like that, Victoria?'

'Yes,' she replied in a whisper, her eyes closed.

David again smacked her hard, and then harder. The precise sound of his palm on her tautened bottom echoed around the room.

'Do you want more, Victoria?'

She nodded without hesitation.

'Tell me you want more. Tell me you want to be spanked some more.'

'Spank me some more, David.' Her voice was soft, a muted cry of crude need.

'Say "please", Victoria!'

'Please, David, please…' she begged through clenched teeth.

How she enjoyed being smacked. Each thwack of David's hand was met with a tantalising whimper of satisfaction.

'Please… *please*!' she begged over and over.

As I watched David's rigid hand alight again and again on the reddening and quivering flesh, I was amazed at what I had witnessed. How could David have been so prescient? How could he have known that the girl longed for correction?

I had had rough sex before, but this was the first time I had watched such orchestrated discipline, and I was surprised by how excited it made me feel.

David passed me the belt. He winked into my startled eyes. 'Now, Victoria, Jonathan is going to belt you.'

I wasn't so sure, but after a confident nod of encouragement from David I swept the belt back and brought it down onto her waiting bottom, savouring the satisfying noise the lash made on her rippling flesh.

'Harder, Jonathan,' Victoria pleaded, 'much harder.' I was enjoying myself, but I was a little worried in case I hurt her, or I went too far. I hit her again, harder this time, as she had requested me to.

'Yes,' she moaned, writhing on the sofa.

'How many lashes do you deserve, Victoria?' David asked, as casually as if he wanted to know whether she took one sugar or two in her coffee. 'Five, ten, twenty?'

'Thirty,' she answered.

I lashed her again with the belt, and then again. I could feel perspiration trickling down my brow as my eyes drank in the voluptuous sight of Victoria's jerking buttocks, and I heard a deep satisfied groan emitting from her mouth with each firm lash. The girl had reached down to her clitoris and was frantically rubbed the swollen nub.

David counted each strike as he stood beside me, his eyes fixed on the flushed bottom of the submissive girl.

'Twenty-nine... Thirty!'

As I stopped, my breathing hard with the exertion and the excitement I felt, David took the belt from me and whipped it down much harder than I had done. Victoria yelped and jerked. And then he stuck again, and again. Victoria was shaking now. I saw her body spasm towards orgasm, her climax precipitated by the intense pain of David's exacting punishment. Her knuckles glowed white as she clutched the sofa and her head lolled back, exposing the stretched sinews of her neck, her face tensed, her eyes clasped tightly shut.

'Now we're going to lick you,' David said hypnotically. 'Would you like us to lick away all the pain?'

She nodded as her body slowly relaxed.

I climbed beside her on the sofa and eased her thighs apart so I had a glorious view of her puckered rosebud and her pink pussy-lips. I grasped her hips and sank my mouth onto her succulent bottom. Air hissed from her lungs as I fed on her tanned flesh. Meanwhile David, who had sneaked his head between her legs, nibbled on her clitoris. Victoria entangled her fingers in our hair and deliriously urged us to pleasure her.

Suddenly David pulled away, unzipped his trousers, hastily rummaged inside his pants, and fished out a huge erection. He shuffled closer and she feverishly fell upon him, instantly devouring his impressive cock with her mouth.

I eagerly took his place between her thighs and slid my finger against her anus, pressing gently until the muscle yielded and my digit sank into her. At the same time I began to frig her with my tongue. She tasted exquisite. From her wet suckling sounds and David's grunts of satisfaction I knew she was using her lips and tongue with great skill.

My own erection was now aching for release. I don't know whether David realised, but we seemed to instinctively change position and Victoria tugged my trousers open and buried her face in my groin. I sighed at the heavenly feel of her warm wet mouth going to work on my cock, lay back, and closed my eyes to wallow in the undiluted pleasure. I was right – she was very skilful, and her skill sent a luxuriant shiver through my body.

'Now, Victoria,' I heard David say, 'I'm going to fuck you. I'm going to fuck you until we both come.'

She nodded her delight, still sliding her lips up and down my bursting cock.

I watched as David prised her legs apart and sank into her from behind with one long lunge. I felt her mouth tighten on me as he entered her. I reached between us and kneaded her breasts as her inflamed crimson buttocks jerked back against David's taut stomach.

He thrust his hips frantically, digging his fingers into her sore flesh as he did so. I had to steady her head so she could continue sucking me as she writhed in a confusion of pain and pleasure.

'Do you like that, Victoria?'

'Mmmm...'

'Do you like me fucking your hot, juicy pussy?'

'Mmmm...'

'Do you like it when I dig my nails into you, like this?'

'Mmmm…'

'Do you like sucking Jonathan while I fuck you?'

'Mmmm...'

As David worked ever harder, a sheen of sweat coating his chest, I could feel my cock swelling inside her mouth. I curled my fingers in her hair and held her still, savouring the feeling.

Then I pulled her off me, afraid I would explode before I had had a chance to enjoy the delight of her pussy. I guided her mouth to my testicles. She licked and sucked while she ran her cool fingers up and down my shaft.

'I'm coming,' David grunted. 'I'm coming...'

Victoria moaned her encouragement, her mouth full of my balls.

At the last second and with an enormous groan, David withdrew and erupted over her bottom, then rubbed the glistening head of his pulsing tool in his own creamy emission and then dreamily between her buttocks. A shudder of pleasure swept through her. She released my testicles and cried out as another orgasm shook her.

Now it was my turn. David and I swapped places. He sat on the arm of the sofa and pulled Victoria's mouth onto his insatiable penis. I knelt behind her, separated her buttocks, and thankfully slid into her quim.

I started slowly, rhythmically thrusting deep, steadily gathering pace until I was pounding away at her mercilessly, remorselessly, my groin slapping her raised buttocks. I pummelled harder and harder and faster and faster. I loved Victoria's muffled yelps of pleasure as I fucked her. I knew my orgasm was upon me, but I couldn't slow to prolong my pleasure. I shuddered and came, my chest heaving as I panted heavily like an unfit jogger…

'Not bad for a country girl, Jonathan,' Victoria purred

softly as the three of us relaxed together. She smiled with genuine affection and kissed me on the cheek, and then kissed David on the cheek, the promised French meal long since forgotten.

That, however, was not the end of the evening's heavenly surprises. As we began our second bout of sex – this time with David lying on the bed, Victoria sitting on his penis and me stooped before her, my hands milking her irresistible breasts and my cock buried deep in her mouth – Victoria's flatmate walked in.

So engrossed were we that none of us noticed the beautiful girl with long dark hair and a complexion as pale as Victoria's standing in the bedroom doorway, watching us, open-mouthed.

I don't know how long she was there, but I do know my cock swelled in Victoria's mouth when I did notice the raincoated beauty, her innocent face a picture of confused astonishment.

'We have company,' David said what I was unable to, clearly unperturbed at being watched.

Victoria didn't respond immediately – not even when the astounded girl asked what was going on, speaking gingerly with an accent every bit as highbrow as Victoria's.

Eventually, though, she did slide my cock from her mouth – with some reluctance, I like to think – and turned to her friend. 'Amanda,' she panted enthusiastically, 'these boys are giving me the best time of my life.'

The girl momentarily looked disgusted and took a retrograde step, but she didn't disappear altogether.

'Oh, Amanda,' Victoria cooed, 'it's fantastic! Come here. Look how red my bottom is. What a spanking they gave me!'

Amanda stayed where she was, but her wide-eyed gaze

flickered surreptitiously down to my rigid cock as Victoria gripped it in her fist. It lurched proudly under the furtive inspection.

'Come here…' Victoria coaxed. 'Come on, they won't bite – well, maybe a little.'

Amanda hesitated as the three of us watched her, and then advanced one uncertain step. From the contours of the raincoat I could tell it contained a pair of large firm breasts, a narrow waist, and shapely hips.

'Jonathan…' whispered Victoria, conspiratorially, 'go and say hello to Amanda.'

I let go of Victoria's luscious breasts and clambered off the bed. Amanda didn't move. She didn't leave. Her mouth remained open, her moist red lips inviting beyond belief. I was hesitant, not believing that Amanda would welcome any attention from me, not wanting to scare her off. It seemed so preposterous; me standing there totally naked and Amanda fully clothed in her raincoat, still buttoned and belted at the waist.

She still did not move, but stared at me with her large eyes, conveying a whole melange of feelings: excitement, fear, amazement, desire.

I could smell the alluring aroma of her perfume. Carefully, I reached out and unbuttoned the top button of her raincoat. She did nothing to object. My cock stiffened even more as I realised the innocent beauty was submitting to my advances. I freed the next button… and then the next. Her hair was a little wet; she must have been caught in a summer shower. The belt was unbuckled and swung free, the last few buttons yielded, and then the coat fell open with a sexy rustle. Underneath she wore a tight black skirt that confirmed my previous assessment of her curvaceous hips, and a white blouse, the top few buttons of which were undone to show a deep and inviting cleavage. Her breasts were indeed large, and looked deliciously firm.

She didn't stop me as I slipped the coat from her shoulders and let it slither to the floor. Barely able to control my excited fingers, but trying desperately to maintain an air of confident control, I quickly opened her blouse and feasted upon the sight of her soft smooth breasts bursting over a lacy red bra.

Still she said nothing, but watched what I was doing with innocent intensity. I undid the front-fastening bra and her fantastic breasts spilled forth. I cupped them, kneaded them. They were soft and silky smooth to my touch. Her eyes closed and her lashes fluttered prettily: the first sign of carnal interest. I pulled her to me and kissed her deeply. My tongue slipped between her pouting lips without encountering any resistance; her lipstick tasted wonderful. Her breasts squashed against my chest as I cupped her lovely bottom through the skirt and squeezed her close. Her firm belly squirmed against my erection and I almost had a very embarrassing crisis. Behind me, I could hear the bed creaking rhythmically and David and Victoria encouraging each other to orgasm.

I pulled Amanda onto the bed beside them, then entwined my legs around her body, my cock prodding her midriff. I slid her a little further down so I could watch Victoria in the last throes of her climax as I did what I wanted. I grasped Amanda's breasts in both hands and slid my cock between them, then moved her head so that when I pushed my cock up, her mouth met the tip.

I could not believe this girl: so luscious, her eyes staring into mine. She was passive and unresisting. I was screwing the breasts of an irresistible girl and I had barely said a word to her.

David and Victoria were still going strong. He was now fucking her doggy-fashion, and both of them were watching me as I continued to push and pull my cock between Amanda's fulsome breasts.

She started to suck me more avidly, her lips awakening on my helmet. Levering my cock from her sumptuous chest, I edged closer to her mouth, my cock bobbing as I moved. She accepted it greedily, licking the head as her sharp nails dug into my buttocks. Then she slid her lips further until her mouth was full and her cute nose nestled into my pubic hair, before slowly and teasingly sliding back up, grazing her teeth against the skin, until she again reached the tip.

I teased my cock from her mouth – she followed it, enchantingly reluctant to let it go – and urgently unzipping her skirt, I rolled it down past her knees and let it slip to the floor. I hooked my thumbs into her panties and sent them the same way as the skirt. I stared, transfixed by the exquisite sight of her lying before me.

At the moment when Victoria and David climaxed, I pushed deep into Amanda's lovely tight pussy. She gasped again, but this time from excitement rather than shock.

David and Victoria disentangled themselves and crouched over Amanda. David held her down by the shoulders and Victoria gently stroked her damp fringe from her perspiring forehead. They watched her reactions intently as I screwed her with fervour.

'Go on, Jonathan, go on…' Victoria urged, drawing a groan from her beautiful flatmate by pinching one of her erect nipples.

David was insatiable. He crouched over Amanda and pinned her arms down with his knees. He then cradled her head in his hands and fed his revitalised cock between her scarlet lips. Victoria leaned close to me and reached between my thighs to milk my balls, her eyes glazed as she watched me pistoning in and out of Amanda's wet sex.

A sudden impulse hit me. I buried my fingers in Victoria's

lustrous hair and pushed her face down. She needed no instruction, and I felt her tongue lap against the underside of my cock as it pumped in and out. Amanda groaned anew around the column of stiff flesh that stretched her lips wide, and rolled her head from side to side, and I guessed Victoria had found her clitoris. I stroked Victoria's back and raised silky buttocks, and then slipped a couple of fingers into her sopping pussy and matched them to the rhythm of my hips.

This was utter heaven! This was beyond my wildest fantasies; probably beyond all of our wildest fantasies. David was a bloody hero for instigating it.

I knew Amanda was close to coming. Her breasts rose as she breathed deeply around David's cock. It was no good, I could hold on no longer. I pulled out and immediately felt Victoria suck me in between her lips. Amanda whimpered deliriously as she came. David pulled free and furiously masturbated, his helmet resting on her glistening lips, and quickly shot his thick cream over her angelic face. The sight was too much for me, and Victoria had to swallow furiously as I drained myself in her skilful mouth.

This was the David I had known. This was the friend I had got drunk with, shared women with. As I lay on my bed and dreamt of all the beautiful girls I might meet in Buenos Aires, I wondered what had happened to him. Could he really have become lost in his greed for money and power, and so disinterested in the joys of the flesh? Both of us seemed so far away now from the young men of those carefree days.

Great sex was what we had wanted and what we had enjoyed. Five failed years of domesticity proved to me that it was what I still wanted. But what of David; what did he want? I no longer knew.

Chapter Four

Buenos Aires was amorphous to me, not only topographically, but existentially; the city spread out before me like my own uncertain future. I did not really know what Buenos Aires could mean to me or what it might do for me; whether I was on the cusp of some mighty significant change in my life, or whether, the fabulous Andrea aside, my time here would pass without consequence or event. I was in unknown territory.

In truth I knew very little about Buenos Aires or even Argentina, little more than what anybody knows: all the tango and polo stuff, the risible generals and the football fanaticism, the attempt at democracy and the prevalence of corruption.

In the next few days I was to learn so much more.

So what did I discover? Well, maybe a more balanced man – a less obsessed man – may have noticed the ferocity of the traffic, the death-defying speed of the *collectivos*, or the occasional niceties of architecture. Perhaps he might have taken pleasant strolls around charming old Palermo or ambled around the more ostentatious streets in the Barrio Norte. He may have laboured with his guidebook in museums and cathedrals, in famous bars and *parrillas*. He may have ventured to Boca, been impressed by the brightly painted wooden shacks of La Camionetta, or studied the fervour of football, its ubiquitous presence in the life of *porteños*. He could have watched the tourists hunt for a bargain in the tat at the old antique markets, before watching the Sunday tango dances in San Telmo.

I did notice much of this, but only in passing, as one notices a mild distraction: for what consumed my interest, as I gradually familiarised myself with the city streets, were women. The glorious wealth of female beauty that filled – nay, congested – the streets of the city. It was everywhere. The city seemed to vibrate on sex. So many types, so beautiful, wonderful combinations of race and age, colour and style. The place was rife with lust. Buenos Aires seemed to thrive on the heady aroma of sexual possibility.

I walked around with my head constantly turned. My heart raced on buses and trains. I stared longingly at girls in bars and cafés. So many women, everywhere, a city choked on lasciviousness. How did these poor boys manage? How could they be blasé about it? I wasn't.

David phoned me a couple of days after I arrived. He woke me from another mildly erotic dream about his wife.

I staggered out of bed, disorientated, confused, melancholic at losing Andrea, even if it was only from the fantasy world of my sleeping imagination.

'Hey, Jonathan. You're here.'

'Hello, David.'

'Things okay?'

'Fine, thanks.' I was struggling to find my voice, to find any voice capable of answering simple questions on a telephone.

'I'm ringing from Santiago. I'll be back in a couple of days. I'm sorry about all this.'

'It's okay.'

'I understand Andrea met you off the plane.'

'Yes, no problem.' I felt like I should say something complimentary about his wife. The situation called for it: a sign of respect for his spouse's hospitality, or at least some comment showing my approval of his choice of partner. But from all the things that I could say about Andrea – and they were legion – none were suitable listening for her husband.

'She said you got on well.'

A vision again of Andrea, the plump, white cheeks of her bottom brightening red under the rough discipline of my hands, came to mind.

'Yes. You're a lucky man, David.'

'I know, I know.' He sounded sincere enough. 'She's going to ring you today. I spoke to her this morning. She wants to show you around town a little. She's been a little tied up.'

I wondered whether David realised the literal plausibility of his last statement. 'No, that's all right. I understand. I don't want you or Andrea to go out of your way.' I wasn't so concerned about David diverting himself from his habitual path, but I wanted Andrea to go as far out of her way as was necessary to repeat our previous encounter.

'Don't be so bloody stupid. I can't wait to see you. There's lots to talk about.'

'Me too, David.'

'When I get back, you have to come to my office. There are some things for us to sort out.'

This sounded vague. What things could he mean? What needed sorting out? I was about to ask him.

'Sorry, Jonathan, I'd like to chat, but I really have to go. See you soon, buster.'

Maybe it was the 'I'd like to chat, but...' line, but this sounded like the same David from the last time we had met: too distracted by business, by making money, ringing me out of some sense of duty, some vaguely half-remembered tie that bound him to call me, out of obligation and civility. I suspected – despite his cheerfulness and all his expressions about wanting to meet me – that his desire to see me was not very strong. In truth, neither was mine to see him: not any more.

Later in the evening, Andrea did call. I had stayed in all day waiting by the phone.

'*Hola*! *Como te va*?' The voice was enough to stir me; so lush, so sexy.

'Hello, Andrea.'

'I owe the apology.'

'For what?'

'I did want to see you, Jonathan. I really wanted, but is some problems. I have been a little *occupado*. I call as soon as I can. I can meet tomorrow for a coffee, if you like. Remember, I have something to prove to you. I give a big surprise, promise.'

I had a fair idea of what she had in mind, but I was disappointed that there wasn't any possibility of seeing her sooner. I craved her body.

'Jonathan, I want to do so many things with you. I really, really cannot wait for the next time.'

It was the last thing she said before hanging up.

The next day, not having to wait for calls, and a couple of hours away from meeting Andrea, I decided to go in search of some of that feminine beauty I had witnessed parading around the streets of the city. Where I would find amenable women and how I would communicate with them with my poor Spanish were true obstacles – but not insurmountable, I thought. There are always possibilities in cities. I had known this for a long time. It was a pity I had wasted five years of my life not taking any of them.

After breakfasting on fresh strawberries and cream – a complementary gift from the obese hotel proprietor, along with a couple of bottles of beer and several cuts of chorizo and ham – I walked down the wooden staircase. A notice informed me that the lift, in true Argentinian fashion, was entered at my own risk, the hotel not liable if I plunged to my death.

On the first floor I noticed one of the rooms was slightly ajar. Nosy as I always am in hotels, I slowed my pace to a crawl to peek inside the door. I was not disappointed, for I got a superb eyeful of the chambermaid's rear as she bent over to retrieve some rubbish from the floor. Her short skirt was raised to the bareness of her tanned thighs, the contours of her fleshy rump clearly visible through the thin black fabric.

She must have heard my footsteps on the parquet floor, however stealthily I had tried to creep past the door. She straightened effortlessly and turned around, revealing her large coal-black eyes and a mantel of glossy dark shoulder-length hair. She held my eyes for a moment, seemingly a little surprised to find me staring at her.

'*Si, señor*?'

I was a little embarrassed to have been caught so obviously leching at her voluptuous body. I mumbled a good morning and left her to the cleaning, a half-smile playing at the corners of her mouth.

One flight of stairs lower and still contemplating the horny sight of the chambermaid's robust buttocks, I arrived in the foyer, where two delightful blondes in thin cotton summer dresses were making their way to the main door.

'Oh come on Stephanie, we're going to be late,' the blonde with the green eyes and the short cropped hair said to her taller friend, as the latter fumbled in her bag for something.

'Look, I know they're in here somewhere. Oh, look, here they are.' Two delightful English girls: the shorter was strawberry blonde, and the taller, more languorous-looking one had flowing golden curls.

The one named Stephanie pulled her room keys from her bag, jangled them in front of her companion, and then dropped them back inside.

I couldn't resist the opportunity.

'Are you two English?' I enquired. Okay, it was a stupid thing to say. They were clearly not Argentinian, but it was the first thing that came to mind.

Both women turned around to look at me, surprised maybe that someone should address them in their native tongue.

They both had separate charms. The short punky one with the tight polka-dot dress and the dark purple eye-shadow looked lively and, although the slimmer, had enticingly large breasts. The taller one, Stephanie, wore a slightly longer floral dress. Her make-up was more discreet and conventional, and she had the most beautiful large brown eyes and an alluring broad mouth with pale pink lips.

'Yes, we are,' Stephanie said, her face broadening to a smile and her eyes brightening as she looked at me.

'Hi. My name's Jonathan, Jonathan Rose.'

'Oh, Jonathan Rose – how English! Hi, I'm Stephanie and this is Frankie.' Frankie looked a little impatient, nodded her hello but did not offer her hand, as Stephanie had done.

'What brings you here?' I asked as I felt the warmth of her hand, holding it in mine for a moment longer than was necessary.

'Oh, we're going to live here. We're English teachers,' Stephanie answered obligingly. 'At least, I hope we're going to live here, if we ever get to find a job.'

'Which is why we're in a bit of a rush,' Frankie added. 'We're already late for our interview.'

'Sorry, I don't want to make you late, girls.' Saying the

word 'girls' to them was delicious, the carnality it intimated in my saucy mind.

'No, it's just that...' Stephanie sounded apologetic.

'I understand. Maybe we could meet for a drink a little later...'

'Good idea!' Stephanie exclaimed. 'We don't really know anybody here, yet. We only arrived ten days ago.'

'Stephanie,' Frankie implored, her gaze directed to the sunny street.

'Our room's number seventeen.'

'I'll call you.'

'Great.'

Frankie didn't look too impressed at the prospect as she herded Stephanie out of the glass door.

I watched them as they strode down the street, Frankie seemingly remonstrating with her friend, perhaps a little uneasy that Stephanie had given her room number to a complete stranger on the strength of his speaking English.

Just as I was about to leave I saw the chambermaid again, bounding nimbly down the stairs to the reception desk. She caught my eye and smiled.

'*Hasta luego, señor.*'

'*Hasta pronto,*' I responded.

What a city: a city crammed full of desirable women. I followed a delectable thirty-something, dressed in a tight and officious-looking business suit, ogling her curvaceous rump as it wiggled its way to the SUBTE, Buenos Aires' underground, but I lost her somewhere on the crowded platform.

I was certainly an early bird this morning. I was plainly in the middle of the morning rush hour as commuters thronged the platform, including another splendid array of female beauties in their formal short skirts, breasts bulging from diaphanous white blouses, bestockinged legs tottering on four-inch heels, make-up expertly applied to highlight their exquisite facial beauty.

So crowded was the platform that I let the first and then the second train pass, before impatience got the better of me and I crammed myself into the nearest carriage with a Black Hole of Calcutta density.

As the train sped into the city centre more and more people clambered onto it. I was forced into a corner by the door where, unfortunately, a miserable business-suited gent insisted on trying to read his paper, obscuring my view of the heaving, sweating mass of desirous women in the process.

I alighted from the train at Catedral on the Avenida de Mayo and entered the first café I could find.

I was pleased to be sitting down after the SUBTE crush. A big-breasted waitress wearing a short black skirt came to take my order and, as she provocatively leant over the table to wipe it clean, her breasts undulated enticingly before my ardent eyes.

What was this city? Latin America was fabled for magical realism, but this was sexual magical realism. The morning was not an hour old to me and I had already been presented with the glorious rump of a chambermaid, dallied with two English girls – one of whom had clearly offered me the potential of sexual encounter – and I was now being given a delicious view of bouncing breasts. And as I reluctantly tore my stare away and turned to the city streets there was more, as slick city women strode past my window, as pram-pushing mothers ambled, as teenage girls and students dressed casually in jeans and T-shirts flitted by.

The signs were good. The signs were very good.

Everything seemed possible; everything that would normally appear fantastic, seemed potentially plausible.

After my coffee and a couple of the sweet croissants *porteños* call *media lunas*, I strolled down the pedestrianised street of Florida, ogling every woman in sight, following rumps and legs and breasts, undressing women in my mind's eye. I sat in cafés drinking more coffee than was good for me and lusted after the clientele and the waitresses in their skimpy skirts and their high heels, alluringly pushing out their already pert rumps.

An hour later I met Andrea in the Tortoni again, but she couldn't stay long. She was covering for another teacher, as a favour, and she only had an hour.

She looked as beautiful as the first time I saw her. This time she was dressed in a simple white cotton dress, her hair held up in a chignon. The craving I had for her was a hundred times worse when I was actually in her presence.

After we ordered, Andrea fixed me with her dazzling eyes and reached over to place her hand in mine. 'Remember, Jonathan, I promised you. I told you, I can tell a man or a woman who likes those special things.' Her voice was light, jocular.

'It's a little difficult to prove, Andrea, if you only have an hour.'

'Yes, today it is, but not impossible. I can show you. You can prove it for yourself.' I looked at her, a little perplexed. 'Come with me.'

We walked around the streets, the sun beating down, making the city's inhabitants look bothered and a little fractious. Andrea's eyes scoured the streets as diligently as my own had done an hour before.

'It's difficult in the street; let's try here,' she said motioning me into a bookshop. We entered El Ateneo, the most famous bookshop in Buenos Aires. It was a serious bookshop, silent and imposing, with an atmosphere something between a library and a church – a little in that respect like the Tortoni where Andrea had first taken me, and the last possible place I would have thought to go to pick up women.

Andrea left me for a moment and I began to flick inattentively through the pages of a slim Spanish novel. She returned a couple of minutes later and, pulling me by the arm, led me to the back of the shop.

'Look there, Jonathan. I am sure. I watch her. I see how she reads. I see how she moves. I am never wrong. Prove me right, Jonathan, prove me right.' She smiled at me, then kissed me gently on the cheek and disappeared out of the door.

I would have noticed the woman Andrea had pointed to anywhere, she was so beautiful. She wore a decorative white sleeveless top that showed off her lightly tanned arms and shoulders, and tight bottle-green slacks. Her cheekbones were high, her mouth abundant, and her lips rosy. A splay of freckles mottled either side of her nose. Her eyes were hazel, and her dark copper-red hair, tied in a clumsy bun, showed off the slender nape of her neck. She was just my type. An air of sophistication and experience hung around her. I observed her from above the novel I had absent-mindedly plucked from a table and watched as her eyes scanned along the bookshelves.

Andrea had left me with a challenge and, as I looked at the beautiful woman, I wondered how I was going to get anywhere close to meeting it, to proving anything. But sometimes – goodness knows why; I suppose it's what we call luck – things happen for us. Events make our desires possible, an opportunity momentarily presents itself and we would be crazy not to take it. The woman selected two Borges novels in bilingual editions and went up to a young teenage shop assistant who – like me, I had noticed – had been perusing the beautiful woman who now approached him.

'Excuse me. Do you speak English?' she asked.

Oh, even better. She was neither a native speaker of Spanish or English. Certainly European; I suspected French.

'Yes,' the shop assistant lied.

'Which book would you recommend?'

The shop assistant hadn't understood. 'Borges is *fantastico*. You take.'

She tried again. 'No, I want to know which is the best.'

Yes, that was definitely a French accent.

He looked nonplussed. Placing his hand on one of the books, he tried to gently tug it from her grasp.

I felt like some fantastic role was being offered to me. This was truly unbelievable. I walked up to the shop assistant's desk and offered my services to the Frenchwoman. As I was asking if I could help, she stared at me straight in the eye, wantonly almost, her lips creasing into a faint ironic smile.

'I think I have, er, some problem here. Have you read Borges?'

I hadn't. 'Yes, of course.'

'Which book would you recommend? You see, I want to read a little about Argentina, the soul of the place. I would like to know where to start.'

I glimpsed her shoulder. I could see the merest edge of her peach bra-strap peeking from the broader white of her blouse.

'Well, Borges—' I was making it up as I went along. I had discarded the convoluted prose of Borges in English, let alone in Spanish '—is a fascinating read, but I would say his territory is less the city where he lived than the more temporal location of literary fashion.'

Where was all this coming from? I was probably

plagiarising some dour literary account I had pilfered and bowdlerised for an encyclopaedia entry. 'Really, if I were you, if it is Argentina you want to get to know, I would try Sabato. Start with *El Tunnel*.' That was the only book I had read by the man. 'Sabato is quintessentially Argentinian, even *porteño*. He deals with all the essential Argentinian themes: love, betrayal, passion, deceit, cleverness and an obsessiveness that can border on perversion.' I was now plagiarising what Andrea had told me about the tango, the first day I arrived.

She smiled when I concluded my spiel. I was pleased with my little speech. I had sounded – however pretentious – quite erudite.

'Sabato. I have not heard of him.'

What a language French is! What an accent she had, drawing out her sentence to twice the length that it would have taken an English person to say it.

I searched along the shelf and plucked *El Tunnel* from it, and then handed it to her.

She studied the cover of the slim text.

'It's a bilingual edition,' I said.

'Oh, *fantastique*,' she enthused, as she read the blurb in English. 'Thank you very much…'

'Jonathan, Jonathan Rose.'

'Jonathan,' she repeated my name pensively, before turning to the shop assistant who was still gazing at the sexy Frenchwoman. 'I'll take it, please.'

'And Borges?'

'No, no – just Sabato.' She looked into my eyes again and smiled, while the shop assistant took Sabato to the cash till.

'And your name?' I boldly asked.

'Beatrice.'

Beatrice, wonderful! Beatrice taking me out of the inferno

of my sexual hunger to the giddy heights of sexual bliss, or so at least I hoped.

The shop assistant returned with her change and we left the shop together.

Over an *aperitivo*, I got to know a little more about Beatrice. She was here with her husband, who had just landed a job in the newly privatised rail company. He was – a necessarily unnecessary piece of information to add – away for a couple of days on business in one of the northern provinces. Beatrice was an academic by trade, but had given up her post to come to Argentina with her husband.

She talked brightly and asked me a lot of questions about myself. I gave her basic scant details, although I embroidered my journalistic experience, talking vaguely about my column in a national paper in England. I said I was on sabbatical here visiting friends, trying to write something.

Beatrice was of that generation who were still impressed by bookish men, by writers. I could see I was scoring points with her. We talked about books I hadn't read. I pontificated on literary theories I barely understood, on ideas I had only half-learnt, regurgitating what I could dredge up from memory from my days as the literary sub-editor of a dismal exam crammer I worked on several years ago.

I ordered a bottle of wine and, over lunch, we chatted some more. I seemed to be on automatic, because my mind was not engaged on the words that emanated from my mouth. I was thinking of Beatrice's firm breasts, of her fabulously small but rotund bottom, of placing my aching cock between those rosy lips and watching her fellate me.

'You must read Cortazar, a fascinating writer,' I babbled, all the time thinking of getting my tongue between the lips of her quim...

'Really?'

'Oh, yes. He lived in Paris, you know, but he is also very much an Argentinian writer, universal in theme, but very underestimated...'

...and then letting her sink her quim onto my cock and ride me while I pinched her firm breasts...

Beatrice listened to me intently as I spoke about Cortazar, occasionally sipping on her wine, her chin resting on her interlocked fingers. I focused on the apex of the triangle her arms made, her elbows resting on the table; that glorious mouth showing her beautiful small teeth, the tiniest of tantalising gaps between the front two that she would occasionally press her tongue against.

As we were finishing our steaks, Beatrice again took up the theme of writing.

'So, Jonathan, what exactly do you want to write?'

'A novel, perhaps.'

'Oh, really?' Beatrice was fascinated, turned on by the rubbish that spewed from my mouth. 'And what do you want to write about?' Still that fantastic French accent, words elongating in her mouth as my prick lengthened under the table.

'Something beautiful.' I audaciously placed my hand on hers, brushing her knuckles lightly with my fingertips.

'Ah, *oui*.'

'But it's hard.'

'Why is it so hard to write about the beauty?' She took an encouragingly long gulp of her wine. I refilled her glass.

'Because it's hard to think of anything as beautiful on paper as this afternoon has been in reality. Good food, wonderful wine, and a beautiful woman to share it with.' I was self-ironising, jokey, but there was a hefty element of truth in what I said. What could be more beautiful than the things I had mentioned, with all that sexual promise hanging in the air?

'You're a smooth talker, Jonathan,' Beatrice said, laughing.

'No, I mean it.' I squeezed her hand.

'And how would you like this wonderful afternoon to end?' she asked, tantalisingly.

'With you as my *postre*.'

She laughed.

We took a taxi back to my hotel. We barely spoke, but we entwined fingers, my imagination working overtime at the delights that seemed to be in store for me, but still not wanting to tempt fate by taking too much for granted. *Postre*! Beatrice was to be my dessert. And what if Andrea was right? What could be more delicious than spanking her firm buttocks with my hand?

I wanted the taxi to go faster. The anticipation was agonising. I looked at the creases her tight pants made around her quim as she sat, her leg teasingly touching mine. I longed for my bedroom and the closed door, longed to bury my mouth in her juicy sex.

At last we were here. I tipped the driver generously, not wanting to wait for change. I took her by the hand and together we climbed the stairs, passing the chambermaid on the way. She looked Beatrice up and down and then half-smiled at me. And then we were there in my room.

Now I could take my time. The urgency was over. I wanted to savour everything, and now the anticipation was bearable because she was in my room.

As soon as I closed the door Beatrice pressed her body against me, her mouth firm on mine, her tongue seeking, probing my lips, my eager mouth awaiting hers.

I pulled her further up towards me, buried my tongue deep inside her parted lips, and grasped her *derrière* in my greedy hands. She kissed me avidly, snaking her tongue around my mouth, then dragging it slowly along my teeth.

I pulled away from her. I did not want a quickie. I did not want this moment to be over so soon and then for Beatrice to disappear into the anonymous streets of Buenos Aires.

'A glass of wine?'

'Oh, yes.' She seemed to understand my hesitation, to share my feeling that an afternoon of carnal pleasure stretching before us should not be rushed.

I went into the tiny kitchenette, retrieved an already open bottle of red wine and two glasses and sat down beside her on the sofa. I filled a glass and passed it to her. Silently she took a sip, and sat quietly as I stroked her tanned shoulder.

Slowly, gently at first, I pulled down the halter-straps of her white blouse, exposing the peach bra. She smiled at me, her hand reaching up to stroke the side of my face, as I freed her firm breasts from the lacy cups and caressed them. I took her glass and placed it with mine on the side table, and then dipped my head and nibbled her already erect nipples.

How fantastic it was! I barely knew this glorious example of womanhood. A light lunch, a little literary banter, and there I was sucking on the pertest of French breasts, Beatrice gasping above me as only French women can gasp.

I retrieved my glass of wine and dribbled a little onto her left nipple and watched the rivulets of ruddy liquid trickle down and disappear from sight beneath the underswell of her mouthwatering breast. She shivered and giggled a little nervously.

I sucked the nipple into my mouth and chewed it lightly, tasting the rich tincture coating her soft and creamy flesh. She stroked my head languidly as I suckled like a baby. I caressed her free breast, rolled the nipple between thumb and forefinger, and was rewarded as she gently shivered again.

'Ah, *oui… oui*,' she moaned as she cupped and lifted her breast for me to feed all the more easily from it. I could feel the passion pounding in her chest. My cock strained uncomfortably inside my trousers for release.

So far I had been gentle, but as she fed more of her pliable flesh into my mouth I couldn't resist a firm nip on the swollen pink teat. She squealed from the shock and inhaled sharply. She arched her back and squashed her flesh harder against my face.

How fantastic! Andrea had been right. She could only be David's wife; both of them sharing an uncanny knack of being able to recognise those amenable to their own particular sexual practices and pleasures.

I rolled my tongue over the erect nipple, soothing the stinging sensation I had caused by my bite, before clamping it firmly between my teeth once again. This time I held it captive for much longer, long enough for me to squint up and relish the confusion of bliss and discomfort on her lovely face.

I squeezed a hand between her thighs and felt the outline of her humid quim through the flimsy green material. She softly moaned her encouragement. I could wait no longer. I wanted to see how far she would go – how far I could take her. Still fully clothed, I lifted her up and got her to kneel on the sofa so her bottom faced me. I slipped my hands around her trim waist and blindly unbuckled her suede belt, unfastened her trousers, and then tugged them down to expose a pair of peach-coloured panties that protectively hugged the firm cheeks of her bottom.

I pulled the delicate underwear aside and licked her white buttocks with long broad sweeping strokes, my tongue flattening on the pliable curves of her rump. Then, crouching lower, I pushed my tongue between her wet labia.

She murmured and ground her hips as my tongue flicked

79

in and out of her tight quim. Her murmurs grew louder as I found and stimulated her clitoris. I could feel her body tensing; an orgasm approaching. This was too quick. I wanted her aroused and I wanted her to stay aroused for as long as possible. I pulled away, leaving her panting heavily on the sofa. The belt was on the floor where it had been discarded. She looked over her shoulder dreamily as I picked it up.

'Oh no, Jonathan…' she protested weakly in her seductive Gallic accent.

I ignored her protestation – as I knew she wanted me to ignore it – and cupped her moist sex in my palm. My fingertips spread out through her pubic hair and I levered her further up, so her pert rump perched tantalisingly before my lascivious eyes. Beatrice's mouth was agape as she contemplated what I was about to do.

I stepped back and coiled the buckled end of the belt around my fist. Beatrice watched me, her lips parted slightly and her eyes bright. Then, as I slowly lifted my arm, she buried her face in the back of the sofa and held her breath. She waited… and then the belt swept down through the warm still air and bit into her raised buttocks. She bucked and stuffed one hand into her mouth to muffle the yelp she couldn't suppress.

'No, Jonathan,' she protested again. 'It hurts too much.'

But I knew she wanted the punishment, her weak supplication only intensifying her pleasure.

Before thrashing her again I admired my handiwork. I could see the clear outline of the belt on her tender flesh. I raised my arm and struck again. My accuracy was surprisingly good, and the fresh angry stripe overlaid that which I had already made. Another shiver passed through the beautiful female. She reached for her bottom to soothe the livid pain, but I pushed her limp hand aside and thrashed her again and again. The excitement was immense as I purveyed the delectable sight of her reddened rump, and watched each jerk of her hips as the belt struck.

'You wanted *postre*,' I panted, once I was exhausted and had dropped the belt to the floor.

'Yes… *oui*.' Her voice was weak. '*Oui… oui…*'

'Turn round,' I instructed hoarsely, and manoeuvred her until she was sitting as I wanted her, perched on the front edge of the sofa. Her lovely face winced at the discomfort in her bottom. 'Now, don't move.' I didn't expect any form of rebellion – I knew she was enjoying the submissive role just as much as I was enjoying the dominant role – but I wanted to maintain a firm control over her.

In my eagerness, and somewhat betraying my pretence of composure, I tugged and fumbled with my clothes. The recalcitrant buttons of my shirt and trousers did everything to thwart me, and my socks caused me to stumble and hop in a most undignified manner. It was still only mere seconds, however, before I stood naked in front of her, my cock pulsing like a living creature just inches from her spellbound face.

'Suck me,' I croaked, my voice doing its own bit to highlight my growing lack of control. Without hesitation she rocked forward and swallowed me completely. I stared down at her gently bobbing head and shuddered with sheer delight. Her hands found my buttocks and pulled my groin tighter to her face as one finger burrowed between them and worried my anus. My lower-belly rested against her hot forehead and her mouth threatened to bring me to orgasm far too quickly.

Trying to distract myself from her magical attentions – just a little – I loosened the clips that held her hair and watched a stream of copper-red cascade down to her shoulders. It shimmered as it settled, and then swayed and caressed her skin as her head moved against me.

Despite my best efforts at self-denial my orgasm approached relentlessly. I felt my balls tighten and the simmerings of climactic release bubbling in the pit of my stomach and at the base of my cock. I had to deny myself the delights of her clever tongue and lips; I didn't want to come before I had fucked her. I spread her out before me. Her head lolled back over the arm of the sofa and her hair swayed just above the floor. Her vulnerable throat looked good enough to eat. She had one foot on the floor, and I lifted her other and draped it over the back of the sofa. A cushion was quickly pushed under her bottom, causing a sharp intake of breath as the material agitated her striped skin, and her hips were lifted in readiness.

I knelt between her spread thighs, took my weight on my arms, and entered her smoothly. She sighed in unison with the sinking of my hips to meet hers.

'Ah, *oui*. Ahhhh...'

She came instantly with a deliciously feminine shudder, and she instinctively reached up and twisted her fingers in my hair.

'Ahhhh...' she sighed again and slumped into the sofa, her breasts gently rising and falling as she relaxed and her breathing slowed.

But I still hadn't come. I flipped her over like a doll and pulled her knees to the floor. I suddenly wanted to sample something I never sampled before. Beatrice looked over her shoulder at me. Seeming to anticipate my requirements, her knees shuffled a little further apart. I nudged my helmet between her buttocks and pressed it against her rear entrance. I watched for a reaction, and saw a faint twinkle in her eyes and a little flickering smile of acquiescence. I grabbed both her wrists and held them together behind her back, and once I knew she was ready, I eased my cock into her bottom with one long slow movement. She was so tight! It was glorious! Her back arched and she let out a guttural groan of ecstasy.

What a sight Beatrice was; her slender back and shoulders glossed with perspiration. I simply couldn't contain myself any longer. As soon as my groin came to rest against her scorched buttocks and I was fully embedded, I came.

As I was seeing Beatrice to a taxi outside the *hospedaje* – with the rather palatable promise that she would return later that night, once her husband had phoned – I saw the chambermaid again. She held a hand to her mouth, blushed, stifled a giggle, and then ran away.

Chapter Five

Frankie had called off, excusing herself with a headache, so I was left alone with the charming Stephanie, who had jumped at my invitation to go out to dinner. I took her to a *parrilla* close to the *hospedaje* and got her life story: a private school education in the Cotswolds, a couple of years teaching in London, and then this, her great adventure, coming to Argentina. She wanted to travel. She wanted excitement.

'What kind of excitement?' I asked.

'Oh, all kinds of excitement,' she said, smiling her broad smile, her wide mouth opening to reveal white even teeth.

As she demurely nibbled on her steak, she confided in me about her relationship with her flatmate. 'Frankie is my best friend and everything, but she can be a little domineering sometimes.' Stephanie leant towards me conspiratorially. 'She's a bit bossy.'

'I suppose it's a little claustrophobic, you and her having to rely on each other so much.'

'Claustrophobic is exactly the word. She doesn't seem to care. She seems quite happy just to stick with me, but I like to meet people – new people, different people.'

My eyes strayed to her fully developed chest. She looked at me expectantly as if I were exactly the type of new person she wished to encounter.

'Where did you meet her?'

'Oh, we met at university. We shared a flat together for a year. I was studying to be a primary school teacher, and Frankie was reading social anthropology. She's very different from me, I mean temperamentally. I'm much more easy-going. Maybe it's the Celtic thing: she's a quarter Scottish. She has some very strident opinions. She always has to be right about everything.'

'Do you argue very much?' I was angling.

'Yes, all the time. Sometimes it's really bad – or it has been, this last week or so.' Stephanie sighed then lightly shrugged her shoulders.

'What do you argue about?'

'Oh, everything. She thinks I'm a bit dippy, you know – that I need protecting because I haven't had her experience of the world. Just because she lived in South America for a year before she went to university. Her attitude can be very annoying. Maybe she is right a lot of the time, and maybe I haven't travelled as much as she has and seen as many things, but that doesn't mean she knows everything, or that what I say isn't valid.'

I nodded in rhythm to the cadences of her speech, as Stephanie unburdened herself in full flow.

'You know what the real difference is between us? I really want to learn about life and people and everything and she thinks that she's already done the lot. She's only twenty-two. I mean, she's just a year older than me and, to hear her speak, you'd think she was as old as Methuselah.' Stephanie had become increasingly animated the longer she spoke, her voice perceptibly rising as she considered her unjust treatment at the hands of her ill-tempered friend.

I liked the plain silk lilac blouse she wore. I could see her nipples jutting out from the soft fabric. She wasn't wearing a bra. I glanced at the triangle of her upper chest, her shirt unbuttoned to just below the top of her cleavage. Stephanie was a delightfully naïve girl, extremely trusting, who just happened to have an incredible body, with the pertest, most mouthwatering chest you could ever wish to

85

see.

'You never argue about boyfriends?' Here I thought I might get onto more profitable territory.

She looked at me, showing mild suspicion. 'No, not really. Not so far, anyway. Until recently I was going steady with Gregory, who was studying mechanical engineering. But Frankie never really liked him. She never said as much until we split up, that is, but it wasn't so difficult to guess. A woman can tell these things,' she said knowingly, but so over-emphatically that it betrayed a certain innocence. 'We only became real friends after I stopped seeing Greg.'

'Why didn't Frankie like him?'

'Frankie never seemed to like any of the boys that I liked. She'd always put them down, saying how immature they were. What she really meant, I suppose, is how immature I was for liking them in the first place.'

'And what about Frankie?' I asked. 'Does she have a boyfriend?'

'Oh no. Frankie never goes steady. It's just not what she does. She has some strange friends, though, really spooky! Sometimes she'll just disappear for days and days. When she comes back she won't tell me anything, but she looks terrible.' Again the conspiratorial glance. 'I think she takes drugs.'

Stephanie drank her wine like water, knocking her head back, draining the last drops from her glass. She was a wonderful temptation, the trustfulness and candour of the girl mixed with the provocative sexiness of her body, her ample breasts, her accommodating mouth, her slender legs leading to full and curvaceous hips.

'You know, I was beginning to think that this whole trip was a mistake. It's so refreshing to talk to somebody else, somebody like you.'

With a touching guilelessness she had laid her hand on

86

mine as I ordered another bottle of wine. Her eyes beamed tenderly, telling me she wanted me, or at least some kind of experience with me: the type of adventure she had forced to the edges of her consciousness. I suspected that it was precisely this department of her sexual self-knowledge where she was mostly charmingly deficient.

A little drunk now, she began to flirt more blatantly, the alcohol emboldening her, making her lose her initial coyness. She smiled, stroking my forearm, then showered me with compliments about how understanding I was, how good-looking: really dishy, she said.

I suppose to Stephanie I was a man of the world: a bachelor who wore expensive polo shirts and linen trousers, who must have lots of beautiful women back home, a sophisticated type of which she had not apparently met many of in London. She was dreaming me, inventing me, and I let her harbour her newly found illusions. I was not about to tell her of my sorry years of professional and personal failure. I would pretend to be exactly who she thought I was.

She asked me if I wanted a *postre*. How could I think of that word without remembering Beatrice; without feeling her body, without smelling her scent, without visualising the string of red welts I had deposited on her bottom? I wasn't interested in *postre*. I was interested in all the interesting things I could do with Stephanie's body and how I could discipline her to obey my every command.

But not tonight. I was still expecting Beatrice to return. There would be another night for Stephanie – maybe many nights. I would aim to give her exactly the education I thought she needed.

After she finished the last dregs of the fruity red wine, I collected the bill, got complimented on being a real old-fashioned gent, and walked her back to the *hospedaje*. She

87

didn't invite me in for coffee, but hinted that she would be interested in coming back to my room. I excused myself by saying that I had an early start and, without making any fixed arrangement, told her I would see her soon.

'Oh, I do hope so,' she said, before leaning close, a little unsteadily, and pecking me on the cheek.

Beatrice came an hour later, dressed in an elegant black strapless evening gown and, as I was soon to discover, black stockings and suspenders and… no panties.

Within seconds of her entering the room, my fingers entered her. I pushed her back against the door the moment it closed. Her head rested against my chest as I frigged her, and she gasped with absolute pleasure. Within seconds her knees weakened and she crumpled against me as an orgasm washed through her. It was incredibly exciting, hearing the occasional guest pass only inches from us in the corridor outside. I'm sure the relative danger had fueled Beatrice's passion to such a pitch.

I carried her to the bed and sat her down, undressed myself, and then stood quietly in the darkness listening to her sucking avidly on my erection. I enjoyed this for long minutes, and then whispered that she should undress too. We slipped between the cool crisp sheets and made love – slowly and passionately.

'You remind me of somebody,' Beatrice cooed as she cuddled into me, her cheek on my chest, the sweet scent of her hair filling my nostrils. Her fingers idly fiddled with my limp penis.

'Really?' I said distractedly as I ran my fingertips up and down her slender neck. 'Tell me.'

'It's a long story.'

'I told you, I'm interested in stories. Who do I remind

you of?'

'You remind me of the first man who really, really taught me the pleasure of discipline.'

'Tell me,' I repeated.

'Well, you did say that you wanted to write about something beautiful. He was beautiful, it was beautiful... *magnifique*. I have tried to write about it myself, but somehow the words are never good enough. I spoil the memory with my useless words, confine the moment, reduce it, imprison its transient beauty. Words are no good for my memory of this man.'

'Let me try to write the story for you.' I had no intention of writing anything. I was merely curious to hear Beatrice, with her fantastic French accent, describe her novel sexual experiences.

'It would make a good story, but sadly not for me. My memory is too precious for that, but I would like you to hear.'

'But if you tell me, you have to tell me everything – all the details.'

'Well, you need the background, first.'

'Go ahead.'

'Okay. My story starts when I was a teenager. I was a very curious girl. I wanted to know what made my parents cry out in the middle of the night, that noise they made which sounded so painful but which seemed to bring them so much pleasure. I would often listen to them. It was impossible not to listen to them, to hear the lash of leather on skin, the satisfied squeal of pleasure piercing the silence of the night.

'I lost my virginity when I was sixteen. It wasn't a good experience or a bad experience. It felt like nothing. A boy from my class who liked me took me down to the river. Neither of us really knew what to do. We didn't even take

89

off our clothes. It lasted a minute, not long enough for me to get much further than the initial pain, that's all. Within seconds he had dribbled inside me. What happened didn't seem to have anything to do with the noises I heard coming from my parents' bedroom.'

'And this man?'

'Wait, before the man, there is one more experience I must tell you about.' Beatrice hesitated a moment, as if searching for the right word, the perfect *bon mot*. 'It happened in my school. I was seventeen, studying to go to university. Two boys were standing by their lockers. Two pathetic boys: one quite strong and muscular with long blond hair, and the other a little shorter, darker. They were my age but immature, both virgins, but they behaved as if they knew everything.

'I was very tired of Albert and Jean, tired of them always saying things to me, telling me how fantastic their penises were. I thought I would try to shame them. I asked them why they talked like they did when they had never fucked a girl in their lives. Albert blushed but Jean laughed at me, trying to be even more macho, telling me that he had fucked lots of girls, much prettier and older girls than me.

'"So you wouldn't like to fuck me, then," I asked. I didn't want to fuck them – not then, not at that stage. We were playing a game, a silly game. I was angry with them. In my childish way, I wanted to humiliate them, to show these two little virgins how sad they were when they talked about women in that way.

'"Any time you want me, I'll fuck you." Jean turned around to Albert, a big smile on his face, his chest pushed out with pride. He thought that the riposte was enough, that the incident was over and the cheeky, insolent girl would go away.

'"You, fuck me?" I said. "You wouldn't know how!"

90

'"You're talking rubbish, little girl," he said, "*Merde*!" he exclaimed. I could see that my outburst had made Jean angry; his face was flushed red.

'"Come on then, take me!" Both boys looked at me as if I were stupid. I was – how do you say in English? – daring them. No – how do you say? – calling their...'

'Bluff,' I offered.

'Yes, bluff, that's the word. "Come on then, take me," I said again.

'"Don't be so stupid! Where can we do it? We can't do it in school."

'"Chicken, you see? You're both cowards. You talk with your mouth, but you don't know what to do with your little virgin penises. Run home to your *mamans*."

'Jean was getting more and more furious with me because he was frightened that I was making him look a fool in front of his friend. "You're so stupid. I don't know whether I want to screw such a stupid little girl."

'"Then stop acting like a big man, when you are a little virgin boy. If you wanted to have me, you would find a way. You're just too scared." I looked at them contemptuously. I thought I had won. I liked the feeling of power over them, watching them blush. I wanted to press home my advantage. "If you were a man, we could go there," I said, pointing to the boys' toilet. "Classes have started and nobody will find us."

'"And what if someone comes, bird-brain?" Jean said.

'"See, you're chicken. Chicken!" I began to mock him relentlessly.

'"Okay then, little girl, let's go," he said, pushing my shoulder.

'I don't think he expected me to move. He was daring me, a kind of counter-bluff, a way of hiding his embarrassment, digging himself out of the hole that he had

91

found himself in. I was a proud girl. I could not refuse. I could not back down, not after everything I had said. A lump came to my throat. He could see me hesitating.

'"Who is chicken now?" he teased, knowing that – how do you say? – the tables were turning.

'I looked at his stupid smug face. I had to do it. I walked straight inside the toilet, my head held high, followed by the astonished boys.'

'What were you wearing?' I asked, wanting to try to visualise the teenage Beatrice leading the two virgin boys into the toilet.

'I had a short pinafore dress, little ankle socks – oh, yes, and my hair was very, very long. I would never cut it. In those days it reached all the way down to my waist, but that day I think it was tied up in a chignon.' Beatrice paused for a moment and kissed my chest. 'Well, we entered the toilet and none of us really knew what to do. I think all three of us were terrified by this stupid game of dare.

'I can remember the strong odour of detergent and the slightest whiff of urine coming from the aluminium trough. I caught my reflection in the long mirror above the wash-basins. The two boys were staring at me from a couple of metres away, their faces bright red under the glare of the neon light.

'We seemed to stand there for an eternity. Jean though, smirked a little, seeing how nervous I was now inside the toilet. I think he expected me to run for the door at any moment. It made me angry; my contempt for that smirk emboldened me.

'"Show me your cocks," I said, mustering as much defiance as I could, thinking that me being so, so...'

'Brazen?' I offered.

'*Oui*, brazen, that they would run away and I could laugh. I would have shut them up for good.

'There was this awesome mingling of fear and excitement. I wanted to run outside, to be free from the game, to be normal again, but also somewhere inside me my curiosity would not rest. I could feel myself getting wet in my panties.'

'Weren't they excited?' Which was how I was beginning to feel, listening to Beatrice's story.

'Oh yes, I'm sure, but remember they were both virgins, and then there was the door. Maybe somebody might come in. They were teenage boys, and the thing that teenage boys fear most is losing face. This takes over everything, even their desire for sex.

'They couldn't refuse to do what I said, not after the challenging look I gave them. If they had run away, they knew that I would have known their secret. I think that it was especially bad for Jean. How could he tell Albert about all the screwing he had done if a girl like me had made him run away?

'After a lot more hesitation they eventually unzipped themselves and pulled out their cocks: Jean first, Albert following. They weren't erect, they were soft and limp. The boy before who had taken my virginity had let me touch him, but that was all. I was amazed at the sight of Albert and Jean's little cocks.

'I didn't lose all my fear, but it subsided – two teenagers with limp pricks do not seem so frightening. They looked a little pathetic, suddenly so shy and embarrassed. So this was really what all that male bravado had been about, a few inches of soft flesh, I thought to myself.'

'I was curious to look at their cocks. It is a strange sight for a young lady to look at males for the first time. I wanted to examine them, to see what they felt like.

'I moved closer. First I took Albert's cock, maybe a little to annoy Jean, the more arrogant one. I stroked it, felt how

93

hot it was between my fingers. Then I took Jean's cock with my other hand and began stroking both together. I was thrilled when I felt them start growing and stiffening in my hand.

'I do not know where the idea came from. I suppose I just wanted to look at them more closely. I kneeled down and gazed at their lengthening cocks, saw how their semen made them shine under the neon light of the toilet. I looked at Albert's first. It pulsed in my hand. Suddenly, I had a desire to take it in my mouth. I pulled back his hood and licked the shiny head.

'I looked at both boys' faces. They couldn't believe what I was doing to them. I am sure in the loneliness of their room they had dreamt about such a thing, but to have it happen to them then for the first time when they should have been studying geography, when nothing very exciting at all should have been happening, must have amazed them. I felt Albert harden in my mouth. His cock had been very little, which is why maybe the thought of kissing it had not been so frightening, but when he got his erection it was so much bigger.

'At first I was a little scared. I thought that he might suffocate me, but my fear faded as I tasted it. For me it was like losing my virginity all over again, to have a penis in my mouth for the first time. And it was better, much more exciting. I peered up and could see Albert's face a little twisted, and then he started moaning.

'I looked at Jean, his prick was quite big too in its erect state. I told you, I was a curious girl. I wanted to see if both tasted the same, so I let go of Albert's and pulled Jean's into my mouth, at the same time sliding my finger up and down Albert's. I thought he was going to come, so I pulled my hand away. It bounced before me, his erection making it spring up again.

'I nibbled at the end of Jean's cock and then, curious again and no longer frightened, took as much of it in my mouth as I could until it touched my throat. Jean put his hands on the back of my head and moved me back and forward. The excitement was making me *very* wet too.

'I was frightened that they would come, and I didn't want either of them to come without fucking me properly. I was enjoying the danger now. So that neither of them ejaculated, I took it in turns, sucking on Albert and then sucking on Jean, and when I thought that they were getting too excited, I would slide off one and suck the other.

'I don't know how long this must have lasted. Time seemed to have stopped for us. Eventually I could not stand it any longer. I was *so* excited by what I was doing, and by them watching me, as I knelt down before them in the toilet. I wanted them to see me, to see everything.

'Just then we heard some footsteps in the corridor outside and we began to panic. My heart beat so fast. The boys, in their fear, began to lose their erections. It was then that Antoine walked in. My heart sank in fear. Antoine was the school bully. Everybody was frightened of him, even some of the teachers. He was a big strong boy with rock-hard muscles, cropped hair, and the cruellest eyes I have ever seen on a human being.

'When he saw what was happening, I saw his face broaden into a big, evil grin. "Ah, what have we here? Little Beatrice, learning to suck cocks. You're a very bad girl," he said, reaching his hand down to stroke the blushing cheek of my face as the other two moved out of his way.

'I had never been so terrified in my life as I was at that moment. I had seen Antoine in action, beating up boys. I knew how strong he was. I knew how cruel.

'He seemed to spend an age just looking at me, peering into my eyes, obviously wondering what pleasure he could have at my expense.

"'Let's have some fun, Beatrice. Let's play a little game."
He turned to the two chastened teenagers. "Tie her up," he
said to them. I think they were as unsure as I was. They
were rooted to the spot, their limp cocks looking very sad.
"Tie her up, there," he repeated more harshly, pointing at
the metal frame of a cubicle door.

'Frightened though I was, I could have pushed past him.
I could have screamed until someone came – but part of
me did not want to resist. Part of me longed for his cruel
treatment. I told you, I was a curious girl.

'Antoine was becoming increasingly frustrated with the
other two, who hovered uncertainly. "Take her!" he growled
menacingly. Both of them took my arms and, removing their
ties, fastened them around my wrists as Antoine supervised
them. "Tighter!" he bellowed at them. I felt the knot of
each tie pulled tight around my skin.

'Antoine went into one of the adjacent cubicles and
climbed on top of the metal frame. There was at least a
metre between the top of the door and the ceiling. "Lift her
up." The two boys, their clumsy hands grabbing me by the
thighs, lifted me up towards Antoine, who secured my
wrists around the frame, until I dangled below. He climbed
down and I was left with my back to the three of them,
staring at the grey walls and the grey pipes inside the
cubicle.'

'The pain in my arms, in my wrists, and my shoulders,
was intense. I felt Antoine's rough hands on my body, lifting
up the pinafore dress, grasping my buttocks and then
tugging down my panties, exposing my bottom to the chill
of the toilet. Antoine hummed to himself as he inspected
my body. The tip of a finger began to slide up and down
my moist pussy lips. "See, the girl likes it. See how wet
she is," I heard him say to the other two.

'I was frightened and humiliated but, underneath both sensations, Antoine was right. I was excited, very excited at the idea of submitting to the will of this bully, to have these three boys see my most intimate places, and to feel that there was nothing that I could do to protect myself. The tickling sensation between my legs gathered intensity. That rude finger was terribly tantalising, brushing against my sex so relentlessly, awakening an itch that I could not soothe. I tried to wriggle down onto it, but it was impossible. Antoine knew exactly what he was doing; knew what sweet agony he was causing me. I clenched my teeth and tried to think of something else, but it was impossible. His finger moved so cleverly on me. The lightness of his touch was excruciating, paradoxically inflicting more pain than I had ever felt in my life. I desperately wanted him to stop, wanted not to be hanging there, but somewhere in my consciousness there was a sharp desire to feel this agony, to understand something of the limits of pain.

'The tickling went on and on, his finger lightly brushing against me. Albert and Jean had been commanded to hold my legs so that there was absolutely no relief I could get from this cruellest of attentions.

'"Stop, please stop," I begged, realising how stupid I was to plead with him, that my supplication would only encourage him to continue. I tried to propel my mind to a place where my body would not feel this tremendous pleasure, like some unquenchable thirst.

'It was a relief to me when he grew bored with his torturous game and began to smack me on my naked bottom. Each stroke from his hand was a salve, a balm to my soul, to feel the hard precision of his palm on my flesh. It was an exact pain. It was satisfying, distracting from the aftermath of my tingling sex.

'I was wet, very wet, invigorated by my humiliation,

exhilarated by my exhibitionism, my bottom being flogged for the delectation of these teenagers. As Antoine continued to spank me, I heard him mutter something to Jean, who crept out of the toilet, to return a moment later. I felt both of my ankles being held firmly, and then something cold and metallic soothing my stinging flesh.

'"Oh, we are going to have some fun now, Beatrice," Antoine said as I shuddered with pleasure at the cooling salve of the metal. He would smack me hard and then replace the pain with the ice-cool of the metal. I was almost delirious – with what? With pain? With pleasure? I no longer knew. My arms ached horribly. My bottom stung. The psychological torture of humiliation and submission made my clitoris throb.

And then I felt the cold metal on my labia.

"What you can do with a bicycle pump!" Antoine burst into a laugh.'

'I don't remind you of Antoine, do I?' I asked, a little perturbed, wondering if it was the school bully that she had recalled after our bout of lovemaking.

'No, not at all.' She smiled at me.

'Anyway, back to the story.' I was enjoying the tale enormously.

'Yes… ah, yes. I could feel the metal pushing hard on my pussy-lips, searching for the opening. I wanted to scream, so intense was the sensation. It filled me, inching further and further inside me. I could no longer distinguish between hot and cold. Both extremes seemed to merge to one overwhelming sensation. It was sending me to orgasm, but Antoine knew what he was doing. He knew that he had complete control over me – even my orgasm. If I was going to come, it would be when he decided.

'The metal pump slid in and out of me. Antoine alternated between rapid thrusts and, when he thought I was becoming too excited, slow pushes.

'Finally, and with Antoine's consent, I came, my whole body shuddering with pleasure as I hung there. I was unable to resist – even if I wanted to – so bound was I by the wrists, my ankles gripped by the other two, my sex impaled on the pump.

'Then, as my pleasure passed, Antoine climbed up and freed my wrists. "Hold her!" he commanded the other boys, who held me so I would not fall. Antoine jumped down and stood before me. "Make her kneel!"

'I was lowered to my knees while Antoine unzipped his flies and pulled out his enormous penis. Administering the punishment had obviously aroused him; his cock was very erect.

'"Now suck me, Beatrice," he ordered.

'I did as I was told. It seemed my willingness to submit to Antoine had encouraged the other two. No longer did they seem fearful of Antoine or shy with me. They touched my bottom and breasts. One of them knelt behind me, and a finger pressed between my sore buttocks and against my little opening. Two other fingers slid into my wet pussy.

'Hands were all over me; on my face, my breasts, my bottom. A penis rubbed in my hair and another pushed between my thighs against my pussy as I closed my eyes and sucked Antoine as well as I could. We were all groaning and my lips slurped on the big cock. Whoever was behind me stabbed his hips and the tip of his cock lodged just inside me. I could not help but groan with delight. But none of us could last long; we were all too inexperienced.

'Antoine ejaculated in my mouth. I felt his salty seed slide down my throat. It was delicious. I wanted more. I could feel myself coming again as the cock beneath my dress spurted too. Most of it coated my pubic hair and thighs. Then, as I flopped against Antoine's sturdy legs my limp hand was lifted and wrapped around the last cock. I heard another grunt and more sperm splattered through my fingers and onto the tiled floor.

'And that was it. I heard them adjusting their clothing and then they left me alone on the floor. The door slammed and their mocking laughter receded down the echoing corridor.'

I looked at Beatrice, impressed by the skill with which she had told her story. 'A good tale, Beatrice.'

She smiled up at me. 'I am glad you enjoyed it.'

'But you still haven't told me anything about the man you said I reminded you of.'

'No, I haven't finished yet. Gerard was his name.'

'What was so special about him, and what's the connection between him and me?'

'Before I get to Gerard I have to go back to those three. They could have had me often – very often – if they had not been so stupid, because I had enjoyed the experience very much. But they could not keep their mouths closed, especially Antoine. He told the whole school about me, boasting about what a big man he was.

'It made my life a misery, a nightmare. I tried to deny everything, but nobody would believe me. I could not walk down a corridor without somebody shouting out something about me, about what I'd done, shouting their filthy abuse at me, calling me a slut. I was the school whore. I am sure that even the teachers got to know about it, and I am sure they believed everything they heard about me, too.

'It was intolerable. It was hell. Sartre said that hell was other people. I knew what that meant at seventeen. I lived it for five months until my final exams when I could leave that hellish place, when I could be known as somebody else other than the girl who let boys take her into the school toilets.

'As I said, when the experience took place, I had taken great pleasure in it. I had enjoyed being submissive. I had enjoyed my humiliation. But for the protection of my sanity, I had to dismiss all positive thoughts of the encounter. I could not separate the pleasure of being dominated from the aftermath of cruel gossip. I had to repress my natural sexual instinct, to deny the sharp sensation of sexual ecstasy I had felt while dangling from the doorframe, or I could not be the total victim of their perverse desires, and at that time I needed to believe I was a victim.

'I became very shy, very withdrawn. From being a bright, lively and fun-loving teenager, I became introverted, suspicious of everyone. Even though nobody knew me in Paris when I went to the Sorbonne, I suspected that somebody, somehow, knew what I had done, or that they would soon find out. I found it difficult to be friendly with anyone. If any boys came close, I would brush them off. And I could not relate to other girls about anything.

'The only thing that I could find refuge in were books, in poetry and literature. Mallarmé and Rimbaud, Proust and Flaubert became my soulmates. I was greedy for words. I devoured books, lived for them, hid myself away from all my shame and regret by burying myself between their pages. I told myself that I would dedicate myself to literature and that I would not let another man get close to me. But deep inside I was desperately unhappy. I had lost so much. Those boys had betrayed me in the worst possible way, and sometimes I would grow nostalgic for the innocent youth that I had been before, that I could never be again.'

'This is, I suppose, where Gerard comes in?' I asked.

'Yes. Gerard was a lecturer in literature. He was the opposite of everything that those boys were. He was kind and gentle, affectionate, sophisticated, intelligent, perceptive – and he was also sixty-three.'

101

'Sixty-three!' I repeated, surprised.

'Yes, but he was still a virile man. He was still very handsome, very distinguished. But it was not his looks. His looks were not important. He was, in the old-fashioned sense of the phrase, a man of letters. Before I had ever slept with him, I was in love with him, because this magician of words had seduced me. Listening to his lectures, listening to him speak intelligently about writing, about life, about everything, he seduced me – at least spiritually – without him even knowing.

'The wonderful thing about Gerard was that he never spoke down to you; he never patronised you. He was always interested in other people's opinions, always listened to what you had to say, no matter how naïve it may have seemed. His hand would reach up to his temples and sweep through his thick white hair, and slowly, he would show you – show you, not tell you – where you were mistaken, how there were other ways of seeing the world. He was a writer, too, a novelist and a short story writer. A beautiful writer: every carefully crafted word breathed his humanity.

'Well, anyway, although most professors saw me as a miserable girl – or a nuisance, as I would often question their interpretations of books that I had read many more times than they – Gerard seemed to take a liking to me. I would often stay behind after his tutorials and listen to him recommend more and more books to me. Then, as we became more friendly, we would go for a coffee. A few weeks later he invited me to dine with his wife at their house. His wife, by the way, was stunningly beautiful, a dark-haired Spanish woman some twenty years younger than Gerard, but equally as kind and understanding.

'I was so happy when I was with them. I felt that they were the family I had never really had. I could not wait for Gerard's lectures, or the intimate little chats we would have after them. I prayed for another invitation to his house.

'By Easter, my dreams were fulfilled. Gerard invited to stay with him in a small *gite* he owned in Normandy. I cannot tell you how happy that made me. His wife was there, too. All three of us would go for long walks in the countryside. And then, in the evening, Maria would cook one of her Spanish specialities and we would talk and talk and talk about everything.

'A couple of days after I had arrived, and having maybe drunk too much wine, Maria asked me about boys, why such a pretty girl as myself didn't have a boyfriend. I tried to say I had not met anyone I liked.

'These were the last people I wanted to tell my sorry story to, but I could not help it. It all came out – everything. Through the sadness that had been hurting me for so long, I told them what had happened with Antoine, Jean and Albert, confessing also to the pleasure I had felt. Before I had finished, I had broken down in a flood of tears.

'Maria, thinking that maybe this was a woman's problem, told Gerard to go to bed. We stayed up for hours talking, she comforting me, sympathising with me, telling me that I mustn't worry, that I couldn't let what had happened spoil my life. That night we slept together. That's all, just slept together, she holding my body in her arms, my head resting against her breast. It was probably the most restful night I had had for longer than I could remember.

'In the morning when I woke up, I felt different, not so comfortable with everything I had confessed to them. I felt a little ashamed that all my secrets were out. They were the people I cared about most in the world and now they knew everything about me, everything dirty and sordid.

'Maria must have sensed my discomfort. She told me that she understood everything, that I mustn't worry, that both she and Gerard thought I had been so brave to confess my troubles, that I had done the right thing and they both felt honoured that I had chosen them to confide in.

'After Maria had calmed me, she went downstairs and I stayed in her beautiful warm bed, eventually falling back to sleep.

'A couple of hours later I got out of bed, showered, and went downstairs in search of Maria, but she wasn't there. I found Gerard in his study, smoking on his pipe so professorially. A book, as ever, rested in his lap.

'"Where is Maria?" I asked, feeling a little shy. Despite Maria's encouraging words, shame still clung to me.

'"Oh Maria," Gerard said, looking up from his book, a little distractedly. "Maria has gone out to leave us alone."

'It was an odd thing for Gerard to say. We never had any secrets between us; nothing had ever been concealed from Maria. She always participated in all our conversations, sharing our interest in literature, making incisive observations that caused both myself and Gerard to pause for thought.

'Gerard went back to reading his book, while I went to the kitchen to fix myself breakfast. A few moments later, Gerard came into the kitchen.'

'"Can we talk?" he said, resting his hand lightly on my shoulder. Gerard had always been tactile with me, but Gerard was tactile with everybody.

'"Of course," I said. I was a little confused. Gerard, normally such a jovial man, seemed a little serious.

'"What do you think I meant when I told you that Maria has left us alone?"

'I shook my head.

'"We both talked about what you told us last night, and Maria said that she thinks we should make love in the way that you like. That is why she has left us." Gerard laughed. "It seems a preposterous idea, no? More Molière than

Rimbaud. An old man, about forty-five years older, propositioning his young, beautiful student."

'I had thought about having sex with Gerard before, but only very casually – as we all think about having sex with just about everybody – but I had dismissed this idea as I had dismissed other casual, fantastic fancies. For the first time in our relationship, I consciously turned my mind to the idea of Gerard as a sexual man, as a sexual man for me. No, the idea didn't seem preposterous. Gerard was an old man, but he looked much younger than his years; he was a sturdy, vibrant man who had kept himself in trim. I felt my blood rushing through my body. My heart pounded as he spoke.

"'Maria thinks it could help you. She's not a jealous woman. We are too close for that. We went beyond jealousy a long time ago. Maria thinks you need to have a positive sexual experience with someone who cares for you, who won't let you down." The more I thought about it, the more I wanted Gerard. My body trembled in anticipation of his touch.

"'I don't want to lie to you or to deceive you. Maria thinks it would be good for you to make love with me. I think it would be good for me. Beatrice, I'm an old man, an academic: a man of books, of learning, of words. Maybe in a few years I'll be dead. I would like for one last time to make love to a beautiful young girl. I cannot think of a young girl I would rather make love to than you. Our tastes, you may not know, are quite compatible."

'Gerard hadn't touched me in all the time that he was speaking; he had just sat beside me at the breakfast table, his soft voice calmly addressing me, as if he was elucidating some intriguing point about Rimbaud.

"'Remember the madeleines, Beatrice? Remember the madeleines of Proust: how he tastes the cake and it reminds him of all the other madeleines that he had eaten before when he was a child. Well, when I was a young man – although you may not believe it, looking at the old carcass before you – but I made love to many beautiful women. What am I saying, Beatrice?"

"'That you want me to be your madeleine?'"

"'Yes, I suppose I do. Just one last time. A taste of the present, fresh and immediate that will allow me to rekindle the exquisite memories of the past."

"'I would love to make love with you, Gerard." I smiled at him, stroking his hand gently with my own.

'He leant over to me, held me in his arms and kissed me gently on the lips, lightly, brushing his mouth tenderly against mine. Yes, I wanted him so badly. I felt that the heavy depression that had settled on me for so long was beginning to lift at last. He kept on kissing me slowly, softly, but I was greedy now. I forced his trembling lips open with my tongue and kissed him passionately, my hand reaching down to feel his hard cock through his cotton trousers.

'I felt liberated at last, free from those horrible boys, free from my own pain and despair, liberated in my need and in my lust.

'I was wearing a knee-length woollen skirt. Underneath, I wore nothing but a little pair of cotton panties. I pulled away from him and leant my bottom against the table so that his eyes rested around my middle.

"'Look at me, Gerard. Look at me!'"

'He reached down to my knees, to the hem of my skirt. Slowly he raised it: first above the knee, then a few inches higher to my thighs, then higher, staring intently at my legs, the tips of his fingers finally reaching the edge of my panties. Then my panties were visible and he could look at the faint dampness of my pussy through the cotton.

'He sank his face into my groin and kissed my pussy

through the delicate material. He breathed deeply through his nose, filling his lungs and inhaling my scent. He cupped my buttocks and held me while I stroked his white hair and squeezed him close. At that moment I felt more affection for that old man than I ever had for anybody else before.

'With surprising strength he lifted me up and turned me over on the large pine table. My skirt was quickly rolled up, leaving my bottom exposed before him. "I'm going to beat you now, my dear. I'm going to punish you, and by punishing you I will banish your pain forever."

'I remained where I was while he left the room. I felt calm and at peace, but I did not have to wait long. He returned with a thick tawse. I could smell the sharp tang of leather in the morning air. He dangled the strap between my buttocks, and made me shudder with anticipation. "I'm going to beat you hard, Beatrice, harder than you have ever been beaten before."

'I closed my eyes and somehow heard him lift the implement and bring it sweeping down onto my vulnerable buttocks. I heard the slap of leather biting into flesh, there was a split second of nothing when the world inside that kitchen stood still, and then the delicious impact ripped through my consciousness. My whole body jerked and the table creaked. I could hear his breathing increasing in volume and pace as I savoured each vicious stroke. The sharp pang of pain, transmuted to the searing heat in my buttocks, suffusing my whole body with an irresistible glow. I badly wanted Gerard to punish me.

'He concentrated on my bottom, each lash sending a delicious shiver through my body, through to the core of my very soul. For variety, Gerard would lower his aim, stinging me on the top of my thighs; the ache in my behind was overlaid with the sharp, bitter-sweet pain burning my thighs.

'I knew that Gerard was getting very excited. He turned me over so I could watch him. I gripped the edges of the table. I looked up at him as he raised my legs and eased them back until my knees pressed against my breasts and he could continue giving me a wonderful thrashing.

'Perspiration was trickling down his grey-white temples and his face was red. He gripped the strap tightly in his hand. I watched it flash through the air, heard the quick clap of the leather on my bottom, on my thighs, on my legs, felt the delicious cleanness of pain. Gerard was liberating me, thrashing out of me all that repressed guilt, all my shame, all my cowardly regrets. I exulted in my pain. Lash after lash purified me, made me feel whole again.

'When he finished thrashing me he dropped the tawse and his mouth descended on my clitoris. Oh, how Gerard loved my little clit! How he loved to suck on it, to lick on it, to flatten his tongue on it, to take it between his fingers and firmly pinch as I shuddered helplessly.

'Eventually, he stood up and pulled his penis from his trousers. It was long and thick. Juice glistened on the head. I wanted to suck him, to suck his fabulous cock, to take it all in my mouth, to feel his seed sliding down my throat – but he was too hungry for my pussy. Before I had a chance to taste him, he was deep within me. Oh, you don't know how fantastic it was for me to feel his loving cock inside me. I had never dreamt of such pleasure. To have that pain in my legs, in my bottom, the red-hot fire on the surface of my skin: and then the rapturous joy of him fucking me. I yielded to the pleasure, and I yielded to the pain.

'I came quickly, clenching him. One orgasm followed another. I came and came, but still Gerard did not ejaculated. He pulled out of me and I just knew what he wanted   .

'I climbed off the table and sank to my knees before him.

I held him in my fist and sucked him into my mouth. Gerard held my head in both his hands and pulled me further onto him. My face touched his trousers, and he held me still. His fingers clamped into my hair. It hurt a little, but I did not care. I heard him groan, and then my mouth filled with his delicious seed. I swallowed greedily, and his beautiful cock twitched and filled my mouth again.

'"*C'est fantastique!*" Gerard sighed above me.

I was mightily aroused now, listening to Beatrice's story. I had prompted her to tell me more and more, to give me every detail of her narrative just as she had willingly taken every drop of Gerard's offering.

Throughout, she had been toying idly with my stiffening cock and, as she reached the climax of her story, she had begun to gently stroke me with her open palm, running her slender fingers up and down my shaft.

'But that is not all,' she continued as I struggled to contain my excitement. 'No sooner had Gerard come inside my mouth, than he picked me up, so strong was he for all his years, and carried me upstairs to his room. I wanted him again; wanted him inside me. My heart ached for him. I needed Gerard. I needed his strong domination… his discipline.

'Once inside his room, with the walls lined by his erudite books, Gerard placed me on the bed and undressed.

'Pulling a few of his wife's silk scarves from the wardrobe, he took my hands in turn and fastened them to the posts of the bed, pulling the silk tight around my wrists. Then he did the same with my ankles, so that it was virtually impossible for me to move.

'It was fantastic to surrender myself to him like that, to feel so totally within his power, so weak, so vulnerable: to become a thing, a toy, an object to do with whatever he desired. And then the *coup de grâce*: as well as binding my legs and arms, Gerard covered my eyes, immersing me in complete darkness so I had no visual distractions: I could concentrate entirely on the pleasure and pain that he would bring to my body.

'I felt something hard being pressed against my vulva, pushing my pussy-lips further and further apart. Whatever it was, it was cold and hard and very thick. I could feel it sliding into my vagina. I was beginning to relax and accept whatever it was when it was suddenly removed and forced into my mouth. It had the shape of a penis – a very big penis. When I lived at home I had found my mother's dildo in a bottom drawer of her wardrobe, so I was not totally innocent about such things.

'I could taste my own juices on the latex. Gerard left the dildo in my mouth. It stretched my lips wide, and my jaw started to ache a little. I could feel him moving away, moving back between my legs. A pillow was stuffed beneath my hips, lifting me to his mercy, and then a strap of some sort was fitted around my waist. Some kind of contraption was being attached to me. I squealed then at the sudden shock, for two dildoes were pushed into me, one in my pussy... and the other in my bottom. I did not like it. I tried to move away, but it was impossible. It was painful to have these two things pressed so hard into me, to feel the intense pressure between my vagina and my rectum. I wanted to scream, but I could not.

'Next, I felt the strap again burning into my skin, lashing across my breasts and across my stomach just above the leather belt that had been fastened on me. It was exquisite torture, not knowing which part of my body would next be engulfed in pain, and not knowing when he would next strike.

'At last Gerard slipped the latex dildo from my mouth, and immediately replaced it with his lovely cock. I calmed

110

and was happy again.

'My head span in my delight. I could not understand it, but as I sucked him the tawse slashed down brutally against my thighs, my shins, and my feet. I shrieked and whimpered around the cock in my mouth, but the beating continued.

'I soon felt another orgasm approaching. To my immense disappointment the cock slipped from my mouth. I searched blindly for it, but then there was movement on the bed, and soft flesh touched my cheeks and squatted over my face. I smelt the humid scent of a woman…'

Beatrice fell silent for a few moments, clearly reliving that experience. Her fist moved more urgently up and down my cock, but I don't think she was really aware of what she was doing.

'And then I tasted female flesh for the first time. Maria lowered herself and I tasted her juicy pussy. I licked gingerly. She was wet and open, and tasted delicious, just as her husband had. I was barely aware of the one dildo being taken out, but I did groan with shock and sheer bliss when Gerard climbed between my thighs and penetrated my bottom with one long push. I could not believe what was happening to me; I was tied helplessly to the bed, I had a beautiful woman using my mouth for her pleasure, a dildo moving in and out of my pussy, and a stiff cock in my virgin bottom.

'It was all too, too much.'

'Magical colours exploded in my head and I came violently. Through my pleasure I was just aware of Gerard coming in my bottom, and Maria writhing a panting as she also came on my face.

'My orgasm was so intense, so debilitating, that the moment it passed I lost consciousness.

'When I awoke, I was nestled between Gerard and his beautiful Spanish wife, clasped between their naked

111

sleeping bodies, their love and their warmth.'

My own cock was bursting as she lazily masturbated me with her beautiful cool fingers. It took long seconds before she came out of her reverie and noticed my critical condition. Without another word she climbed on top of me, eased herself onto my grateful erection, and fucked me. Her breasts swayed and bounced above my greedy eyes and I grabbed her taut buttocks. I pushed a finger between her buttocks and massaged her anus. The muscle resisted for a while, and then the tip of my finger popped just inside and she ground down onto the double penetration.

We came together. Beatrice squealed and I grunted as I exploded inside her tight cunt, and then she flopped onto my chest and our breathing slowed in unison.

We lay together in the darkness.

'Gerard taught me everything,' she whispered sweetly, when I thought she had fallen asleep. 'He taught me how to look at what happened in the boys' toilet as a fortuitous experience, and to divorce the pleasure that I had experienced from the sordid betrayal that followed it. He got me to tell him every single detail and showed me how I could tell the story. If it had not been for him, I could never have described it to you in the way that I have.

'There were never any limits between us – nothing. He was as free with my body as I was with his.'

'You never really said why I reminded you of Gerard,' I prompted.

'Oh, what you said in the café about wanting to write something beautiful. It was so Gerard. Also you share the same tastes. I only have sex with very beautiful and very interesting men.'

'And what happened to Gerard?'

'Oh, Gerard is still alive, although he is in his seventies now. He wrote a very beautiful book about me. You see,

112

one of the reasons I cannot write about my life with him is that he wrote about it so perfectly.'

'What was the book called?'

'Of course the book was called *Madeleine*. I was his madeleine, as you are mine, to some extent. Sex, so Gerard thought, takes us back to the beginning, sweeps us across space and time, reveals our true identity to ourselves. It is the fabulous moment of self-discovery, but only if we make love honestly, generously, willingly; if we bring pleasure to the totality of who we are, in all our contradictions of pain and pleasure. It is the joyous state of epiphanic self-realisation.'

'Do you still see him?'

'Yes, when I can. That is why I am a little depressed to be here for six months. I know that he desperately misses me. He writes such beautiful letters. I love him. He encouraged me to come here, promising me that the thought of seeing me again would keep him alive.'

I looked at her through the darkness. She knew the question I wanted to ask her.

'Yes, I still do make love with him. He doesn't have the strength that he did fifteen years ago, but he can still please me immensely. I still like to accept his seed in my mouth. I feel like I am swallowing him down: his life, his history, everything good about him. And he still knows how to discipline me, to punish me how I need to be punished.'

'And what about your husband – does he know?'

'No, of course not. He is a kind man, an interesting man, but his interest in sex is a little conventional. I love him in my own way, but he is not Gerard. He does not have the same life-force. I married him precisely because I knew that I could still continue seeing Gerard, that my husband would never suspect that he was more than my friend and mentor.'

113

We fell asleep after talking, with her head resting on my chest, and when I awoke in the morning, like a dream – like a fantastic dream – Beatrice was gone.

Chapter Six

David called the next morning.

'I'm stuck, Jonathan. I'm not going to be back until next week. They're flying me straight to Rio, and then on Sunday I'm in Bogota. It's too crazy, boy, too fucking crazy. I've been looking forward to seeing you and they put me through all this shit. Don't worry, I'll be back by next week.' His voice rasped down the line at breakneck speed, giving me no chance to interrupt him.

To be honest, I hadn't given David much thought. I was more interested in the conversation that had preceded it: Andrea's invitation to visit her dance studio in San Isidro, on the northern outskirts of the city. I was glad that David, for whatever reason, wasn't going to be present.

'Hang on until I get there. You're staying for another couple of weeks?' David continued.

'Yes, I'll hang on, of course, but I was thinking of going travelling—'

'Where to?' interjected David.

'North, maybe. I quite fancy a look at Rio, or maybe Peru, or I was...' I was irritated that David had obviously forgotten my plans. I had written to him twice outlining my intention to stay in Buenos Aires for only a couple of weeks before heading off to explore the rest of the continent. Obviously I wasn't uppermost in his priorities.

'Don't forget, I've got plans for you, my son,' he said, breaking in again in his mock-cockney accent, picked up in those prelapsarian days of easy fuck, before Marie and domesticity got their claws into me.

'Plans?'

'Hey, I've got to go now. They keep me busy, these bastards. Hang on in there!'

When I returned to my room the maid was already there, the soiled sheets of my previous night's romp with Beatrice gathered together in the corner of the room. The maid wore a simple short red dress that showed off her luscious legs and the curved outline of her panties. I never know why women don't like their panty-outline to be seen. To me it looked very erotic as I stared at the delineated crescents of her pert bottom.

This was a saucy girl, I suspected; with her impractical high heels already pushing out her rump, she seemed to arch her back a little further upward, so that if she was to lean any further over I would be able to glimpse a little of her knickers.

She knew I was standing behind her, watching. She greeted me with a casual '*hola*', before continuing her chores, her eyes remaining on mine much longer than civility required. As she continued sweeping each shove of her arm made the hemline of her dress sway, tantalisingly giving me a microsecond view of the tops of her thighs. She started to hum gaily, before breaking off to ask me in Spanish if I liked music.

'*Si, muchissimo.*'

'And dancing?'

'Of course.'

She stared at me and then slowly looked away, smiling to herself. She seemed to work very slowly, unnecessarily slowly. Eventually she gathered up the dirty sheets from the corner of the room and, with a cheery '*hasta luego*' and another lingering smile, she was gone, closing the door behind her. I collapsed onto the bed, exhausted after my

exhilarating night with Beatrice.

San Isidro lay six or seven miles out from the centre of town. I took a ride of death with a grumbling, horn-tooting, lane-hopping, taxi-driver and arrived there at about three in the afternoon.

This was a rich area: leafy, ostentatious, the same chaos of architecture but lower level, Spanish villas competing with mock Tudor. From what I had heard, the area was a strange mixture of artistic chic and retired military, old aristocracy and business tycoons, with a few wealthy ex-pats thrown in for good measure.

The dance studio was located in a quiet tree-lined street. A huge whitewashed house with Georgian pretensions and enormous lattice windows stood before me, its grandeur making me double-check the address that Andrea had given me.

I walked through a broad manicured lawn up to an imposing oak door, rang the bell and waited. An oldish distrustful maid, obviously expecting me as she asked no questions, led me into a luminous atrium. I followed her swift strides to a leather sofa at the back of the room where she motioned me to sit down.

As I alternated between gazing at the decor – the glass ceiling, the walls decorated with Modernist paintings, the impressive chequered floor and so forth – and the window behind me, which gave a splendid view of a garden that stretched as far as a football field into the distance, I saw Andrea appear from a room to my left.

'Jonathan!' she exclaimed, her arms stretching out to embrace me. She wore a light green dress which hugged her ample figure and which was cut low enough for me to see the parting of her abundant breasts. 'You got here okay?'

'Yes, no problems. You look ravishing.'

'*Gracias, señor*,' she said, self-consciously fluttering her long eyelashes. The green dress certainly suited her, setting off the honey-blonde of her hair.

'Do you want me to wait?' I could hear the strident rhythm of a tango coming from the room behind Andrea.

'Well, I thought you might like to watch. I am sure that you will enjoy the show,' she said teasingly. 'But first, tell me about the French girl.'

I had already told Andrea about my success with Beatrice. I elaborated a little for her delectation, rounding off my tale by again expressing astonishment that, after the briefest of perusals, Andrea could infer the Frenchwoman's sexual tastes with such accuracy.

'You know, Jonathan, sometimes I amaze myself. I think it is because I understand the sexual complexity involved. Is far too easy to divide the world into the submissive and the dominant: is *mas subtil*. Like me, maybe there can be elements of both. It helps that I am a dance teacher and therefore a student of movement and gesture. I saw how that girl reached for a book, saw how she flick through the passages. She was a submissive *classico*, but there are so many types. I have known powerful men who love to be dominated and others who love to dominate. *Es muy complicado*, but today I have for you... Never mind. You see for yourself.'

She led me through a panelled door to the delightful wood-floored room where she had been giving her class. It was a fantastic room, with high decorative ceilings, and terracotta-painted walls. A chaise longue was at the far side, below a broad window which let in plenty of air and light.

'Sit there,' she said, 'and wait.' She looked me over, a glint in her eye, before she left by a side door. From the

118

other side I could hear the murmuring of whispering voices.

Two minutes must have passed before the door reopened and Andrea entered with another gorgeous woman with jet-black hair tied at the back in a wooden band. She wore a simple and plain but elegant black dress, with high slits in the side that reached up to her stocking-tops. Her beautiful chest was slightly smaller than Andrea's, but still large in proportion to her narrow waist. Her legs were long and slender.

She smiled at me a little coquettishly as she entered, revealing a lovely generous mouth and huge dark eyes.

'This is Claudia,' said Andrea theatrically, as Claudia bowed slightly in my direction. 'Claudia, this is Jonathan.'

'*Encantado*,' the young beauty said, offering her small hand to me. However *encantado* she was, she could not have been as enchanted as I was, gazing into the darkness of her eyes.

Andrea turned to the sleek music system behind her, gently took Claudia by the hand and waited for the music to start. Both women stood silently and completely motionless.

As the accordions began and then the strings followed, the women started dancing energetically to the pounding rhythm of a tango.

I cannot describe in words how erotic it was to watch those two beauties dancing together. Andrea was obviously taking the male lead, Claudia expertly bending to the will of Andrea's body. Her flesh became pliant and then rigid, depending on the demands of the music. The movements of her limbs were dextrous and purposeful; Claudia's head was held erect and then, as Andrea forced her back seemingly with the force of her body, Claudia's head arched backward, showing the tensed sinews of her neck. Both women's breasts seemed to heave in unison with the throbbing beat of the strident music.

At one stage of their little *pas de deux*, Andrea lightly clasped Claudia's buttock in her hand, as Claudia once more tossed her head back in melodramatic defiance of her mock lover's embrace. Then Claudia, raising her arm, grasped Andrea's hand in her own, before Andrea spun the young girl around the room, first in jaunty movements to the left and then the right, before completely twirling her around, giving me a tantalising glimpse of the fine lace embroidery of her black panties and the tawny skin of her thighs. The dance was highly arousing. I studied every swirl of their skirts, every agile movement of their arms and legs, every rhythmic thrust of their voluptuous bodies.

As the music came to an abrupt halt, Claudia slid down Andrea's outstretched legs, seemingly placing the full weight of her torso onto her partner, before collapsing on the floor, her rigid hand reaching upward to clasp Andrea's thigh then her fingers sliding down to just above the knee, before slowly bowing her head, in what I assumed was some symbolic imitation of death.

'Bravo,' I applauded, clapping as quickly and as loudly as I could. Both girls looked over to me, smiling and laughing, bowing and curtsying, interspersing their appreciation of my applause with bright smiles and kittenish chuckles.

Andrea put her arm through Claudia's and walked over to me.

'You were fantastic,' I enthused, still clapping.

'I hope so. We've been practising for a long time.' Andrea was a little breathless after her exertion on the dance floor.

'You are both astonishing.' My eyes flashed from one to the other, amazed to have had such a wonderful personal performance from two such virtuoso performers, two such sexy women.

120

'Come on, let's have a drink,' Andrea suggested, as she began to get her breath back.

Andrea led us through to another room, a living room of some sorts. It was smaller than the ballroom, with a plush red leather sofa and a fireplace. The lighting was more subdued, the curtains half-drawn. Claudia sat on an armchair by the unlit fire while Andrea went to fetch drinks from a table in the corner of the room. I was aware of Claudia's eyes resting on me as Andrea poured us both cognacs. I caught her glance momentarily before she awkwardly deflected her gaze.

'What a place you have here,' I said, admiring the book-lined walls, the ornamental hearth, and the antique table from where Andrea fetched our drinks.

'I do not always work here. It is normally down there, near the garden shed,' she said, laughing. 'This is the house of my father. He is away in Europe for a few months, so I have this place to myself.'

'I thought you came from Cordoba.'

'I do. But when my parents separated, my father came to live here. We are very close. He is very good to me. It is not every father who would build you a dance studio in his back garden,' Andrea said laughing, before excusing herself to go to fetch ice.

'Do you speak English?' I asked Claudia, as soon as Andrea had absented herself.

'A little only.' She answered my question demurely. 'I study for a few years in an academy, but I forget so much.' I noticed a gleam of perspiration on her throat, stretching down enticingly to the swell of her young breasts.

'She can speak very good English, much better than me – only that she is modest,' Andrea said as she returned with the ice. '*No es timido, solamente modesto.*'

Claudia laughed, holding her cognac glass a little

121

awkwardly, nervously.

'What do you do, Claudia?'

'*Soy estudiante...*'

'In English, Claudia,' Andrea encouraged.

'*Lo siento*. I am sorry,' she corrected herself. 'I am a student.'

'Of the tango?'

'Of law.' Her beautiful eyes flashed me the warmest and most inviting of smiles, as she momentarily lost her social discomfort.

And so we passed an hour, chatting amiably. Andrea told me that Claudia was the best tango dancer she had ever taught and how over the last few weeks they had become such good friends. Claudia looked happy, although still a little nervous, obviously appreciative of the attention and respect the older woman gave her. Claudia, in her turn, told me that Andrea had been one of the best tango dancers of her generation – something David had never mentioned.

We all began to laugh more easily, helped by the liberal measures of cognac that Andrea poured. Claudia lost something of her initial timidity. I told them both a little more about my life, about my relationship with Andrea's husband, my job and life in London – although I missed out some of the more recent dismal details.

So the time passed pleasantly and the mood slowly changed. Andrea played some more tango music for us, enthusiastically commenting on the verities of each piece we heard. I wouldn't say that any of us were drunk; I wasn't – merely intoxicated by the grace and beauty of the two very different women who sat before me – but perhaps if Claudia hadn't been fuelled a little bit by booze, she wouldn't have got up to do an encore of their previous dance with Andrea.

I watched, as amazed as I was before. The girls swirled and twirled before me, if less stridently than before, no less erotically.

When the dancing stopped they fell together in a heap on the sofa, laughing again, smiling into each other's eyes. Andrea bent to kiss Claudia gently on her cheek. When she pulled away, she kept her arm hanging lazily around her shoulder.

'You are very beautiful – *muy hermosa, carina.*'

Claudia smiled at Andrea, her face open, her eyes wide in admiration of the older woman.

'And you have a lovely body, *señorina.*' Andrea lightly ran fingertips over the quivering breast of her voluptuous student.

Claudia sat up, back straight. '*El señor!*' she said, looking in my direction, surprised that her mentor should be so indiscreet with a man present.

'Oh, I am sure he like your breasts, too,' Andrea said, laughing. Claudia flushed red with embarrassment.

Andrea's arm was still around Claudia. She moved it slowly down the lithe girl's back. I sat next to Claudia, my cock hardening in my pants. She looked anxious, her newly gained confidence receding behind an edgy apprehension.

'Relax, Claudia,' Andrea murmured hypnotically, but Claudia's body remained stiff – not as stiff as my erection, but stiff. 'Relax, *carina.*'

However nervous the girl seemed, she made no attempt to remove Andrea's hand, which continued to stroke the small of her back.

'*No te gusta el señor?*'

'*Si, me gusta.*'

'*Es guapo, no?*'

'*Si, es guapissimo,*' Claudia said, looking into my face. So, she liked me and I was good-looking, but Andrea was going to have to do a little more if I was going to get my hands – and, my God, did I want to! – on her ravishing young body.

'*Entonces*?'

'*No entiendo*.' Claudia did not understand the situation, why she was being touched in such a way, and why the Englishman was looking at her so lustfully.

'We like you, Claudia. We like your body. I would like to teach you something a little more interesting than the tango. Would you like to learn?' Andrea's open palm was now stroking Claudia's breast, brushing gently over her nipple. 'Would you like to learn?' Andrea repeated. The girl was breathing heavily.

Claudia looked at her friend and then to me. Andrea continued with her seduction. 'You told me that you like to try new experiences...'

'Yes, but this is different. I am not sure...'

Andrea silenced Claudia, kissing her firmly on the lips, before Claudia managed to pull away, gasping for air.

'*Es mi novio. Le quiero.*' She loved her boyfriend. How could she be unfaithful to the love of her life?

'We will not tell him,' Andrea said, reverting to her competent English. 'He will never know anything.' I nodded in agreement. Claudia looked at me as if I were from outer space, worried, frightened of what we might do. She had never found herself in such a situation before. Andrea's caressing touch and the taste of her mouth had excited the girl – as was obvious from the protuberance of her nipples through the velvet of her short dress.

I placed my hand lightly on her stockinged knee. Her body was rigid under my touch as I caressed her leg from her knee to the supple flesh above her stocking-tops, edging the hem of her dress further up her beautiful silky skin.

'It will help you, Claudia.' Andrea's hand was stroking

her nipples through the black dress. 'Men like a woman who knows what to do. We will teach you how to make him happy.'

Andrea reached over to kiss Claudia again, finding her lips closed as before. Eventually, under the coaxing pressure of the experienced woman's tongue, Claudia weakened, her mouth opening slightly.

What a sight it made, watching these two paragons of female beauty kissing. Their lips fastened together; Andrea's tongue flicked in and out, then strayed to Claudia's full lips, moistening them as she held the girl by the nape of her neck. Eventually she forced Claudia's mouth harder onto her own, and Claudia gradually surrendered to passion, her legs relaxing, becoming pliable under my touch and the pressure of Andrea's lust.

Once Claudia had relaxed her clenched knees, I rolled the palm of my hand up and down her dark stockings, over her thighs and under, finding the thick seam at the back. The tips of my fingers explored as far as her stocking-tops, and then further to the bare flesh above. Claudia's eyes were still on me, still wary and suspicious.

I got down to my knees, my heart pounding with the excitement of having two beautiful women above me on the sofa. I ran my tongue the length of Claudia's stocking, all the way down to her ankle. Gently, I removed her high-heeled shoes before my tongue's return journey, all the way back up to her stocking-tops. Claudia still flashed concerned looks at what I was doing, clearly wondering what I intended to do, although she no longer tried to free herself from Andrea's increasingly passionate embrace.

I pushed her dress up further, carefully inching it higher, until I could see her prettily embroidered lace panties. I didn't touch her at first, but just stared at her panties, the flesh of her chestnut-brown thighs, and the enticing swell

125

of her pussy lips through the material. I savoured the promising delights that awaited my fingers, my tongue, my cock.

I touched her gently through the teasing material. I could feel the dampness through the lace. Andrea was now on her knees on the sofa, flicking her tongue in and out of the girl's mouth, her glorious green-clad rump perched up before my greedy eyes.

I strayed further between Claudia's legs and, softly stroking her lace-covered pussy-lips with one hand, I lifted Andrea's dress with the other, exposing a pair of skimpy green panties. I pulled the panties down and gazed at the tiny aperture of her rear passage, while continuing to stroke Claudia's young quim.

I sank my teeth onto Andrea's naked flesh, and she wriggled with delight as I bit into her rump. I was so excited to be reacquainted with the unique taste of Andrea's skin. Andrea reached behind, pulled her left buttock so her cute rear entrance opened before me, and I accepted the invitation and pushed a finger into the tight passage. At the same time I massaged Claudia through the panties and felt her getting wetter and wetter.

As I continued to frig Andrea's bottom, I carefully – not wanting to break the spell and scare the girl off – ventured to explore inside her panties. I slid a finger beneath the elastic and into her soaking pussy. Her mound was almost hairless. She flinched again, but this time she was not recoiling nervously from me but emitting a shiver of delight.

Andrea suddenly reached down behind the sofa and produced a silk scarf. Quickly bringing Claudia's hands together, she expertly wound the scarf around her forearms, teasingly at first, tickling the girl's skin, before pulling the silk taut around her wrists. She made a tight knot from which Claudia would find it impossible to escape.

Claudia's eyes opened wide in amazement, as did her mouth. But, before the beautiful girl could complain, Andrea quickly gagged her with another scarf she had gathered from behind the sofa.

However much the girl had relaxed under our attention, she again tensed and stared incredulously at her teacher. She seemed frightened, betrayed. Her hands were bound and she was completely defenceless against our amorous intentions.

'*Quiero besar tu cono,*' Andrea cooed, having completed her task. 'I want to kiss your quim.' She knelt beside me on the floor, hooked her thumbs into Claudia's lacy panties and slipped them down her stockinged legs.

And what a quim the girl had! Her light covering of soft hair shimmered before our eyes, her rose-pink pussy-lips swollen with anticipation, the petals of her sex opening before us. Her hands were fastened tight, and her legs were easily controlled by Andrea and myself. She had no option but to put up with whatever indignities or pleasures we were about to bring to her.

Andrea pulled Claudia's moist sex-lips apart to reveal the deeper red, and then raised the girl's legs in the air a little, pulling her towards the edge of the sofa a little more, exposing the most delightful little rosebud I think I had ever seen.

I kissed her thighs as Andrea nibbled her erect clitoris, causing a reluctant quiver of sensual delight to surge through the girl's body.

As Andrea licked and chewed more vigorously, I positioned a fingertip against Claudia's bottom and pressed on her taut anus, bringing a little confused whimper from her as it sank just inside.

Claudia began to cry: with fear or pleasure, I do not know. I wormed my finger further and further inside her. She sighed through the gag, and instinctively tried to squirm away from our tormenting. She twisted and writhed, pressing down on my intrusive finger and Andrea's vibrant tongue. She was trying to resist us, but only succeeded in intensifying the physical pleasure we were bringing to her. We rocked her body to the crescendo of orgasm, as we expertly stimulated her. However much she wanted to resist, she knew it was futile: she could only yield to the strength of her pleasure.

She came, squealing through the gag, her mouth open around the little bundle of silk, her body furiously twitching in the most delightful sexual spasm I imagine she had ever had.

Andrea obviously knew that this was just the start of the girl's pleasure. Sitting Claudia up, she unzipped her black dress, undid the shoulder straps and pulled it over her head and her bound arms, exposing her ripened, rounded breasts enclosed by the matching black bra.

Andrea removed the flimsy piece of underwear. She took both erect nipples between thumb and forefinger and pinched them hard. Claudia flinched and nibbled her lip, recoiling from the intense pain. She was passive in her hands, submissive, too mesmerised by the actions of her tango teacher to offer us any resistance.

Then Andrea silently bid me to stand, unzipped my trousers, and slipped her cool fingers into the waistband of my briefs. I nearly came there and then, so erotic was her touch. But I managed to control myself and watched as she pulled my erection out into view. Claudia's eyes widened at the sight of it. Andrea pulled back my foreskin and stooped to lick the swollen head, flicking her tongue along the underside before sliding her tight lips over my helmet. She knelt again, cupped my buttocks, and pulled me towards her until her mouth was full and her nose nestled in my pubic hair.

Hell, she felt good!

When she was satisfied with the rigidity of my cock, she took it out of her mouth, signalled for me to kneel on the sofa, and guided my cock towards Claudia's waiting wet lips as I removed the gag.

'Take…' she breathed sensually.

Claudia looked unsure. I suspected she had never sucked a man before.

'*Toma*…' Andrea urged. Claudia hesitated a little longer, and then leaned forward a little and tentatively pressed her lips against my bursting helmet. Andrea held it still, and gently massaged the foreskin back and forth. I breathed deeply, trying to control myself, wanting to savour such exquisite bliss for as long as possible, looking down at the beautifully innocent girl, a look of confusion and uncertainty and joy on her clear face. She tickled me by ever so slightly rubbing her lips across the tip of my cock. I watched her tentatively lick at a little pearly emission. Andrea carefully cupped the back of Claudia's head and urged her to take more of me into her mouth. Her glistening lips parted further and I slipped deeper. Andrea also cupped by bottom and inched my hips closer to the spellbound girl.

It was wonderful to watch the young student learning the craft of fellatio: to watch her head bob up and down and her mouth fill with my cock, its tip rhythmically distending her cheek as she used her lips to fuck me with increasing confidence and vigour. I closed my eyes and listened to her wet suckling, and then felt Andrea's lips join her student's on my shaft.

I knelt over them. Andrea turned Claudia until she was kneeling on the sofa before me. I felt like some kind of god, looking down upon two perfect females as they fellated me. As Claudia worked I reached down and undid the band that held her hair in place, and watched her beautiful raven hair cascade down over her shoulders.

Andrea broke away and delved behind the sofa again. She lifted a small leather whip into view.

Claudia couldn't see what was happening behind her, but she certainly felt the harsh lash on her buttocks. She jerked and her eyes closed tight as the whip swept down again and again, inflaming her tender flesh. Each time the whip cracked she yelped around my cock and tried to tug herself free from the oppression of my controlling hand.

Andrea looked impassive, but I knew that, underneath the dispassionate exterior, she was enjoying herself immensely. One swipe followed another. I could see deep red marks on the upper curve of Claudia's bottom. She sucked with even greater fervour. It was almost as if she found the rhythmic motion of fellatio a kind distraction from the keen pain of the whip.

'Now for the fucking,' Andrea said, discarding the whip and unzipping her dress, revealing again those glorious breasts with their delightfully pointed nipples that I remembered so well from my first day in Buenos Aires; that I would never forget for the rest of my life. Her tiny green bra lifted and squeezed them together. Oh, and the beautiful sight of her moist pussy-lips.

She gently pulled Claudia onto the thick patterned rug and, pulling a plump cushion from the sofa, placed it under her bottom. She spread the girl's legs wide before me. I could see the wispy triangle of hair. Her expression was servile as she peeped up at me. Her pouting lips glistened with a little of my pre-come. I knelt between her shapely thighs, a worshipper before the mount of her love.

I could wait no longer for my prize, and so I lifted her silk-encased legs up and supported them behind the knee in the crooks of my arms, grasped her thighs just above

130

her stocking-tops, and slid into her with one long lunge of my hips.

I started to move slowly, savouring every moment of the gorgeous girl, but she was too, too much, and gradually I began to thrust faster and faster.

'Ah, *si… si… si…*!' Claudia moaned beneath me. I could see Andrea was taking great pleasure in directing the performance.

'Ah, *si...*!'

I could resist the Latin beauty no longer; I was coming. I felt Claudia's body tense around me as my orgasm erupted from my jerking balls. As I ejaculated she came too, eyes closed, moist lips slightly apart, the elegant fingers of her bound hands clenching and unclenching on her flat stomach; a lovely feminine orgasm that left her gasping and murmuring her pleasure.

As I knelt on the carpet, still embedded in the delicious Claudia, my breathing gradually slowing towards normality, I gazed down at her. Her cheeks were glowing healthily, and her eyes smiled up at me from under lowered lashes. She looked more than a little at peace with the world.

'I never think it could be so exciting, Jonathan,' she said sweetly. 'Thank you.'

After we had all showered and dressed, Andrea and Claudia prepared some food. We ate our dinner on our knees in the living room.

Claudia had lost all of her sexual inhibitions; she seemed to have no desire to revert to the shy girl I had met in the late afternoon. Andrea had been right again: Claudia had enjoyed her pain immensely. She talked brightly and laughed easily, every now and then reaching down to gingerly feel the glowing ache of her tender behind.

After dinner, Claudia telephoned her parents to tell them

that she was going to stay over with her dance teacher. Andrea then took us both upstairs to what appeared to be the master bedroom, sparse but comfortable, the king-size bed plenty big enough for three.

As I undressed, Andrea pulled Claudia's panties down before my eager eyes. She pulled off Claudia's dress, leaving her naked, and then removed her own dressing gown that she had put on after her shower. The two beautiful females stared into each other's eyes the whole time, caressing each other, stroking breasts and buttocks. Andrea cupped Claudia's pussy as they kissed.

'Lie on the bed,' Andrea said. Claudia obeyed and spread herself out on the silk sheets. 'Another show for the English gentleman,' Andrea said, looking at me, thoughtfully reaching down to the wispy curls of her own sex.

Andrea held Claudia's hand and moved her inert fingers to her own clitoris. 'We want to watch you,' she whispered huskily. 'I love to watch a girl feel her own body. It makes me so wet, Jonathan, so wet.'

Claudia did as she was told, and tentatively rubbed her clitoris. Andrea and I knelt on each side of her on the soft mattress. Andrea lifted Claudia's head, and I fed my fresh erection into her mouth. Her juicy lips opened dreamily; she seemed to be behaving instinctively now.

'Claudia,' Andrea whispered hypnotically, 'put your finger in your bottom. We want to see you do it.'

Claudia, clearly now enjoying masturbating for us, did as she was told without hesitation. She inched her glistening finger from her clitoris and stretched a little to find her anus, and then pushed the straightened digit into her back passage.

Without warning, Andrea lashed the girl with the cord of her dressing gown. Claudia tensed. Her mouth was still on me and her finger frigged her own bottom. Her body writhed under each substantial blow, tossing from side to side under the lash, as Andrea aimed for the tips of her breasts, for the exposed lips of her sex: for the most vulnerable places that would bring most pain to her student.

The thrashing was relentless. Claudia's eyes scrunched tightly shut in her delicious pain, her mouth clamped tight on my cock. I took the swollen tips of her breast firmly in my fingers and pinched as hard as I could, intensifying Claudia's agony, all the time watching the cord descend on her tender body and her face flushed in her tantalising torment.

After exhausting herself, Andrea nestled between Claudia's thighs and touched her lips to where Claudia's finger had so recently been. A shiver ran through Claudia's beaten body as Andrea manipulated her swollen clitoris with her skilful tongue.

So far, Andrea had been the dominant one in our little *ménage à trois*, but I now wanted to take control, to play out my own fantasies with these two fantastic creatures.

I pulled Andrea onto the bed and then rolled Claudia on top of her. Neither of the girls seemed to mind the extra *frisson* of pleasure as I positioned them wherever I wanted. Andrea took Claudia's ripe breasts in her hands and massaged them lovingly.

And now I had what I wanted: Andrea lying on the bed with Claudia stretched on top of her. I entered Andrea and fucked her as I masturbated Claudia, incredulous to have two such breathtaking females squirming with pleasure beneath me.

I eased my hips back and forth and watched Andrea roll her head from side to side. But there was another prize I wanted. I managed to roll the two of them over, so that Claudia was on her back with Andrea on top, her beautifully rotund bottom raised before me.

I began to screw Claudia. I masturbated Andrea, and then slid a lubricated finger into her tight anus. I forced my finger as deeply as I could into her bottom, rotating it, making her buttocks quiver as I continued grinding into Claudia.

And then – oh, what joy – I pulled out of Claudia and squeezed my cock into Andrea's tight rosebud.

'Oh, yes… take me in my *culo*… oh, yes.'

She was so tight, so beautifully tight.

'Oh, yes…' she urged me on to greater efforts. I felt her relax a little more, and gratefully sank deeper into her bottom until my pubic hair was cushioned against her buttocks. I held her hips and fucked her with short sharp stabs. She loved it!

Andrea and Claudia came together, and so unbelievable was the sight of them and the feel of the tight rectum squeezing me that I erupted a split second later.

The three of us curled up together and I drifted into an extremely contented sleep.

But this was not the end of the excitement for me. I don't know what time it was, but I awoke and felt Claudia gently shaking my shoulder. As I stumbled to consciousness in the half-light of a nascent summer dawn, I saw Claudia put a finger to her lips in a shushing gesture. She took my hand and pulled me up, then led me to the door and into another room where a single bed was positioned under the window.

I was not yet fully awake – in fact, barely awake enough to be aroused by Claudia's breasts shimmering in the early morning light.

She pulled me down onto the narrow bed and whispered in my ear. 'Please, I want you to do it to me like you do it to Andrea. *Por favor*. Please, Jonathan.'

I looked down at my sadly flaccid penis, and she

understood my immediate difficulty.

'*No hay problema*,' the little temptress whispered, and lowered her face to gather my flesh into her warm wet mouth.

Boy, was she irresistible! I would defy any red-blooded male to deny himself the pleasure she could bring with her lips, and tongue, and teeth.

In no time her handiwork had produced an erection that speared proudly up from my groin. And now I was actually being asked to bugger her virgin hole. I had died and gone to heaven!

Claudia smiled at me, and then turned and knelt on the bed, presenting her rounded bottom to me expectantly. Suddenly I felt a little surge of panic; I didn't want to hurt her, and I didn't want to disappoint her.

Again the clever girl seemed to understand my predicament, for she peered over her shoulder and said softly, 'I am ready for you.'

I stroked her smooth buttocks, and then noticed for the first time that she had already anointed them with some kind of cream. She must have visited the bathroom and prepared herself before waking me.

This was a young lady who knew what she wanted! And how to get it!

The springs of the little bed strained as I positioned myself and it took our full combined weight.

'Are you ready?' I asked, and saw her nod, her shoulders hunched and her head hanging down slightly. I pushed a finger into her bottom without any resistance. It was definitely tighter than Andrea's. I could wait no longer. I prised her buttocks apart and replaced my finger with my cock. Her back arched and I could feel the extra girth stretching her rectum as I plugged her. I could tell she was in some discomfort, but she made no complaint. I began to pull out of her to give some respite, but she bravely stopped me.

'No… please…' she begged. '*Mas*…'

I halted my retreat, and instead pushed against her again until I filled her to the hilt. I paused, allowing her time to grow accustomed to the new sensations, and gradually her little moans of uncertainty became little moans of delight.

When I thought she was okay I started to move. The springs squeaked as my hips drove back and forth with increasing vigour. Claudia squirmed with pleasure and pushed her buttocks back against me, meeting my forward thrusts and making our flesh slap together in the silence of the early morning. I watched her sink her mouth into the pillow to stifle her sobs of delight, and I knew she didn't want to alert Andrea; she didn't want to share this new experience with her dance tutor.

Her arms tensed and she gripped the bed covers tightly.

I spread her buttocks wide and gazed down at my greased cock pounding into her poor stretched bottom. Claudia grunted and her hanging breasts jerked every time my balls swung against her tensed thighs. We were both perspiring heavily with the effort of our coupling.

At the last moment I pulled Claudia back up against my chest. The action deepened my penetration even further and her head lolled back onto my shoulder. Her mouth opened in a silent scream and she shuddered in my arms. I cupped her breasts and pinched her nipples as my sperm flooded her tight rear passage.

I held Claudia like that for a long time, gently rocking her and kissing her temple and cheek. Her fringe was damp on her forehead, and she quietly mumbled words I didn't understand. Her soft buttocks molded themselves tightly into my lap, and the glove of her rear passage hugged my spent cock affectionately.

As I knelt there in the crisp dawn, with such a beauty enfolded in my arms, I thanked God or fortune or whatever it was that had led me to such delights, such a realisation of half-imagined fantasies, such exquisite joy. In short, that had led me to Buenos Aires.

Chapter Seven

What a difference sexual satiation can make to ones surroundings! Before I left London and Marie I had despaired of the place, of its congestion of cars and people, its dirt, its aggression; of its shoddy streets and the coldness of its winters; of the depressing morning faces that greeted me on the inevitably delayed tube. Buenos Aires was no less dirty. It had its squalor and its gloomy Monday faces, but here I felt alive, liberated. I loved the city. I could not but help feel a sympathy, which I had never done for the people of London, for the washed-out faces that often passed me by on the streets: the chronically disappointed. Most of the time I didn't even notice them, so frequently was my head turned by a beautiful face, a pert rump, a slender leg.

How could I feel anything but warmth or sympathy for a place that had given me so much in such a short space of time, that had offered me Andrea, Beatrice, and Andrea with Claudia, and that maybe offered me so much more? How could it not compare favourably to the dismal city where I had spent so long repressing my lust for the sake of supposed monogamous bliss, releasing myself with a mechanical conjugal fuck or a lazy bathroom wank? It was easy to conclude that at last I had found home.

I woke up again in mid-morning, back in the double bed with two delightful females looking up at me and giggling as they licked on my stirring cock. What had happened to me that fate, after slumbering for so long in my life, had given me this? If this was what Buenos Aires was going to be like, I never wanted to leave… never.

I made love to them again, alternating between the youthful Claudia and the more experienced Andrea. I screwed them, wondering when all this might be taken away from me; when the great god of chance, having given me so much pleasure, would suddenly withdraw his favours from me. It added intensity to every thrust of my cock.

I did everything that day; saw everything. I could do with them what I wanted, take them whichever way I pleased.

By the evening Claudia had to go home. She couldn't explain her absence from the family hearth any longer, and besides, she had a date with her boyfriend. Lucky man, I thought, knowing what Claudia now knew. I would have died for a woman at nineteen as experienced in carnal pleasures as Claudia had now become.

I knew that I too had to depart. Andrea had an evening meeting, although she wouldn't tell me much about it. I didn't want to go. Why would I want to leave that perfect paradise, that garden of earthly delight that San Isidro had been to me over the last twenty-four hours?

I couldn't have done anything else by that stage. Anyway, I was too exhausted, but that wasn't the point. Not the whole point. I liked Andrea. I liked her spirit, her attitude to life. I wanted to stay with her, to nestle my head between her breasts. San Isidro was like a cocoon for me, a refuge from everything bad that had ever happened to me. I did not want to sneak off back to my lonely *hospedaje*. But, with a vague promise that Andrea would call me in the next few days, I sloped back to Palermo.

I have prevaricated and procrastinated for long enough. Now the time has come. I must tell you what I haven't so far told you. I must struggle to find the words, to fill the gaps, to explain, as much to myself as to anybody else, what happened. I must write about Marie.

I met Marie, my wife of four and a half years and my lover of five, through David. She was his long-standing girlfriend. Not his only one, for David always had lots of 'entertainment' on the go at the same time, but Marie was the woman he always seemed to go back to, the woman that I – and everybody who knew David – thought he would eventually settle down with, maybe even marry.

In those days I thought she was such a beautiful woman: she had a stunning curvaceous figure, limpid green eyes, a delectable crop of cool blonde hair, a broad generous laugh and a smile that could send shivers down my spine. Marie was a wonderful combination of Celtic passion and English *sang froid*; she had a calm inner certainty that was so refreshing compared to many of those girls I knew, full of insecurity and repression. This, of course, was before her passion developed into a passionate obstinacy and her *sang froid*, to maintain the cod French, transmuted itself to a kind of careless *ennui*: from being feisty and free-spirited she became bored and bitterly angry, at least with me.

Victoria, vividly recalled in these pages, gave David and I our first taste of what David used to call 'extreme love', but she was not our only experience: not the only woman to savour the delights of a tanned backside or a gagged mouth, my prick in her quim while David rode her from behind. We developed a penchant for mutually thrashing and rogering accommodating women. There was Cynthia from the office, Isabel, a Spanish girl, Frederique from France, a couple of barmaids we favoured with our cocks and our whips and, when willing women were thin on the ground, a couple of East End tarts we picked up from my own locale.

Yes, I'm sure you know where this is heading: how one seemingly disconnected paragraph relates to another, the logical progression of C following B following A...

And how I loved Marie! How I dreamt of her, fantasised over her alluring body with my sad hands, and even sometimes in mid-hump as I screwed some office temp fresh from typing school. Yes, even as an Annabel or a Tracey or a Lucy sucked on my shaft, Marie would force her presence into my thoughts and, closing my eyes, I would dream it was her mouth on me, her lips milking me dry, her hands squeezing my aching balls.

It was not that I didn't have plenty of opportunity to see her. This was my problem: she was David's girlfriend, the real one, the one we thought that deep down, despite the carnal dalliances he frequently enjoyed, he loved. He even referred to the others as his 'bits on the side', a meaningless diversion from his true path, his real love. This was the problem because I suppose I was still his best friend, the one who shared his secrets, and was expected to keep them. I was the one who got to know the sordid details, the petty frustrations, the grand ambitions and, most agonisingly for me, the companionship of his girlfriend. My problem was that even before we became a threesome, we already were a threesome, so to speak.

Neither of them ever minded me tagging along. And Marie seemed to like me. It was often at her instigation that I found myself in their company. She would ring me at my office, inviting me to dinner, to pubs, to wine bars, to football matches, to autumnal parks and expensive restaurants. All the time, of course, with David there too. Sometimes I dreamt that it would just be me and her, but it never was – not then.

Apart from the fact that David had got to her before I did, he was more eligible than I. David was the high-flyer, not me. He was working for a national women's magazine, writing features about the rich and famous, running around the most chic restaurants, flying to the most exotic

Caribbean islands. And all the time I still ambled around flower shows, reported the latest road fatality or dredged up the dreary statistics of juvenile crime from my East London poverty-stricken patch. The only features I got to write were not on the super-rich or the over-talented, but on some third-rate and mind-numbingly dull local historian or, worse, the retired park-keeper.

Maybe I digress a little, but this is how it was. David, always having greater confidence and drive than I, fêted screen stars and alternative comedians while I, standing on rain-sodden doorsteps, requested snaps of newly deceased sons and daughters from grieving parents. What did I have to offer Marie compared to what David could give her – apart from the tepidity of platonic friendship?

So we three became a gang of three, occasionally with an interchangeable fourth, one of the current women in my life who invariably, once screwed, would be forgotten. What would be the point of making any commitments when I loved Marie, loved her like an infatuated schoolboy, loved her to the point of obsession? By necessity, I obviously had to hide my feelings, but my love concealed, festered, grew, nurtured itself, became almost ridiculous.

David and I had not stopped our games. Only two weeks before the incident I am about to relate, a certain buxom Belinda had obliged our always eager cocks in the back of David's car, pulling us off simultaneously so we spurted onto her face. This was a secret we obviously kept from Marie. Nothing of our fondness for the *ménage à trois* was ever mentioned to her – until that night.

That night!

We rolled back to David's place in St John's Wood at about two in the morning. We were all quite drunk. We had been celebrating my thirtieth birthday. It was a mark of my affection, of the closeness of our relationship, that I

142

should wish to pass my entry into my fourth decade with David and Marie.

We had had dinner in one of my favourite Soho restaurants. The evening had been lively, bright with our laughter, and we had polished off more wine than was good for us.

Back in the apartment, David had insisted upon opening a bottle of champagne that Marie had bought to mark the occasion. We guzzled the bubbly and giggled like schoolchildren.

Marie looked spectacular that night, her shining blonde hair caressing the small of her back, her make-up as expertly applied as always, delineating the naturally well-defined features of her face. She wore a short sequin dress, low-cut, her ample breasts crammed together, accenting every heave and undulation of her alabaster chest. She managed to look both elegant and sexy at the same time.

The conversation, as it often did, turned lightheartedly to sex, with David regaling us with half-true anecdotes of the sex lives of the celebrities he had brushed against. Marie, also decidedly in the know about the fashion world – she too was a high flyer, working as the deputy fashion editor on the same magazine as David – spun a more credible tale of one designer she knew who couldn't achieve orgasm unless she had sex with at least two men.

David and I both laughed, a little uneasily perhaps, thinking about our own shared fetish. David, although not exactly an expert in *haute couture*, made some barbed comment about how horrible the woman's designs were and the conversation turned to another topic, although related to sex, not specifically concerned with the fancies of the disparaged fashion designer.

We were drunk, it is true. It is also true that, in my booze-clouded frame of mind, I wanted something to happen. I could not spend the rest of my life in unrequited love. Sooner or later the situation would have to come to a head, even if it meant disgracing myself, or losing David's friendship for ever.

There was a slight lull in the conversation as David, rather unwisely, opened a fresh bottle of wine. Marie sat on the sofa beside him, her knees pulled up to her chest. I could see the marble white of her thighs. She was never shy with me, often conducting conversations with both of us as she lay in the bath, the door ajar. Or sometimes she would flounce into the room in her underwear, asking either of us for advice about what dress she should wear.

'I'd like to try it, sometime. Why not? I've done most other things, but I've never done that,' Marie said, slightly slurring her words, as David passed us each a full glass of white wine.

'What? What are you talking about, my little peach?' David asked, having half-forgotten the topic that she had earlier raised.

'You know, I'd like to have sex with two men.'

'Oh, we're back to that, are we?'

'Well, you know, it could be interesting in the right circumstance. And with the right men, of course.'

'I don't know whether I would really like to do it with another man,' David said rather hypocritically. I raised my eyebrow, knowing only he could see.

'We're not talking about you doing it with another man, numbskull. We are talking about two men doing it with one woman.'

'No, that's what I meant. I don't think I could do it with another man there.'

'But you have, darling.'

David looked at me, fleetingly, unobtrusively. He was obviously thinking the same thing as me, wondering if

Marie had somehow learnt about our little secrets. Liberal and liberated though Marie might be, neither of us, I am sure, thought then that Marie would have approved of what we did. She must have known about the occasional dalliances David had, but she never pushed it, never forced him to confession. But furtive shags with secretaries or the occasional willing starlet was of a completely different order.

'What do you mean?' David asked, rather defensively.

'Izmir, David. Don't you remember Izmir?'

'What's the secret?' I interpolated. I knew the story – David had already told me – but I wanted to hear Marie's version.

'We screwed at twilight in Izmir, on what David assured me was a secluded beach. After we finished my bottom was covered with sand. Sand gets everywhere, you wouldn't imagine, so I don't recommend the great al fresco fuck. Anyway, when we finished we turned around and there, on the not so distant sand dunes, silhouetted by one of the most fantastic sunsets I have ever seen, were ten or more inbred locals staring down at us. I wondered whether they were going to give us a round of applause.' During her little story, a little glazed though they might have been by the consummation of so much booze, her eyes peered straight into mine.

'Exactly,' David said conclusively. 'This is my point. Do you think I enjoyed all those geeks staring at me? And if I didn't enjoy it then, why do you think I would enjoy it now?'

'I don't believe you, my man. You're telling porkies about your porky.'

'Rubbish!'

'Remember Charlotte's survey? Remember how many men fantasised about seeing a woman with a full mouth and a stuffed pussy? Men love that sort of thing.'

'I'm not "men" dear, I'm only one man. And anyway, the problem with Charlotte's little sex surveys, though national she may claim them to be, is that not only does the frustrated girl make up all the questions, she also makes up half the answers too.'

'No, no, that was *bona fide* and you know it. You're hiding something. Come on, you can tell me. You're not normally so coy.'

'I'm not coy, you daft tart, but give me one man – me – and two women any day of the week. You forget how greedy I am.'

'Do you remember that party we went to last year? Do you remember the scene in the bedroom with Louise Fisher and those two models? You didn't exactly turn away then.'

'I never do for a free show.'

'So, you prefer to watch, you sad bastard.'

'Maybe, maybe not.'

'I saw how greedy you looked, especially when the CP began.'

'I was curious.'

Marie gave him a long, hard, disbelieving look. 'And what about you, Jonathan?' Marie asked, elegantly rising to her feet. She retrieved the bottle of wine and poured more of it into my fluted glass, spilling almost as much again on the carpet. 'Surely you're not going to be as obstreperous as that lying sanctimonious bastard?' she said, laughing.

'I've never really thought about it.'

'Liar.'

'I mean yes, I've thought about it. I think about everything, but...'

Have you done it?'

I paused for the slightest of moments.

'Aha – yes, you have. Who did you do it with? Not him? Please tell me it wasn't him.'

Maybe David thought Marie was getting too close to the truth. The bonhomie of the conversation had darkened a little as Marie's persistent questioning of us and her drunken assertions had added an air of tension to the evening. David certainly looked at me severely. He was angry, I suppose, that I was not the accomplished bluffer that he was. Trying to deflect the conversation, he said, 'If I recall that survey it was women, not men, who fantasised about doing it in threes.'

'You're not telling me you wouldn't like to do it, too? Men like to do it and they like to watch. They're much more visual than women when it comes to sex. But of course women like the idea of being taken by two men. Maybe they don't like the practice, but the idea: yes. I do,' she said, looking at me.

And so the conversation progressed. Marie refused to let the subject rest, and David grew a little irritated at her persistence.

Marie suddenly rose again and walked over to me, rather unsteadily. She sat on my lap. It wasn't so unusual for her to do this. We had an agonisingly tactile relationship. Well, agonising for me, at least, considering my feelings for her, to be that close and yet so far away. To smell her perfume, her skin, to feel her hands around my waist or resting on my shoulders was, to say the least, a bitter-sweet experience.

'Well, birthday boy, if I ever was going to do it, I wouldn't mind one little bit if it was with you.' She flopped her arms around my shoulders and kissed me full on the mouth, probing my lips and gently nibbling my tongue. She had never done this before. I could taste champagne and the sweetness of her lipstick blending with her moist tongue.

I did try to resist her. I was a little embarrassed at her display, not wanting to offend David. Now was not the time to pledge my devotion, not with Marie drunk and lecherous.

'She's a good kisser, your old lady,' I said, trying to maintain the levity of the situation.

'You're drunk, woman,' David said. I was not convinced he was being wholly jocular.

'Mm, just a kiss for the birthday boy,' Marie said, pulling away from me, looking over at David, and then sinking her tongue forcefully into my mouth again. Without warning she reached down and stroked the bulge in my trousers. 'Oh, big boy,' she breathed seductively, flitting her fingers lightly along the uncoiling length.

David looked decidedly agitated by now. He obviously didn't want to show his anger, but he clearly didn't like what he was seeing. I wasn't so sure either that this was such a good thing. I felt embarrassed that David knew I had an erection because Marie had embraced me.

'Come on, Marie, time for bed,' David said getting to his feet.

'Oh, I like the sound of that,' Marie purred, gazing into my eyes, grasping my cock tighter and giving it a squeeze.

'You've drunk too much,' David reiterated, as fearful as I was that things were getting out of hand.

'Of course I'm drunk, David. It is one of the advantages of drinking a lot. And one of the advantages of being drunk is that you can do wicked things and then forget about them, excuse yourself in the morning. Being drunk is perfect.'

David stood behind her and tried to put a hand on her shoulder, but she shrugged him off. She licked behind my ear, her hand now brazenly rubbing up and down my cock through my trousers. I didn't know what to do; my arms lay listlessly by my side. An intractable desire swept through me. I wanted to hold her, to take her, to tear her dress apart to pull off her panties and screw her as hard as I could. To screw all that love, all that frustration, the bitter regret, the sad nights of loneliness, the numerous pitiful wanks. I wanted to screw her with all that, to stuff her with my love for her. David looked at me imploringly, but there was very little I could do.

'Come on, David,' Marie said, turning to him, 'I want to screw the birthday boy and I want you to watch – or, better still, to screw me as well. I told you I wanted to have sex with two men. What other two men would I really want to do it with, apart from you two? Look, Jonathan's game. You should feel his dick.'

Still massaging the embarrassing lump in my trousers, she reached over and unzipped David, and pulled his limp penis into view. David didn't stop her, but merely stood like an imbecile before her.

She stroked him, running her forefinger and thumb down his shaft. 'Oh David, don't be like that. Let's play.'

'No,' he said firmly, turning his back on the scene.

Marie stood up angrily and left the room. David turned back to me, said something about her being too drunk, and tried to hide his embarrassment behind a pained smile.

I thought that that was the end of the matter. I assumed that Marie had gone to bed but, two minutes later, she returned and deposited a cardboard box in the middle of the floor, triumphantly turning to David and asking: 'What's this then, David? What's this?'

It was a rhetorical question because it was easy to see the contents of the box that David had hidden away from Marie. There were whips and gags and blindfolds, and I could see the glossy sheen of some specialist magazines that I think David utilised to aid his imagination during our sexual bouts.

149

David was furious. 'You – you had no right!' he stammered, his eyes narrowing vehemently.

'So punish me, David,' she goaded defiantly. 'Punish me like you punish all the others!' She pushed against his chest. She was taunting him, tempting him.

'I don't want to punish you,' he said softly, his voice weak.

But Marie was insistent, and prodded him again in the middle of his chest. 'Are you a hypocrite? Come on, David, let's share your filthy secrets. Come on, spank me.' She knelt on the patterned rug, lifted her perfect bottom, and pulled up the skimpy sequinned dress, exposing a pair of sweet red panties. 'Come on. Spank me, darling. I want you to,' she said more softly, more invitingly.

The sight of his lover, lewdly and provocatively offering her bottom in what he assumed was an attempt to humiliate him, made something snap in his mind. He grabbed her firmly by the upper arm and pulled her to a dining chair. 'Okay then... okay,' he panted. 'You want this, Marie? You want to play? Then let's play. Kneel over the chair!'

'Oh, you're so masterful,' she mocked, but sexily draped herself as he had instructed.

She looked over her shoulder to see what he was doing. 'Put that on her,' he said to me, his hand trembling as he passed me a blindfold.

I fixed it tightly over her eyes. David roughly pulled her panties down to her knees, revealing the firm globes of her bottom. He rummaged in the box and found a thick leather strap. He coiled it around his hand, and then without warning, he swept it down across her exposed buttocks.

I had never seen him hit anybody so hard. Marie was stunned by the pain. Her head snapped back with the force of the lash, and her beautiful bottom quivered beneath the impact. A pink blotch rose immediately.

Before the shock had worn off and she could utter a sound he struck her again, just as hard.

'Owww…' Marie protested, but she didn't move to protect herself; she was clearly loving this brutal treatment. I stood beside David, watching her magnificent white buttocks redden with every awesome stroke.

After six thrashes Marie said quietly, unable to hide the tremour in her voice, 'That's enough.'

'No, it isn't,' David said spitefully, turning his disappointment with Marie into a bitter anger. 'You wanted to play games, so now you have to take your punishment. Remember, it's the rule: you have to do what I say.'

'I don't know…' Marie said, her previous confidence dissipating rapidly. 'Perhaps we should—'

David retreated to the box and fetched a pair of handcuffs. It was too late for Marie to resist by the time he had snapped them around her wrists and attached her outstretched arms to the legs of the dining room table.

'David, stop it,' Marie pleaded. 'What are you doing? You're hurting me.' At first this had been a silly, if painful, game. It was her way of getting back at him for needing the box of implements and not finding more than enough satisfaction in just her. But the game was now over, and David was just being mean and spiteful.

'You don't know how much this hurts me, too. You see, Marie, I know you want this. I've always known you wanted it. I've tried to fool myself into thinking that I was wrong, but I wasn't, was I, Marie? I'm sorry – I can give it to you, but I can't respect you.'

I noticed that the blindfold was damp with Marie's tears. David's eyes, too, were rheumy with alcohol and bitter sadness. It seemed like a moment of truth in their relationship, a culmination of so many things that had gone on before that I had no knowledge of.

'So, Marie,' David continued, his voice mingling sadness with anger, 'I am going to give you what you want, but know that I never wanted to – not with you, anyway.' He turned to me. 'Hit her hard, Jonathan,' he said, handing me the thick strap.

He knelt and unzipped the back of her dress, down to where the hem of the skirt was folded up around her hips. It peeled open to expose her unblemished flesh, and then he ripped off her red bra. I knew her lovely full breasts had tumbled free, but from where I stood I could only just make out a little of the profile of one. I watched with envy as David cupped them, tenderly at first, and then I knew he had pinched her nipples painfully for she tensed and moaned with pain. He looked up at me. 'Thrash her, Jonathan... thrash her!'

The sight of her kneeling over the chair before me, bound and blindfolded, was too much to bear. Again and again I brought the strap down on the fleshiest part of her already flushed behind.

'You want this, Marie,' David taunted quietly, his mouth close to her ear. From the way she groaned I knew he was still pinching her nipples. 'Come on, don't lie to me. Tell me. Tell me how much you want this...'

'Yessss...' she moaned, the sadness in her voice overlaid with an insistent lust. 'Yes, yes, yes...'

I brought the lash down, the pain of each stroke reverberating through her body, a thunder passing through her, her moaning in time to the rhythm of the leather.

I observed the scene, trying to distance myself from the love that I felt. I saw her lustrous hair swaying against her shoulders as she gently shook her head in torment. I saw the glint of metal around her wrists and heard it softly chinking. I saw the black blindfold, stretched tight around the back of her head. And I saw a sheen of perspiration coating her skin. I felt such a mixture of confused emotions; of desire, love, and sadness. I swept the strap down again on her already beaten buttocks, in an attempt to block out all the tenderness and frustration of my passion.

Marie moaned. I reached between her legs and felt the moistness there. I found her clitoris. It was too much, and she instantly writhed and squealed as an orgasm swept through her.

David released her from the handcuffs, and then dragged her from the chair and onto the floor. He knelt down on the carpet beside her. 'Fuck her, Jonathan. Fuck her.'

Marie was still blindfolded. Needing no second invitation, I lay flat and pulled Marie's limp form on top of me. I penetrated her easily, and holding her trim waist, I slid her up and down on top of me.

As we were screwing, David pushed her down until she was squashed against me. Her velvety breasts felt glorious as they massaged my chest. He fed to fingers between her lips and made her suck them noisily. Then he pulled them out and leant over her back. I couldn't see what he did next, but from the cocktail of shock, discomfort, and joy freezing her beautiful face, I knew he had pushed the lubricated digits into her bottom. Her eyes closed and her mouth opened. I couldn't have been happier, for the unexpected intrusion made her writhe all the more and grind her cunt down onto my lucky cock.

'Fuck me Jonathan...' she panted in my ear, her breasts heaving on my chest. 'fuck me, please...'

I watched David squat behind her. He pressed on the small of her back, which tilted her bottom slightly and aided my penetration nicely, and then I felt Marie tense and knew exactly what he was doing. He winked at me as she clamped her mouth onto my shoulder. He moved slowly for what seemed an age, and then paused, his fingers buried into her fleshy buttocks, and I guessed he was fully lodged in her bottom. Indeed, I knew he was, for I felt his hairy balls sway around the base of my cock. Marie coiled her fingers in my hair, not realising quite how hard she was pulling and how painful it was for me. But I didn't care; it all added to my immense pleasure.

What a fantastic rhythm we managed to set between us. Her joy crescendoed as we increased our tempo. As she screamed at the moment of orgasm, I came too, and watched David's face contort as he did the same.

Five long years later, I can hardy believe that anything like this happened, that the woman I left had anything in common with the Marie of five years before. How could that Marie, who had so thoroughly enjoyed having two men fuck her, have been the same woman who would brush me aside in our domestic bed, or dismiss me with a hand-job as mechanically as if she was doing a domestic chore? It can't all have been me.

David and Marie eventually went to bed. I did not follow. I got the impression that, after this incident, I certainly wouldn't have been welcome. We had all gone too far. We had stepped over the mark, crossed boundaries that maybe shouldn't have been crossed.

I wondered what they thought as I slept on David's sofa and Marie and David lay in the room next to me. For my part, I was confused. I had enjoyed the sex with Marie very much – the fact that she was submissive added to her attraction – but it didn't necessarily mean that I was any closer to my goal of stealing her away from David than I had been before. Perhaps, in the broad light of day, it might seem that I was further away. By participating, by allowing myself to participate in this little orgy, I might be banished from their company. What had happened had changed completely the nature of our relationship. Nothing could be the same between any of us any more.

But my thoughts about my relationship with them were secondary to my suspicion that the events of that night had irrevocably changed the bond between them. I remembered David's words as he towered above the handcuffed girl, telling her how it hurt him, telling her that he could no longer respect her.

Marie was the first one up, next morning. She woke me, pecking me on the cheek as she usually did when we met or we were parting from each other's company.

'Come on, sleepy-head, time to get up.'

I looked at her beautiful face as I forced myself to consciousness; and, as I shook off my slumber, every earth-shattering detail of the night before was recalled from my memory before her sparkling eyes. 'Last night,' I mumbled.

'Last night things got a little out of control. I'm not sorry I did it. I wouldn't have liked to have gone through life without being acquainted with you sexually, or receiving a thrashing like that. But once is enough, big boy.'

She pecked me on the cheek again and smiled down at me.

'Marie...' I wanted to tell her then. I wanted to tell her that I loved her, that I was prepared to give up everything for her, even my long-standing friendship with David. I knew it would hurt him to be deceived by me, but the love I felt for her was too overpowering. But I couldn't say anything. The words locked inside me refused to come out.

'Look, David is in a bit of a funny mood about this. He's a bit angry. He's a bit angry with you and with me, too. I don't think he has much right to be, but that's the way it goes. He's like that sometimes. The thing is, I don't think it's a good idea for you to hang around here today. Look, I'll sort everything out. I don't really see what the fuss is. We had a great one-night stand, but you know what David's

155

like. He can be a real sanctimonious git sometimes, a bloody hypocrite. Just go, Jonathan. I'll give you a ring in a couple of days, or David will... but not now, all right?'

Things didn't exactly work out like that. I didn't hear from either of them for a fortnight. An agonisingly long fortnight for me, as not only had I thought I'd lost my best mate, but more importantly – much more importantly – I had blown it with the woman I loved. I drank myself through two weeks, hovering by the phone, resolving to ring one of them and then at the last minute letting my resolve weaken.

It was Marie who broke the silence first, bursting through my door at four o'clock on a Sunday afternoon, her eyes red. She was distraught, restless, unable to stay in the same position without agitatedly flitting from one place to another. Nor, at first, could she speak.

'What's wrong, Marie?'

'It's David. He's gone round the twist. He's off to Argentina.'

'What?'

'He's off to bloody Argentina. He's been headhunted. He's got a job with some cable company. He's leaving in two weeks, and... and he's not taking me.'

The story came out slowly, disconnectedly. He had told her that it had nothing to do with her, but that he wanted to work in a different environment. It certainly had nothing to do with what had happened between the three of us, he assured her. That was just a sign that something was wrong. He didn't love her, and that was that. What he loved was his freedom.

I knew that David could be ruthless. I had seen evidence of it in his working life, but all this seemed unnecessarily cruel. I surmised that he had been prompted into this action by the events of that night, whatever he had said to Marie:

that somehow he naïvely separated women into two categories, the ones that did and the ones that didn't, and that Marie had fallen from saint to sinner. In truth, I didn't know.

There certainly wasn't any real reason to go to Argentina professionally. Even if he didn't want to take Marie, some cable outfit in the far-flung corner of the world seemed a considerable second-best to a man like David, who was maybe weeks away from being offered a weekly column for one of the more respectable broadsheets.

Marie wanted me to try to talk some sense in him.

Maybe I should have been happy. With David out of the way I could pursue Marie. There were now no obstacles in my way, especially if David had dumped her. There could be no guilt on my part – well, apart from that night.

But happy I was not.

Marie's disconsolate state was an indication of how much she cared for David. At best I could be rebound material. I also suspected that, over time, Marie might come to blame me as much as she blamed herself for what had happened and that, far from bringing us closer, David's departure was going to drive us further and further apart.

The next day I called him at his office and arranged to meet him that night. He had sounded friendly on the phone, breezy, light-hearted, both of us having veered away from the subject of my birthday celebration, David's imminent departure, or Marie's grief.

We met in one of our usual Soho pubs.

'Okay, let's get the shit over with first,' David said, even before I had had a chance to say hello. 'First, you and me are mates, all right? I hope that whatever has happened or whatever will happen, we will stay mates. Secondly, I'm going, it's decided. It was decided a month ago. I didn't want to tell you then, because I was told to keep it under

157

my hat. This has nothing to do with her and nothing to do with you. I've had to make some tough decisions. I've always had to make tough decisions. I don't want to stay with Marie any more. Look, there are things you don't know, and things it is no longer my place to tell you. Anyway, there is always a time to move on and this is it. This is a great chance for me. You know that I've always wanted to see Argentina. I've got relatives there. My mother was half-Argentinian, and this is my chance. Also, this company I'm going to work for are going to be big, very big, and I have a chance to be part of it.'

That, in essence, was the tersely delivered speech. There were several things that didn't really fit together. For one, David always told me everything about his career, so I was surprised that I hadn't been told about the Argentinian job. He also knew that I could keep secrets from Marie, so there shouldn't have been any problems about that. Thirdly, he still hadn't convinced me that a job in Argentina, or the filial connections he had with the place, were enough to make him leave his current comfortable position on the ladder of journalistic fame.

'You know something else about that night?'

'What?' I asked cautiously.

'We planned it. I planned it. I asked Marie if she wanted to and she was keen, but it was me who persuaded her. In fact it got to the stage where I almost had to badger her into doing it. I suppose it was a kind of leaving present. I know how much you like her. A kind of handing-over ceremony: I was Britain, you were China, she was Hong Kong. She's all yours now, if you want her.'

I had never thought of David as being so callous. Yes, it was true, as I later learnt from Marie, that David had once asked her what she thought about the idea of all of us having sex together, but it had never amounted to any kind of badgering. It had only meant that because they had so openly discussed it, if she actually initiated it, then maybe David wouldn't be so shocked or offended. And, that night, he certainly hadn't seemed very happy about it.

I was surprised to hear one year after he had departed for Buenos Aires, and for all of his talk of freedom, that he was engaged to be married. I was even invited to the wedding. He always invited me to go to Argentina, in every letter or email he sent, but, short of money and without any great urge to do so, I never went.

David's departure heralded probably the happiest time I had ever known in my personal life. With Marie, I went from platonic consolation to passionate lovemaking in two short weeks. There was no room for her to harbour any grudges against me, so full was her mind of bitterness for the betrayal that David had committed against her. The 'bastard' was seldom allowed to enter our conversations. Nor was much of our previous shared lives together ever mentioned, particularly that night. Our pre-lives were blanked out. They became a forgotten history.

There were – and I don't thank David for this, as I see him as being largely responsible – conditions to my being with Marie. They became apparent in a very short time. There were to be no extra-maritals, because if I was going to have her then we would have to be married. If David hadn't told her about all the things that we had got up to when he was dumping her, then I don't think she would have been so suspicious on that score. I pledged my troth, and six blissful months after David's departure we were wed in a Camden registry office. David, not surprisingly, was not invited to the wedding, but he sent me, at least, good wishes for our future life together.

And yes, the first year of our marriage was fantastic. A fucking bonanza. Every spare hour of our lives saw us screwing, this way and that, exhausting our bodies with carnal pleasure, sating our lusts in some of the most savoury ways possible known to man or beast. Why would I want to look elsewhere? Why would I settle for second-best or second-rate when I had the best, most fuckable woman in my bed every night?

For one thing, I was too tired. Sometimes my cock would scream for rest, for a break from the relentless gymnastics we put it through. She was sexually insatiable.

However, our sex life, although prolific and interesting, was, compared with what I had witnessed on the night of my birthday, largely conventional. Maybe Marie was in some kind of denial, but there were to be no more whips or chains, no more games of submission or dominance. But that didn't matter. I was so happy to at last have the woman I loved. I couldn't believe my luck.

So what happened? How did we go from this glorious honeymoon period of constant sex to the dismal state of sexless stasis that preceded our break up? It certainly had little to do with me. I was, for all the exertion and the demands made on my winking friend, always keen. It was Marie who became disillusioned. Like the old housewife stereotype, she cried off with headaches and tiredness, or cited the demands of her job for lessening her libido.

We would take recuperative holidays on the continent and, for a week, things might return to bliss or at least near-bliss, because we never quite got back to that early stage. Partly because Marie never stopped working. Her laptop, like a needy child that had to be looked after, always accompanied us on our vacations. As soon as we returned normal service would be, or in our case wouldn't be, resumed. And while frequent threats were made to me if I should ever stray from the marital bed, the marital bed ceased to be a fun place to be. However, foolishly, I kept

160

my word. I shouldn't have believed my luck!

I have since realised exactly what my problem was. When I was David's friend, and even after as platonic comforter, my salary bracket or the absence of professional drive or ambition was never a question. The fact that I could make her laugh, care for her and later, when we lived together, fuck her senseless, were considered more pertinent factors in our relationship. But as time wore on and wore us out, my lack of professional success and my apathy began to become an irritant in our relationship.

As she went from one classy magazine to a classier magazine, as her income soared at the same rate as an IMF debt to a developing world nation and mine didn't, she lost interest. It was as simple as that. Power and money and success fired her libido. She was dominated by it in all meanings of the word. That had been the attraction of David.

Regaling her with tales of traffic victims and the tediousness of flower shows did not arouse her. I lost out in the 'being a real man' stakes; my pulling power did not come via a cheque book or the number of people I had under my professional control. On top of that, I was not allowed – although when the sex stopped I constantly dreamt about it – to have anybody else under me or on top of me at all.

All I had wanted was Marie: her mind, her wit, her charm, her pussy, and probably in that order. And what Marie had wanted was a man who could turn her on by dropping the right influential names and by reciting all the noughts in his bank account, whipping her into an orgasmic frenzy as much with his power and influence as with, I suppose, his whip.

The last scene I have to painfully recount, the incident of the garden shed, was not about Marie accidentally being found in want of additional attention. It was the clearest, most obvious and degrading way that she could find to tell me I was a loser, that she didn't want me. And what she did want was me, to all intent and purpose, to fuck off *tout de suite* from her life for ever.

She didn't need to fuck the bald secondary-school teacher from next door at all. As she was to tell me, saving me little of the details, she had already been shafted that day by some go-getting executive who had got from her everything he wanted, and everything I hadn't had for such a long time. Those business trips, increasingly frequent as our relationship wore on, were fatuous excuses for gratuitous and gratifying sex. All this was related to me in the post-match analysis of her tool-shed hump.

It made everything perfectly clear: her reluctance to lie naked with me in bed, the pyjamas necessary, I suppose, to hide her scarred bottom; her constant self-criticism about her clumsiness when I would occasionally find bruises on her body. How naïve I was! How trusting! How stupid!

She knew I would come home at that time. Perhaps it was the Russian roulette turn-on, the fifty-fifty chance that, in early December, I would look for her in the garden shed, that I wouldn't see cardiganed Arthur escort my beloved to the little wooden hut and there on the little workbench that I never used, among rake and hoe and spade and lawnmower, little Arthur would get his biggest surprise since the local authority let him have early retirement at fifty-one, a fact he would laboriously inform me of every time I talked to him.

I saw it all from the bedroom window. I saw them enter and, with the aid of a speedily retrieved pair of binoculars, I saw my girl arch over the workbench and Arthur take his antique cane, bending it slightly, before bringing it down on Marie's aroused flesh. Marie was the embodied reality of thirty years of Arthur's schoolgirl fantasy life. Thwack! His eyes bulged with pleasure. Thwack! Her bottom wriggled before his astonished gaze, her hips pressed against the rough wood of the workbench. Thwack, thwack, thwack. Six of the best.

Marie turned over, pulled down his pants and sucked on his ancient member. Perilously, I had had to balance one foot on the marital bed and the other on the dressing table, to give myself a good view of the little incident.

After she had sucked on him for a good time, she climbed back onto the bench and pulled her skirt up around her waist, giving Arthur the most delicious view of her pantyless crotch. I saw Arthur's eyes taking it all in, basking in the sight of her moist quim, in those beautiful folds of sex-flesh that I not so long ago had lost my mind to. I saw Marie parting the cheeks of her bottom and slipping a finger into her anus, in and out, slowly and patiently for poor Arthur's delectation.

Poor Arthur nothing!

She had never done that for me for three years and, after tonight, she never would.

I saw Arthur slurping on her, her little finger going in and out of her bottom all the time. I saw Arthur sitting on the little stool in the garden shed and Marie planting herself on him, rocking up and down, Arthur's dick going in and out of her wet sex. I saw Arthur's whole body stiffen as he shot his seed into my wife.

In short, I saw enough to never want to see bastard Arthur or my bitch of a wife ever, ever again.

Chapter Eight

When I got back from my adventures with Andrea and Claudia, I called on the two English girls, but they were not in their room. I couldn't get any sense out of Señor Albertini, the portly hotel owner. They hadn't vacated the hotel, but he did not know how long they would be gone, or where they had gone. He merely shrugged a lot and raised his eyes to the ceiling.

Neither had David rung, or, if he had, Albertini wasn't saying, the septuagenarian barrel. Even the delightfully saucy chambermaid, usually a ubiquitous presence in the hotel, wasn't around that day.

I spent the next few days alone, wandering the streets of Buenos Aires, having morning coffees in *confiterias*, afternoon strolls in parks and museums, occasionally taking buses and trains to the outskirts. I sipped on beers in the shade to shelter from the ball-breaking summer heat of the city.

I tried to get to know the city to distract my mind, though it never really worked, from the wealth of beautiful woman who were as ever-present as the sweltering summer heat. I walked into every bookshop, hoping I would meet another Beatrice. In every *confiteria* I would search for potential pre- or post-prandial lovers. Every street filled my mind with erotic possibility.

So for a few days I was a little sad and lonely, but really I had no reason to be. I had had the best sexual time I could remember. I knew more would follow, that Beatrice might again show, that Andrea definitely would, hopefully with Claudia in tow. Stephanie would be back and, this time, I would give her what she wanted. My chambermaid danced lasciviously before my eyes every day. Surely something more would happen there, too.

Three days passed before I received another telephone call from David:

'Jonathan, you have to hang on. The bastards have got me not knowing if I'm coming or going. I have to fly to Caracas, then to Miami, then I'm in New York for the weekend. I won't be back until next Thursday by the earliest. Sorry, but don't go anywhere. I have plans for you, sunshine. Plans for us. Hey, I've got to go now. Thursday, next Thursday, the twenty-fifth. I'll pick you up in my car, okay? Take it easy. *Ciao.*'

And that was that.

The next day I had a quick call from Andrea:

'Hi, Jonathan.' Her voice was breathy, sexy, intimating all the pleasures we had had and all the pleasures I still hoped were to come. 'How are you?'

'Fine, and you?'

'Busy, busy, busy. Look, I am in town today. Would you like to meet? I have got a couple of hours. In the Tortoni, yes?'

Yes, please!

Andrea looked as stunning as she always did, casually dressed in a white T-shirt, tightly stretched across her breasts, the delicate lace of her bra visible beneath, her mouthwatering nipples prodding through. A navy blue mini-skirt highlighted the natural sheen of her slender legs.

What impressed me less was the scruffy twenty-year-old pony-tailed youth who was sitting beside her, his dark eyes fixed exclusively on Andrea. It was only when she stood to greet me that he slipped out of his reverie and glanced at me.

'Hello, Jonathan,' Andrea said, before reaching over and kissing me on both cheeks. I felt the suppleness of her breasts momentarily pressing against my chest. 'This is Rodolfo. He's my student. A great tango dancer. Do you remember meeting Claudia?' she asked, without any trace of irony. Andrea, I was beginning to understand, for all her natural charm, was a consummate actress as well as a skilful dancer.

'Oh yes, Claudia.' Of course I remembered Claudia.

'Rodolfo is her boyfriend.'

Rodolfo stood up clumsily, betraying all the youthful gaucheness of an adolescent, which, if Andrea's description of him was accurate, miraculously disappeared once he began to dance.

'Hello, sir. Pleased meeting you,' Rodolfo spoke in his faltering English. 'I am sorry sir, but I must to depart now. I have a date with, with...'

'Your girlfriend.' Andrea helped him out.

'*Si*, my girlfriend.'

'Oh, I'm sorry to hear that.' It sounded as if I was sorry to hear he was seeing his girlfriend. Some Freudian slip, perhaps! I didn't like the idea of Claudia, or for that matter, Andrea, playing with this boy, when my prick was itching to get into both their pussies again. Of course I wasn't at all sorry to see Rodolfo go. I wanted to get him out of the way as quickly as possible. I wanted Andrea exclusively to myself.

After Rodolfo had, as clumsily as he spoke and stood up to greet me, rather over-theatrically kissed Andrea on the cheek, he departed. I turned to her, held her hand in mine and asked, 'Does Rodolfo know?'

'Come, Jonathan, do you think I would tell it to him? Of course he does not know. Although he may be a little suspicious if she practices some of the things that we taught her. We did not leave any marks, did we?'

'I don't think so.'

Andrea smiled at me before she continued, 'But also perhaps Claudia may be suspicious too.' Andrea winked at me saucily.

'You mean, you've been giving him some lessons, too?'

'I am a teacher, Jonathan. I love my job *muchissimo*. There is much satisfaction to know that as they have sex tonight, they will perform so much better, thanks to me. I will have brought a lot of pleasure to both of them. Rodolfo has natural potential, but he did not know how to – how do you say? – stay the course. Now he is a little better.'

'Of course, you know he's infatuated with you. I could see it in his eyes, the way he looks at you.'

'Well, it is nice to know, Jonathan, that as he makes love to his girl, he will give a thought to his teacher. Infatuated though, no. He loves Claudia. I know it. There is also a professional interest here, as well. Those two could be the greatest tango dancers in Argentina. They have much talent: much, much talent. The better they make love together, and the more they learn about the discipline, then the better they dance.'

It was a great feeling to be pulling that stretched white T-shirt over her head, and then to unhook her bra, exposing once again those fantastic breasts. It was great to lift each juicy sphere to my lips, to take them in turn into my mouth, to flick my tongue all over the flesh and then take her nipples between my teeth, making them wet and hard. It was great to feel the pressure of Andrea's hand on my neck, pulling me closer and closer to her heartbeat. And it was great to hear her sighs and moans as she enjoyed every teasing nip and tug on her teats.

167

We hadn't stayed in the Tortoni for very long. She had a treat for me, she had said, producing a key to an apartment one of her friends owned, but seldom used. The flat was on Callao, in the heart of the city.

As soon as the door closed behind us I feasted hungrily on her breasts and ran my hands up and down her skirt, tugging the hem up and brushing my knuckles against the damp gusset of her cotton panties. I found the zip at the side, pulled it down, and the tiny skirt slithered to the floor. I turned her and pushed her against the apartment door, and then spanked her cotton-covered buttocks. It was fantastic. She whimpered and her fingers clawed at the door. I savoured the sight of her bottom quivering under the rapid impacts of my palm. The afternoon was hot and we were soon panting heavily.

She was too much; I wanted to fuck.

I stopped hitting her and allowed her to lead me into a plush bedroom. I sat on the bed and she stood silently before me. Hooking my thumbs inside the waist of her panties, I slowly teased them down her silky thighs.

Unable to resist any longer, I cupped her bottom and buried my face in her wispy blonde pubic hair. Her fragrance was like a drug to me. At that moment I could have eaten her. I licked at her light hair, and felt her juicy lips peel open. She was ready for me.

'I don't have much time, Jonathan,' I heard her say above me. Her fingers were in my hair, pushing me gently away.

That was a shame, but it added an exciting urgency to the afternoon; made it somehow more illicit. I would have preferred to savour Andrea at my leisure, but a quick screw was better than no screw at all.

I undressed hastily. Andrea's eyes were on me the whole time. My cock was furiously erect. When I was as naked as she was, she sucked me until happy with my rigidity, and then lay back on the bed and stretched her arms above her head. I took the hint and quickly fastened one wrist to the bedpost, using her panties, and the other I secured tightly with her bra. I pulled her hips down the bed so that her stretched arms ached, and then slid my cock into her waiting pussy. There was no time for finesse. We came together. Every thrust of my hips had her revelling in her climax; her face flushed red as she shivered with a joy.

Before leaving, she turned and kissed me. 'You know, Jonathan, you are very lucky in that hotel.'

'Oh? Why's that?'

'You have not noticed? The pretty maid... she is one of us.'

The girl had been driving me crazy for days. Every day she came in to clean my room, no longer waiting until I absented myself as she did with all the other guests. And every day she seemed more seductively dressed, her skirts skimpier, her shirts stretched tighter over her firm pear-shaped breasts.

At first, and with English modesty, I had vacated my room for her, thinking that she would not like to be watched while she did her chores. Later, I left because she aroused me so much that I was a little frightened that I wouldn't be able to keep my hands off her. I imagined headlines about international incidents, and being bunged up in some Godforsaken Argentinian slammer on goodness knows what charges.

Without wishing to sound arrogant, it had seemed clear though, even before Andrea's comments, that the maid was attracted to me. Not just because of the sexy clothes she wore, but the way she would move, the way her bottom would sway provocatively, and the way she always seemed to notice a speck of dust – so small I could never see it – on the floor near me, and would drop to on knee to pick it up and give me a tantalising view of her shadowy cleavage. I swear she was always braless.

She would wink at me, too, sometimes as she asked me about what I did with my time in Buenos Aires. She also liked to talk about the other occupants of the *hospedaje*. She seemed particularly intrigued with discovering more about Frankie and Stephanie.

The day that I had gone out to meet Andrea, I had offered her a coffee and received a life story. She came from Salta in the North West of Argentina. Her uncle – not her real uncle but a friend of the family – was the proprietor of the hotel and he had offered her work. She wanted to study, to improve her English, to live abroad. Her sister was in Miami and she was going to visit her in the autumn.

She talked affably but, as the clock ticked by and I was aware of my date with Andrea, I had to ask her to leave. She seemed disappointed, her parting *hasta luego* more wistful than normal.

The next day, she came into my room as usual, nine o'clock on the dot, dressed in a beautiful short white cotton dress that hugged her delightful breasts and barely covered the top of her silky coffee-coloured thighs.

'Where you like me to start, *señor*?' she asked sweetly.

At first I wasn't sure if I imagined the suggestive tone in her voice, but my penis was already stiffening beneath my towelling dressing gown. I had to sit down on the edge of the bed so as to disguise the tent that was quickly developing.

'Where would you like to start?' I rebounded the question. She smiled saucily, her eyes twinkling as she glanced at me.

'In the bathroom, then.' She took her mop and bucket into the *en suite*, and I followed, leaning against the

170

doorframe with my hands in the pockets of the gown so as not to be discovered.

How Andrea knew about the maid, I knew not. She had only seen her for the briefest of moments that first day when she dropped me off at the *hospedaje* but, by now I had total confidence in her powers of sexual divination. And I had every intention of finding out for myself at the first possible opportunity if she was right again.

I watched the lovely maid mopping the linoleum floor, sweeping the wooden pole from side to side, the hem of her dress swaying tantalisingly as she did so.

'You're a very beautiful young lady, Anna.'

'*Gracias, señor.*' She turned her head, flashing another white smile at me, her silky black hair sweeping across her face as she did so. 'And you, you are very handsome man,' she said coyly.

'*Gracias, señorina.*' I replied.

I could have stayed watching her like that for an eternity, the beautiful blackness of her flowing hair silhouetted against the brilliant white of her dress, her rump now swaying more frantically before my greedy eyes as she scrubbed the brass of the taps. I could see the tips of her breasts rubbing against the stark white porcelain as she crouched over the bath to clean it. I wondered whether she was simply doing her duties conscientiously, or whether there was something more purposeful to her movements. Whatever her motives, she was turning me on, very, very much.

My heart thumped excitedly in my chest. My cock was fully erect beneath my hands. I wanted to fuck her there and then.

She turned and looked at me. Her bright eyes studied my face, and then they slowly roamed down and came to rest where my hands were plunged into my pockets. I blushed, certain that the evidence of my excitement was blatantly poking towards her. The cute smile drifted from her lips, and an expression of uncertainty and curiosity clouded her face.

The front of her dress was a little wet, and I almost groaned, so tempting was the sight of the near transparent material moulded like a second skin to her breasts. But what would she do if I made a move, if I walked over and touched her? I could sit her bottom on the edge of the basin, pull her legs around my waist, and fuck her there and then. Or I could push her to her knees, open my gown, and feed my cock between her sweet lips. But what if I was reading the situation wrong? What if she ran from the room screaming? I could very easily find myself in all sorts of trouble. Maybe I was wrong. She was young and coquettish. Perhaps she didn't realise just where things were heading. Perhaps she really wasn't aware of the affect she was having on me. She was certainly old enough and sexually mature, and she behaved in a sensual way that bespoke of some knowledge of carnal desire, but what if this was as far as she wanted to go? What would happen if she was appalled and disgusted if I were to make a move? I had to consider the possibility that I had been wrong: that Andrea, on the law of averages, couldn't be right every time.

She was driving me crazy. My heart pounded, my cock throbbed, and still I hesitated. I have never liked rejection and only the most worthless scum of mankind would force themselves on a woman who did not want to be forced. This idea had always repelled me, and lust was no excuse. For me sex, however varied, however strange or perverse, had to bring mutual pleasure, even if this was through the intermediary of sharp pain.

So I held back as she went back to work and her buttocks

rippled before me inside the tight cotton dress. I didn't want to talk to her. I wanted to feel the nubile firmness of her body, to part those thighs, to smack the beauty of her curvaceous bottom.

When she had cleaned the bathroom I thought the moment had passed. The bathroom was small, and where perhaps I could be most intimate without actually touching her or raising suspicion as to my motives. I remained in the doorway as she passed me, still desperately trying to hide my erection. I had to move slightly to let her pass and, for the briefest of moments, I felt her cotton-clothed body brush against me.

It was just a moment, but I couldn't help but feel that that touch was meant, especially as she could have asked me to move from her path, thereby avoiding any contact at all. She smiled at me too as she did it, her eyes sparkling, her mouth slightly open, showing those perfectly white and even teeth.

Did she know what she was doing to me? Had she any idea just how sexy she was?

My mouth was dry. I was regressing to a fumbling, tongue-tied schoolboy.

I stared down at her as she hovered, and then she moved on, but as she did so her hand brushed lightly across my erection. It could have been an accident, but I knew it wasn't.

Her eyes held mine confidently. 'Thank you,' she whispered.

How can I describe that moment? It happened. It showed that she was every bit as knowing and as willing as her body and all her innocently suggestive gestures had implied. She was not merely leading me on. She was not about to report me to the authorities if I dared touch her.

I knew my moment had come as she leant over the bed,

straightening a corner of the sheet, tucking it under the mattress. I sank to my knees behind her and lifted the hem of her short white dress…

And oh, what a surprise! The darling wasn't wearing any panties!

She didn't say anything, nor did she move as I gazed at the firm ripeness of her bottom. I gently placed my hand on one of her buttocks and felt its soft satiny texture. I did the same with my other hand. She did not look back, but I heard her emit a little surprised gasp. She still did not move as I pulled the cheeks apart, and spied the little button of her tight anus. I placed the tips of my fingers between her legs and softly stroked the moistened velvet of her quim.

She was sighing as my fingers explored her, lightly and gently at first, but gradually more urgently. Her bottom squirmed on my palm. Her sighs increased to a discernible pant.

Adding another finger, I put my other hand back onto her bottom and rocked her up and down, and stared at the fantastic sight before me. Her white cotton dress was rolled around her waist. Her back arched and dipped as she rested her elbows on the bed, and her rich dark hair swept the sheet as she abandoned herself to the pleasurable sensations simmering through her body. Her upper body heaved and she rolled her breasts and nipples against the mattress. My fingers were slick with the copious evidence of her enjoyment.

I stood up and smacked her without warning. The little minx didn't complain, but moaned slightly and wriggled her bottom to show her approval. I smacked her again, each smack bringing a cheeky wiggle of appreciation from her, encouraging me to put more force into the next spank. I did as she wanted, and soon her buttocks were a mass of pink blotches.

Without wanting to break the spell, I hastily leant across to the bedside unit and picked up my hairbrush. Feeling a strange desire to be just a little sadistic, I pressed the bristles onto her scolded flesh, and then into the deep valley between her buttocks and against the taut entrance to her rear passage. She absolutely loved it, and flopped forward onto the bed.

I knelt between her thighs and eased the handle of the brush into her sopping vagina. I pumped it back and forth and watched her squirm helplessly, her fingers clenching and unclenching in the freshly laundered sheet, and her neat teeth nibbling the crisp cotton to keep herself from moaning too loudly and bringing someone to investigate. Her bottom looked so cute and vulnerable, so I slid the brush from her, pulled her buttocks wider apart, pushed the wooden handle against the tight aperture, felt a moments resistance, and then watched it sink down into her.

What a sight!

She gasped and writhed as I eased the implement deeper into her rectum. I guessed this was the first time she had been penetrated so rudely; I was sinking my brush into her virgin bottom. Her eyes remained tightly closed and her face was a picture of blissful concentration as she accepted the joys I was bringing to her.

I left the brush sticking up from between her buttocks and slipped my dressing gown from my shoulders. Her hips lifted willingly as I guided them up and slid a pillow beneath them. This new position made her more accessible to my desires. A flicker of disappointment clouded her face as I removed the brush and dropped it to the floor, but she squirmed happily as she felt it instantly replaced by the warmer and much larger tip of my cock. She held her breath beneath me, not knowing which orifice I wanted, and to be truthful, I was torn between the mouthwatering promise of both. I waited for a while, watching the anticipation building in her expression, and then dropped my hips and smoothly entered her sex.

She sobbed quietly as my groin slapped down onto her spanked bottom and my weight squashed her into the bed. She was still clothed, and this only added to the eroticism of our coupling.

I kissed her cheek avidly. It was hot, and the tiny tears of joy that meandered on her flesh tasted a little salty. She twisted her head and I found her tongue, and we muttered incoherently together as we kissed. She felt so small and helpless beneath my broader frame.

She moaned rhythmically with every downward lunge of my hips. I managed to squeeze a hand between her and the mattress, and savoured the feel of her lovely ripe breasts through her thin dress. With a little reluctance I withdrew from her tight sex, but I had other fish to fry. She seemed to sense my intention, for she stiffened uncertainly. But I was not to be denied now. I blindly fumbled for her buttocks with my free hand, pulled them apart, nudged the tip of my cock around until I felt it against her rear entrance, and then sank into her beautifully tight bottom. Her back arched, with surprising strength, in unison with my penetration, until her breasts were lifted clear of the mattress and I was able to maul them unhindered. She held herself up for a few seconds, and then slumped down again and came. It was all too much for me too, as she shuddered on the end of my cock, and I ejaculated deep inside her clutching bottom.

When she had gone, after cleaning the rest of my room as I lay smugly watching her from the comfort of the bed, I dozed, happy in the realisation that I would be able to see Anna every day. Perhaps, though, I would never derive quite the same amount of pleasure as I had that first time. It was an unforgettable experience, but the seduction had been as powerful as the sex. But she was a rare young beauty, and I was pleased enough to know that she had invited me to her room that night.

At seven-thirty, I knocked on her door. Anna was waiting for me, still wearing the same figure-hugging dress that she had worn earlier. She must have known how sexy it made her look.

Before I could even say hello, she lifted her index finger to her lips and, making a shushing noise, took me by the hand and led me into her cramped room.

'I have to be careful. I do not want any of guests to see who I am with. If Señor Albertini discover I am with another man, he try to throw me onto the street. Fortunately he away at the moment, so I can show you all, but I still must be careful. The guests can be terrible gossip.'

I was intrigued by what she said about showing me everything, but I surmised that she was meaning to reveal more and more of her firm young body – and I wasn't complaining about that enticing prospect.

I tried to take her in my arms, but she resisted. 'Later, *señor*, later.' I felt a little put out; a little hurt. I hated rejection.

She led me to a little table in the centre of her room and pulled off a tablecloth to reveal a little spread that she had made in my honour. There were beautiful cuts of cold meat, a plentiful bowl of salad, a good bottle of wine and a small cake crammed with *dulce de leche*, the sweet caramel that is so popular in Buenos Aires.

'First we eat and then we go down. I have key.' She picked up a key that lay on the table, showed it to me, and then placed it in the tiny side pocket of her dress.

'What are you talking about, Anna?'

'Later. First we eat. Then I take you to Señor Albertini's room.'

'Why Señor Albertini's room?' I glanced around. True, there wasn't much space and Anna only had a single bed, but there was certainly enough room for a repeat performance of our morning escapade.

'Everything later, Mr Rose, but now eat.'

We ate in silence, intermittently broken by Anna wanting to know about London and England, and me occasionally trying to raise the issue of Mr Albertini and why we had to go to his room. But I gained no further information. Anna merely told me, in her enchantingly broken English, that all would be revealed in due course.

Most of the time, though, she merely smiled at me, or giggled a little to herself, reaching over the table to take my hand in hers.

I wasn't totally convinced that it was a good idea to explore Mr Albertini's abode, no matter what interest it might hold for me, for the same reason I had harboured fears of seducing Anna. I had heard enough stories and read enough in the newspapers about the Argentinian system to be wary of it, and to fear participating in any illegal activity. I was also a little suspicious of what Anna was up to, and why exactly she wanted to show me her boss's room, and what precisely she wanted me to do when we got there.

When the meal was concluded, Anna said, 'Is now time. Follow me and be quiet.'

She walked me back to the reception area and, instead of going up the stairs as I had suspected she would, she walked past the main staircase to another set of steep narrow steps that led down to a cellar. Anna walked down first and then stood at a big wooden door. She struggled to turn the key in the lock.

Once she had eventually managed to open the door, she flicked the light switch to reveal a room almost as large as the atrium in Andrea's father's house. At the farthest end was a bank of television screens, fifteen in all, stacked in three rows, a thick partition of wood separating each layer. In front of the screens was a large black leather sofa. On the wall nearest the door through which we had entered, were three or four filing cabinets, a desk, and a large gilt-edged mirror. The only other pieces of furniture were a huge double bed, a little bedside cabinet and a commodious armchair.

But apart from the shock of seeing so many televisions, the greatest surprise was a huge collection of video cassettes lining the wall on shelves between the bed and the bank of screens. There must have been something close to five hundred.

I was amazed. The room was clean and orderly, although the weak electric light and the large space in the centre gave a dismal atmosphere to the place. It was however, compared to the humidity of the rooms in the hotel above, comfortingly cool.

'What on earth...?' I stammered in English.

'I will show you, but first you need to know history of Señor Albertini. He is not nice man. He was army officer and is a police informer. Many people suffer because of him. All you see was paid for by army during time of the *junta*. Albertini was given much money to provide surveillance in his hotel.'

'He was a spy?'

'He was spy for the army.'

'And who did he spy on?'

'He spy on the army. A lot of officers, usually – how you say? – lower-ranking, would stay here and Albertini would keep eye on them,' Anna said pointing to the television sets.

'You mean—?'

'Yes, of course. Every room has hidden camera, and not just one. Albertini could get to know every secret in his hotel. He was useful tool for blackmail – for everything underhand that you could imagine. Sit down.'

Anna went to the collection of videos and randomly selected one from the pile. She inserted it in a machine that rested under the wood panelling where the televisions were stacked, picked up a remote control and pressed a button.

All fifteen screens flickered into life. A shock of electronic snow suddenly turned to blue and then two people could be seen fucking on a bed: an elderly silvery-haired man and a young woman in stockings. The woman was on all fours and the old man was lunging at her from behind, occasionally smacking her plump bottom as she jerked on him. The camera must have been placed high in the room as it angled down onto the bed, but then another camera took over, showing a side perspective. You could clearly see the man's cock pounding into her.

'When all was over Albertini keep the cameras,' Anna continued, as I tried to come to terms with what I was witnessing; not just a couple fucking in front of hidden cameras, but the wider implications of this discovery. 'Now he watch for pleasure mostly. We do not often get army people here now. He like to watch, that is all, although occasionally he blackmail a man having an affair, or a lady enjoying a little naughty afternoon fun.'

On the screen, the old man and the beautiful woman with pendulous breasts had now been joined by a third woman who had climbed under him and was licking and sucking his balls as he continued shafting the kneeling woman.

'We get many whores in here. Albertini is a pimp. He

nearly have me as a whore. It was three months after I arrive. I have made friends with a man I have met in the botanic gardens. A nice English man. We have become lovers. I would sneak him into my room in afternoon when I think Albertini is taking his afternoon siesta. One day Albertini invite me into his room. Wait…'

Anna switched off the video just as the silvery-haired gent was coming over the buttocks of the woman on all fours, his semen dribbling down onto the chin of the blonde who lay underneath.

Anna placed another video in the slot. Again the snow, the flash of blue, and there was Anna in a skimpy denim mini-skirt, outstretched on the bed, her skirt pulled up over her buttocks, and there was... My God! There was David, bringing his hand down to crack upon the lovely girl's bare bottom!

'So, he sit me down and show me this. What do I think I am doing letting men spank me when I should be working, and what would my family think if they ever see it? he say. And if I am not a good girl and do what he tell me, then I will be in serious trouble.'

'Like what sort of trouble?' I asked, as if I didn't know.

'He go to my family and tell them all.'

As I listened to Anna my eyes remained transfixed on the screen. David had taken a long riding crop and was lashing the girl across her buttocks and the small of her back. Anna, tethered to the bed, could do nothing but flinch at every stroke of the whip. David lashed her lascivious rump and then the back of her legs, as mercilessly as I remembered him beating Marie...

'So, what exactly he want me to do? I ask him. I was so shocked, so frightened, I could not think straight. He make me go to him and lie across his lap. Then he spank me hard until my bottom is black and blue. Then he push me on the

181

floor and hold my face near his penis. Señor Albertini is not a handsome man. I did not enjoy licking him. An old fat man is not like a good young man like you. He pull out of my mouth and come all over my face. I did not like him.

'You must remember I was new to Buenos Aires. I have no family here and no friends. I was frightened of being put onto the street. Those first few weeks after he show me the video, he did what he want to me, and I let him.

'He would come to my room at night when I am sleeping and pull the bedclothes off me and beat me with his belt. Or sometimes he pull my half-awake body over his lap and spank me on the bottom, then sneak his hand between my legs to see if I am wet. When he see how excited I am with the surprise beatings, he smack me more.

'Or sometimes when I am cleaning a room, he would barge in and lock the door and then, saying nothing, he pull out his cock, make me kneel, and push it in my mouth until he come.

'All was filmed, was always filmed. He would invite his friends to come and watch. I remember a nephew of his called Luca. He is much younger, about my age. When they are watching me, growing more excited, Albertini would call me down here. I have to stand in front of them while Albertini lift up my dress and pull down my panties, their eyes all the time staring at me. Then Albertini would push me onto the bed and make me suck Luca while he spank me with his belt.

'Maybe they make me a rude girl, but I cannot say that I did not enjoy sucking Luca while, at same time, I feel the sting of Albertini's belt on my bottom.'

Now Anna, emancipated from the leather straps, was straddling David, his prick pumping in and out of her, her face tensed in pleasure as he dug his fingertips into the soft flesh of her bottom...

'One time Luca bring a beautiful girl down to the room. I do not know where he find her. They make me watch as they undress her. Luca let his uncle cup her bosom and suck her teats, while he ease down her panties. The girl is enjoying it and seemed to have no inhibitions, until Luca drag her to the bed and tie her wrists to the bed, pulling her rump up so she lay before me. Albertini give me a cane. I know what they want me to do. It was such a surprise and such a thrill to hit the girl. I think she enjoy it because, after the first shock, her shrieks would be followed by a moaning.

'It make me so wet. It is almost a relief when Albertini push me on top of her and, tugging my panties down, fuck me from behind. I can feel the heat of the girl's bottom against my skin while Albertini have me. I come almost instantly, forgetting how disgusting the man who is screwing me is, watching Luca in the girl's mouth...

'As I said, I was frightened of Albertini, but the sex, especially when Luca was there, was good. I was naïve girl and, no matter how horrible Albertini was, at least I discover pleasures that I never dream of. I would have continued, but Albertini want me to be his whore.

'That was last straw. I tell him that if he did not leave me alone, I will go to his wife. He is so frightened of her. She own much of the hotel. I tell him if he think about doing anything more bad to me, he should not, because I take some of the videos and give them to a friend. If anything strange happen to me then she would show them to her father, who have a high position in the government.'

On the screen Anna was now on all fours as David rode her from behind, those beautiful breasts dangling down, swaying as he screwed her as hard as he could, pinching her firm teats. between his fingers...

'He hit me. He slap me across the face. But once he do it

he never dare to do it again, and he was more frightened of me than I was of him, no matter how many connections he still have with the army.'

David could wait no longer and, withdrawing from Anna's juicy quim, he shot his seed over her red bottom.

'So, we strike a deal: he will let me work for him, he will give some money to buy a *casita*, and he will expect nothing from me but my work. And, in return, I will not tell his wife. So far it has worked, but I know how furious he will be with me if his secret is discovered. This is what I am frightened of.'

Anna had taken David's sated cock into her mouth and was sucking it eagerly, the expression on her face showing how desperate she was to make it hard again so he could go on fucking her...

'*Basta*,' Anna said, as she pressed the remote control and the screen fuzz returned. 'I have something else I would like to show you.'

Another video was inserted into the machine and there, to my astonishment, was Beatrice's creamy posterior in full view of the camera, and me pumping in and out of her back passage.

'That looks interesting,' Anna said, smirking at me as I rutted against the French beauty.

I had never watched myself performing before, but my fascination with the show was tempered by the outrage I felt, knowing somebody had secretly filmed me in such an intimate moment.

Soon fascination and outrage gave way to lust as Anna craftily lowered my zip, pulled my cock from my pants, and began to lick it reverently. I savoured the sensation and watched the elegant Frenchwoman reach back between her thighs and weigh my swinging balls as I thundered away at her tight anus. I could remember just how good it

184

had felt, and the cheeky lips and tongue now busy in my lap were combining with the graphic memory to quickly bring me towards an orgasm.

And then the video changed. This was obviously a compilation of edited highlights as I now watched Frankie and Stephanie lying on their double bed, Stephanie lounging back in a diaphanous slip, and Frankie crouching between her thighs, licking the length of her sumptuous pussy.

'Oh, Frankie, I don't know...'

'Shush. You like it, you want it. Forget the little prick,' Frankie hissed, interrupting her slurping ministrations just long enough to silence her friend's minor rebellion.

The "little prick", I took it, referred to me. This was obviously very recent footage.

I couldn't believe it. Not that Frankie had a penchant for female flesh, but that I was watching those two adorable girls in such an intimate position. Decency and my own distaste for prurience should have made me leap to my feet and switch it off, but it was difficult to move with Anna's head bobbing up and down and her tight lips sinking to my balls and then slowly rising again to my bursting helmet. I reached across her curled-up form, wormed my hand beneath her skirt, and slipped my fingers inside the moist folds of her quim.

Stephanie was groaning with pleasure now, her face flushed, her glistening sex held before Frankie's excited eyes. Frankie had a large dildo and was teasing Stephanie with it. The whole scene was now soundtracked by Stephanie's feeble protests and Frankie's firm assertions that her friend loved every second of it.

I lifted Anna up, pulled her astride my thighs, and sat her on my twitching erection. I cupped her breasts through the thin dress and pinched her budding nipples.

The dildo was well embedded in Stephanie by now.

Frankie was frigging her friend and sucking on her clitoris at the same time. Stephanie's slip had been discarded, and her perspiring breasts rippled with the pumping movement of Frankie's arm and the dildo.

Anna rode me as I watched the screen over her shoulder. I was lifting her up by her beautiful bottom and letting her slip down again onto my lap.

Frankie had another dildo. She moistened it in Stephanie's nectar, and then slowly manipulated it up Stephanie's back passage. The lovely victim was now plugged both back and front.

I could feel Anna's body tensing, her thighs tightening against my hips and her arms hugging my neck. The gorgeous girl buried her face on my shoulder and clung to me like a limpet. I slid a finger into her behind and tickled just inside her anus. She loved it, and drove down harder and harder onto me.

Stephanie was wailing. Her body suddenly jerked as she came. Frankie was relentless. She ripped off her own clothes and then planted her sex on Stephanie's face. I could just make out Stephanie licking her friend as Frankie arched her back and squeezed her own breasts in her delirium.

Anna orgasmed on top of me, but I hadn't come. She quickly climbed off me, took my cock in her hands, and masturbated me as hard as she could, her generous lips hovering just above my helmet. I looked down from the screen, from Frankie rolling her sex around on Stephanie's rigid tongue, to watch my sperm erupt powerfully into Anna's hungry mouth.

Chapter Nine

I spent the night sleeping in Anna's youthful arms. She had sworn me to secrecy about Señor Albertini's cellar room, but she understood perfectly why I might not want to stay at the hotel any longer. Albertini was coming back that very day, and the privacy that had been afforded our own first encounter could not be guaranteed after his return. I kissed her tenderly and left her room as the sun rose in a cloudless blue sky.

The biggest surprise of the previous evening had been seeing David administering a thrashing to Anna. When I thought about it, though, it wasn't so strange: David had booked the hotel for me before his departure and, knowing David, it was not so unusual that he should be on such intimate terms with one of its personnel. I only wondered whether Andrea also knew of his penchant for whipping chambermaids.

I started speculating on the nature of David's and Andrea's relationship. They were, in the old cliché of domestic bliss, made for each other. Their powers of sexual divination, Andrea's taste for submission and his for domination showed an uncanny horse-and-carriage compatibility. But he had shunned such sexual congruity with Marie. Something must have happened to him when he had come to Argentina. It wasn't so difficult to imagine Andrea effecting such a change, considering how she had hurricaned through my life since I had arrived here.

It was Andrea who came to the forefront of my mind as I considered where I should now go, not wanting to provide free entertainment for Señor Albertini and his cronies. After I had showered and breakfasted, I called her.

'There is no problem, Jonathan. I know a place. Another friend of mine. I was so stupid not to think of it before. She has an apartment they are not using at the moment. They are away on business. They will not be back for a couple of weeks: well, ten days. I should have offered it to you before,' Andrea said to me after I told her that I had had to leave my present domicile, although I didn't mention all the sordid details. I suspect she imagined some affair of the heart, or rather some entanglement of the loin.

'Oh, the place in Callao?'

'No, not there. Is even more central than that. Do you remember the *cemeterio* at Recolleta?'

'Yes, I do.'

'Is very close to there.'

'Fantastic.' It was fantastic, although one might not think that such close proximity to a cemetery would be. This was the most expensive area of the city, where I had wistfully sat at La Biela in the shade of a parasol and watched an exquisite promenade of rich and beautiful women pass by. It would be perfect.

'I will pick you up at three.'

I settled my account at Albertini's and took a walk down to Plaza Italia, a bustling square close to the hotel. I found a smart *confiteria* in which to pass the time.

I wondered about Albertini, the voyeur extraordinaire. I imagined his beady eyes gawking at the video of me and Beatrice, and wondered how the two English girls must have thrilled him!

As I had shafted Anna, the video had stayed on until the end of the scene: Stephanie was forced to lick Frankie while Frankie sat on Stephanie's face, reaching down to stick the largest of the two rubber dildoes in her quim. I was sure they wouldn't like the idea of Albertini watching them in one of their most private moments, either.

I could have gone to the authorities but, as I said, the authorities frightened me. And Albertini, with all his connections, could create a lot of problems for some troublesome Englishman. I was sure too, that the portly owner was not averse to sharing his secrets with the local constabulary. They seemed to control most other areas of crime; why not vice?

So who else could help? I didn't know enough about the press here, or who to contact. And being a journalist, I realised that I needed some more concrete evidence than a mere accusation told to me by a chambermaid. I doubted that Anna would provide me with a tape, and I also suspected that my nationality wouldn't have been of much help to me.

And thirdly, there was, of course, Anna. I had promised that I would not disclose any of Albertini's secrets. I didn't want to cause her any trouble, after everything that had happened between us. She had, so she had said, shown me for my own benefit, although I suspect that she also got a thrill out of screwing me and watching the other two English occupants of the hotel.

The only positive thing that I thought I could do without landing myself – or her – in any kind of trouble, was to warn Stephanie and Frankie. I should try to get them to change their hotel, as I was about to do. I decided to contact them as soon as they returned.

Walking out of the café, I let myself drift into a kind of reverie. I was so content to be in Buenos Aires. The hot sun beat down on the asphalt; the day was exhaustingly humid, uncomfortable, energy sapping. People strode around languorously, hoping for the clouds to break and the air to cool, cursing the weather like English people curse the rain. The pollution seemed to sit heavy in the air – cars and *collectivos* belched their fumes into the muggy city heat, but I was happy. I never wanted to leave. What I wanted to do was to leap in the air with joy. I was meeting Andrea again in the afternoon. What bliss! Never in my wildest imaginings had I expected to experience what I had experienced. Fantasy had nothing on the reality of my time in Argentina.

Andrea tooted from below my room and I watched her climb out her car, wearing a tight scarlet dress, her eyes searching the window of my room for me, smiling as I waved. David must be mad, I thought, as I descended the stairs with my luggage.

Anna was waiting for me in the reception area. I kissed her goodbye on her lips, then promised to ring her once I knew exactly where I would be staying. She looked a little sad to see me leave, knowing that there would be no more flirting in room twenty-two – or at least not with me.

What a delightful feeling, going from one gorgeous woman to the next, leaving the beautifully young lusty Anna for the older, wiser, more experienced Andrea. Marie and my bloodhound loyalty now seemed even further than the temporal and spatial distance that I had put between us.

A million miles. A million light years!

Andrea leant over and kissed me firmly on the lips.

'You're looking well, Jonathan,' she said, turning an amused gaze upon Anna, who stood watching us from the porch. 'I think I can see why,' she said, before I had a chance to reply.

The apartment was on the ninth floor, giving a splendid view of the city: a skyscape of towering glass, and further

190

beyond, the silver-grey of the River Plate. There were two lavish white-walled bedrooms, a luminous living room leading off to a broad balcony, an all mod cons kitchenette, and a dining room with a huge oval oak table in the centre. I didn't know who owned this place, only that they were friends of Andrea's, but they must have been extremely rich.

Unfortunately Andrea could not stay; she had an appointment with her mother, who was in town for a couple of days.

After she had gone I made myself comfortable, familiarising myself with the house. Later, I went for a stroll around my new *barrio*, but not for long. The sweat dribbled down my back and my shirt clung to me. I was too debilitated by the heat. I longed for air conditioning and cold beers, and to freshen myself with a good shower.

When I returned, I called the hotel and managed to contact Stephanie. They were back! Of course, I wanted to warn both of them about the shenanigans at the hotel, but I also wanted very much to see them, especially after the performance I had witnessed on the video in Albertini's clandestine room.

Would they come and meet me in La Biela? Would they dine with me? I would pay, of course. I knew that they were a little worried about their money. I wanted to see them. I made that clear, but there was also something I needed to talk to them about that couldn't really wait. Stephanie was intrigued, but I wouldn't tell her anything more. She happily accepted my invitation.

'Remember to bring Frankie,' I said, imagining the wicked time that I hoped all three of us were going to have that evening.

It was dusk by the time the two girls arrived. Stephanie wore a simple cream dress, strapless, low-cut, and stretching across the plumpness of her breasts. Her fair wavy hair hung down to her shoulders. Frankie wore a tight black leather skirt and a white blouse tied in a knot at her midriff, her breasts heaving inside the satin material.

I kissed both of them: Stephanie first, feeling the warmth of her cheek as it rested on mine, and then Frankie, a little more perfunctorily.

'So where have you two been?' I asked, as soon as we were sitting at an outside table. The place was crowded and we were lucky to get a seat.

'To Iguazu, the waterfalls. They were fantastic!' Stephanie enthused. 'I've never seen anything quite like it. We also spent a few days in Brazil, on the beach.'

'I thought you were worried about your money.'

'Well, I got a little windfall. Daddy sent me a bundle of money in the post, and we've also both landed jobs at the British Consul. We've been ever so lucky.' Stephanie spoke as if everything in her world was rosy – had always been rosy. There was something rather unnaturally undamaged about the girl, something so perfect about her inhabited world of niceness and decency that made me think she longed for some kind of severe chastisement, if only to give her life some balance.

Over our *aperitivos*, Stephanie continued to enthuse about her travels, the sunny Brazilian beaches, the magnificent power of nature she had witnessed amongst the waterfalls, and the fortune of having obtained a job at the British Consul. Frankie sat silently, staring at me and her friend with a slight whimsical smile on her face, that intimated more boredom than mirth.

I knew I had to be careful. Having my wicked way with Stephanie might not have been so difficult, but getting

Frankie in on the act might be very hard. I wanted her, too. I wanted her tight body; those achingly adorable breasts. I did not need Andrea's help this time: even without the consolidating evidence of the video, it was so obvious that the girl was a dominatrix. I didn't yet know, however, whether she had any interest in me at all. She certainly didn't seem to find me very attractive.

I made plans in my head, thought about lines I might drop into the conversation, and dismissed tactics as soon as they appeared in my consciousness. I had to be careful. I had to be clever.

Over dinner I attempted to talk to Frankie, to get her to open up to me. I asked her the usual generalities; about her family, what she had studied, where she had travelled to – but her answers were always brusque, to the point of being rude.

'So what was all this urgency about wanting to see us?' she asked, when she had become tired of my attempt at friendly interrogation.

'I think it would be a good idea if you left the hotel.'

'Oh, yes? And why is that?'

'Look, I found some things out about the place – some bad things.'

'Really?' Stephanie gave a little gasp of surprise.

'What things?' Frankie sounded dismissively suspicious of me.

'I can't really say. I promised not to tell. All you need to know is that Albertini, the man who runs the hotel, is not a good man.'

'No, he's a fat sexist bastard – but then again, you can't go running away every time you meet one of them,' Frankie said, a smug grin forming on her face.

'There's a bit more to it than that. He spies on people.'

'Is that so? And how do you know all of this stuff?'

'Look, I was told—'

'Told by whom?' There was an aggressive look to Frankie's face as she spoke, her antipathy to me fuelled by wine and the preceding couple of Martinis she had gulped down.

'Listen, Frankie,' Stephanie interrupted, 'if Jonathan says we should move, I mean if he really knows something and he can't tell, then we should take his word.'

'I'm taking the word of no one,' her friend said calmly, swigging back her wine.

'The man is a pervert. He has cameras in the rooms. I know: I've seen them.' I was getting a little angry at Frankie's attitude towards me – understandable though it might have been, considering that she was jealous of Stephanie's attraction to me.

A brief silence followed. The atmosphere was heavy; there was a game going on between Frankie and me. We were competing – or rather, she was competing. I wanted the entertainment to be all-inclusive.

'I have to go to the bathroom. Excuse me.' Stephanie got up to leave the table, casting an angry glance at Frankie, clearly annoyed at the irritating behaviour of her friend.

I was glad when she had gone so I could tell Frankie the whole truth. She would have to believe me.

'Listen, Frankie. I know what I'm talking about. The chambermaid showed me this little room downstairs when Albertini was away. I wanted to warn you that he has videos, lots of videos. I've watched them. There are cameras hidden everywhere. I checked myself. They're in the light fitting, the air vent; tiny things designed for military surveillance...'

She only looked half-convinced.

'I've seen you,' I said, carefully, still not sure of how she would react. 'I watched you and Stephanie. I saw everything. "Forget about the prick."' I mimicked her accent. 'Do you want all the details? I am only trying to protect you both, that's all.'

'And did you have a good view?' Frankie retorted, trying to give an impression of nonchalant dismissiveness. 'Maybe it's you who's been spying on us.'

'I didn't have to tell you. I didn't have to say anything at all. I just wanted to warn you, that's all. What you do is up to you.'

'You know what I suspect?'

'What?'

'I suspect that you are every bit as big a bastard as Albertini is.'

When Stephanie came back the conversation reverted to England. We talked of what we missed about our homeland. In truth, I had to exaggerate, because there wasn't anything that I really yearned for. I already had more than enough of what I wanted here and, being a greedy man, I still hoped for more.

Being placed in the far corner of a room with blaring tango music blanking out any external sound, we hadn't noticed that, outside, the heavens had opened. As we left, the rain was crashing down on the parched pavement, cooling the muggy air.

What a blessing this was! I had been trying to get the girls to come back to my place for a night-cap and, although Stephanie had been more than keen, Frankie in her dour manner had wanted to take a taxi home. But with the rain lashing down, and a distinct absence of taxis, it made my borrowed apartment seem a much more logical alternative.

And this rain was no ordinary rain: this was torrential. Thunder roared above our heads and fork lightning dramatically illuminated the night sky. Even though the apartment was only two blocks away, by the time we reached it, we were all drenched.

On the way up, Frankie even managed to smile a little at her discomfort, while Stephanie laughed heartily at the state she was in, although I found it very enticing. Her dress clung to the contours of her body and the sumptuous curves of her breasts were clearly delineated through the cotton. Her lovely blonde hair was sopping wet, the rainwater dripping down from her forehead to her nose, her face hued with the green and black of running mascara.

And Frankie was no less alluring. The wetness of the rain had made her nipples erect through her blouse and her midriff was covered with a sheen of water.

Once in the apartment I went to get towels so the girls could dry their hair, and then drinks to warm their shivering bodies. The rain lashed against the windows and thunder rumbled in the distance. I intentionally left the lights off, and the orange glow filtering through the windows from the deserted street and the occasional clap of thunder created just the atmosphere I wanted. The rain poured down the glass and cast a continually moving shadow on the interior wall opposite.

'I'm soaked through,' Frankie moaned.

'Look, why don't you take a shower?' She looked at me suspiciously but relented under Stephanie's encouraging gaze. I went into another of the bedrooms and fetched her a silk dressing gown, which probably belonged to the lady of the house.

As the bathroom door closed behind Frankie, I began to undress excitedly.

'You don't mind, do you?' I said to Stephanie as she dried her hair with the towel. I was pulling off my slacks, making no attempt to hide the bulge in my briefs.

'No... I...' Stephanie stammered, a little nonplussed: amazed, perhaps, that a man should be blatantly showing off his semi-erection to her.

When I was down to only my underwear, I walked over to her. 'You should take off your clothes as well.'

She stood, fixed to the spot, staring up into my eyes. At that moment there was a deep roll of thunder and a splinter of lightening which, added to the tension in the room, made her flinch.

'Here, I'll help you,' I said, putting my hands under her dress and pulling her skimpy panties down to the knee with one quick tug. However amazed she was at my audacity, she didn't resist and, when her little white panties lay at her ankles, she accommodatingly stepped out of them.

'Jonathan?'

My hand slid under her dress and felt her hot quim. The tips of my fingers probed her moist lips.

'You like this, Stephanie. Let's not pretend,' I cajoled the surprised girl, slipping the tips of my fingers further into her. 'You want this just as much as I do, don't you?'

'But, Frankie...'

'What about Frankie?' I stroked her and gently kissed her lips. I felt her knees weaken.

'Oh, Jonathan,' she moaned.

Suddenly and forcefully, I pressed down on her shoulders and pushed her to her knees. I liberated my hard penis from my briefs. It speared up, twitching before her spellbound eyes. I watched triumphantly as her moist lips peeled ever so slightly apart.

'Suck me,' I urged. She was clearly reluctant, probably surprised by the breakneck speed of events, and unsettled by the insistent nature of my actions and the pressure of my fingers on her shoulders. I repeated my injunction. She obeyed, and I luxuriated in the feel of her tentative lips closing over my helmet. I touched the back of her head and guided her further onto me. Closing my eyes, I relaxed and enjoyed... If only Frankie could see us now. That would teach her a lesson for the way she spoke to me earlier.

I could have remained all night with that beautiful girl kneeling submissively before me with my cock lodged firmly in her mouth, but I had other plans. The presentation had to be perfect if my little project was going to be successful. Frankie was still in the shower; but for how much longer?

I roughly pulled Stephanie off me, her suppliant eyes looking up. She started to protest at her harsh treatment. 'Jonathan, what's wrong? What are you doing?'

I instantly thought of David and how authoritative he could be; persuading a woman into submission. 'Stephanie, you must do what I tell you. You know it's what you want.'

'Jonathan, I'm not so sure that you—'

'Stephanie, be quiet,' I demanded. She obeyed immediately, pouting in a childish sulk.

I raised her up by her elbows and guided her to the sofa. I pushed her down into the softness of the upholstery and sat beside her, placing my hands on her shoulders and pushing her down so she lay on her back looking up at me.

'Jonathan...' she beseeched softly.

She was going through a charade, because she could have walked out of the apartment at any time. Or she could have screamed for Frankie to come, but she did neither of those things. She preferred this simpering, pleading performance, precisely because she knew I was going to be ruthless with her. It was the rule of the game; her own meagre self-justification for wanting to be disciplined.

I knelt astride her soft breasts, and cradling her head in my hands, I watched her lips part to accept my cock into her mouth again. I thrust my hips towards her face and watched my cock slide further inside. Her hands came up and pressed unconvincingly against my stomach, in a vague display of resistance.

'You will do it, Stephanie, because you want to do it.'

Her hands flopped down again onto my thighs, and she began to massage them in time with the milking motion of her mouth.

I gently touched her flushed face, and could feel my helmet prodding her stretched cheeks from within. With wide twinkling eyes she stared up at me, clearly amazed as she was at last following her natural submissive instincts. With increasing confidence she gradually sucked me with more gusto; without any hesitation or regret.

I heard the shower fall silent, but I suspect Stephanie did not. Judging by her increasing enthusiasm for her task, she was unaware that Frankie was probably dry by now and in all likelihood slipping into the silk dressing gown.

It was time for the next stage of my plan.

I quickly, and to Stephanie's obvious surprise, disengaged my cock from her extremely talented mouth, climbed off her, and before she could protest I sat down, hoisted her over my knee, and pulled her dress up to expose her lovely bottom.

My timing was perfect, for the door opened and Frankie, dressed in the silk gown, walked in, and stared in amazement at the scene that greeted her.

I looked at Frankie's shadow, just as the thunder rumbled again and silvery light flared on her profile, and then I smacked her friend's fleshy buttocks with the palm of my hand. Stephanie flinched at the strike and rolled nicely on my erection. I repeated the action, this time slapping her much harder, and all the time staring into Frankie's transfixed eyes, gauging her reaction.

Frankie, who wore her youthful world-weariness heavily on her sleeve, could not believe what she saw. Nor did she quite know how to react. I hoped she would do exactly

199

what I encouraged her to do.

'Look, Frankie. Look at Stephanie. Isn't she beautiful?' I struck the perfectly positioned bottom again. 'She's for you, Frankie. This beautiful creature is waiting for you.'

I suspected she wanted to fight against the lust that was obviously sweeping through her body. I am sure that part of her did not want to weaken, that there was an angry bitterness in the core of her soul because I had stolen Stephanie from her. I was sure this was the battle raging within, as I spanked Stephanie again.

'Frankie. Look, she's waiting. She's waiting for you.'

Frankie's eyes were glued to Stephanie's blushed bottom.

'Come on, Frankie… enjoy yourself!'

It was all working like clockwork. As if entranced, Frankie walked to the sofa, close enough for me to reach out and grab her by the wrist. 'She's very beautiful. Look at her bottom.' I let go of Frankie's wrist and tanned her friend again. 'Let's have her, Frankie. Let's take her, you and me. Let's punish Stephanie.'

I was excited but very nervous. I knew that at any moment the spell could be broken, that Frankie could decide that the game had gone far enough. I decided not to overdo it, and so I gently massaged Stephanie's sore bottom. She sighed at the soothing motion of my hand, and from the mellowing look in Frankie's eyes I sensed I had done the right thing and that her necessary acquiescence would now be forthcoming.

'Let's tie her up, Frankie,' I carefully ordered. 'You tie her legs.' How delightful that was, to try to dominate a dominatrix!

Frankie stood for a moment, running her fingers over the silk belt, still unsure, still hesitant.

'Come on…' I encouraged again, fighting to maintain an edge of authority in my excited voice.

Slowly, Frankie moved closer. She slipped the belt from the loops of the gown, and began to bind Stephanie's ankles together. I rolled Stephanie onto the sofa, found my trousers and removed the belt, and then used it to secure her wrists.

Stephanie put up no physical resistance, but she did look amazed at what was happening to her.

'Jonathan, stop this,' she pleaded weakly. 'Frankie, tell him to stop this.'

'Stephanie, be quiet,' Frankie said firmly. 'You know you want to be punished. You know you like it, so stop pretending.'

'Tell us you don't really want this to happen, and we'll stop,' I added, confident of her total submission. 'Tell us, Stephanie. Tell us to stop.'

Stephanie didn't make a sound, but merely hid her face in the cushions.

'If you complain from now on, we'll ignore you,' I said.

I signalled to Frankie and together we lifted Stephanie, carried her into the bedroom, and tossed her onto the bed.

In the half-light I searched the wardrobe for belts and, finding half a dozen or so, pulled them out and put them on the bed. Stephanie made no more protestations. She did tug on the belt binding her wrists, but only succeeded in pulling it tighter, and she tried to lever her ankles from the silk cord, but it was impossible; Frankie had bound her every bit as expertly as I had done. I smiled at my accomplice.

I returned to the closet and, finding a chiffon scarf, used it to gag Stephanie. I fastened it tightly over her mouth, and then stood back to admire our handiwork. She looked absolutely gorgeous, tied and helpless, her dress a tangled mess of material which barely concealed her charms from our hungry eyes.

We both picked up a belt and began to alternately and

201

methodically lash our victim across her thighs; not viciously, but just enough to let her know who was in charge. Attempting to avoid the bite of the leather, Stephanie managed to squirm onto her front, but only succeeded in presenting us with her glorious rump. It represented a target just too appetising to resist. We rained lashes down on her white silken flesh, as the rain lashed down on the window pane. Stephanie squirmed under our blows, confusedly trying to seek relief from the pain that I knew she so desperately craved.

'Let's blindfold her, too,' Frankie suggested, searching the wardrobe for an appropriate scarf. Having found one, she pulled it roughly around Stephanie's head. She could not see now. She would not know where the next lash was coming from.

I manoeuvred Stephanie into a kneeling position, so her beautiful bottom perched up before us. I'm afraid I was just too weak to deny myself any longer. I allowed Frankie to welt Stephanie's lovely bottom a couple of times, and then I ordered her to untie her friend's ankles. Oh, how I loved being in control, to be able to do what I wanted with the two girls, as Frankie complied with my demand without question. Once the silk bond was removed she struck her friend with a couple more calculated strikes on the tops of her thighs, and then I climbed onto the bed, pulled Stephanie's legs apart, and shuffled closer. Clutching her succulent buttocks, I prised them apart and revealed her cute anus and her wet sex-lips.

I glanced at Frankie, and revelled in the fact that she was completely immersed in the sexual charge that pervaded the room.

I had conquered them both. How satisfying that realisation was.

'Now, Stephanie,' I whispered into her ear, the silk

blindfold dancing lightly against my lips. 'I'm going to fuck you.' I felt the mattress sink as Frankie climbed onto it, and knew she was watching us closely. I straightened up, kneeling tall, opened Stephanie with my left thumb, and aimed my cock with my right hand. My helmet nudged between her soaking lips, and then one quick stab of my hips and my groin slapped against her welted and blotchy bottom. Her head rose and her blonde hair swept her back as I gripped her hips, held her as tight as possible, and ground against her lithe form.

I was in no hurry. I took her slowly with long steady strokes, each one bringing a smothered moan as Stephanie delighted in her pleasure after receiving so much pain.

'Do you like watching, Frankie?' I croaked, aware that my voice betrayed my mounting passions.

Frankie said nothing. Her eyes were frozen on the erotic tableau before her; her delirious friend groaning and bucking her hips, her breasts swinging within her dress as she rocked back and forth, and the point where my glistening cock pistoned in and out of her body. Lightening crackled outside the window and for a second the contours of our perspiring bodies were a flickering contrast of phosphorous white and deep shadow. Frankie inched closer, breathing lightly, and slid one hand between our legs and one between her own. As Stephanie and I headed towards our mutual orgasms Frankie masturbated with increasing urgency, and circled my driving cock tightly with her forefinger and thumb.

Stephanie slumped into the mattress and came, and the sight of her rapturous friend took Frankie over the edge too. I let myself go immediately, and my cock pulsed within the tight ring of finger and thumb as I discharged deep inside Stephanie.

We removed all of Stephanie's bondage and dozed

together for a while, our limbs entwined and our fingers idly stroking and exploring. Once I had recovered I rolled onto Frankie. There was no resistance; indeed, she welcomed my approach.

We kissed passionately as Stephanie lay beside us, her eyes closed and her breathing slow and relaxed as she continued to repose.

This was a more languid screw. I entered Frankie, and we gently rolled our hips together. It was a complete contrast to my previous coupling, but no less enjoyable. Having ejaculated so recently I was able to maintain control for a long time. Frankie orgasmed quietly in my arms a number of times before I tensed, wormed my tongue into her welcoming mouth, and came inside her.

The storm outside had abated and the rain no longer lashed against the window, just as the storm in the room had abated.

Stephanie murmured in her sleep and cuddled into the two of us.

Frankie smiled up at me in the darkness. 'Oh, Jonathan,' she purred sleepily, 'that was just so, so nice.'

Chapter Ten

If I recall everything I did in the following days, I would never finish telling my story. Too many tails, so to speak, for the tale. It was an incredible time. Never had I had one like it before in my entire life, and never maybe will I have one like it again.

A brief résumé: Frankie and Stephanie were guests in my borrowed apartment, both together and separately. Then, once I rang Anna, she came and, at length, pleasured my length in a surprising number of skilful and imaginative ways. And then of course there was Andrea who, now her mother had gone, found that she had much more time on her hands, and more and more often, me in her hands. Claudia also called round and, although she did not have much time, gave me a delightfully deft blow-job after I had made her bottom red raw with my belt.

And David.

What happened to David, my initial reason for coming here? From our several telephone conversations, it seemed that in nearly four weeks the man had visited every country in the world except for Argentina. I had berated him for stopping me from travelling, as he continually pleaded with me to hang on until his return, but this was a little disingenuous on my part. In truth, I was having such a good time that the thought of travelling anywhere – even outside my borrowed apartment – seemed nonsensical. I was pleased that I had visited the city and seen its sights in the first couple of weeks, or my anecdotes of the place would have been unsuitable except for the most bawdiest of my friends.

In truth, before David's call, I was, for all the sexual gratification, beginning to get a little depressed at the prospect of my imminent return to dreary, wintry London. Reality was starting to slap me in the face. I had no job, no long-term place to live, nor much money, and a CV that was less than impressive; my future prospects did not look good. Andrea talked about several possibilities of working in Buenos Aires, but I was still a little unconfident about my Spanish, and nothing that she suggested sounded very realistic at a time when I needed to be very realistic indeed.

There was David, of course. If anybody was in a position to offer me a job, then it was he. But I had despaired of seeing him. Anyway, there was this pathetic thing I still uselessly harboured inside me called pride: I thought I could not live comfortably working for David, nor did I wish him to pull any strings for me.

No, it was most definitely time to face facts, maybe to grow up. Buenos Aires had been fantastic to me. It had cured itches both sexual and existential, and made me realise that more was possible in life, in all sorts of ways than I had thought. I had even begun – although it is something I thought I would never totally lose – to think of Marie in a less negative way. The bitterness resided but maybe didn't take up as much space as it had done when I had been so fresh from her betrayals.

So refreshed, I most certainly was. It was the resignation part I was finding difficult: resigning myself to London, to mediocrity, to cramped bedsits, to dirty tubes, and a greater degree of sexual abstinence than I had had here. But Buenos Aires was a holiday and all holidays must come to an end.

So David rang two days before I was to depart:

'Hello, Jonathan.'

'Hello David,' I said apathetically. David's jet-hopping

206

and the certainty that I wouldn't see him were two things I had definitely resigned myself to. 'Where are you this time?'

David chuckled. 'I'm here, you bloody fool, in Buenos Aires. Look, they wanted me to fly to Santiago again, but I told them no way. I've had a mate here for four weeks and I haven't even had a chance to see him, not to mention the necessity of reacquainting myself with my wife.'

I had only some three hours previously reacquainted myself with his wife, thrashing her soapy body in the deluxe shower of my luxurious apartment.

'Great. Can I see you?'

'Don't move. I'll pick you up in twenty minutes.'

To give David his due, he did look completely shagged out, his face unhealthily ruddy and worn, his eyes red and a little listless. It was not age that was being unkind to him – he was still handsome – but his gruelling schedule had definitely taken its toll.

Seeing him that night was the first time in my life when I stopped envying him his success. As David always said – at the time I thought it had been with mock modesty – it was a question of swings and roundabouts. Maybe I wasn't doing so badly, after all. For all my lack of ambition and wealth, if you were going to put money on the coronary stakes, you would get better odds on David than you would on me.

He drove me in his BMW up to San Isidro, apologising for the absence of Andrea who had had something on, she had told him, and couldn't cancel because of the short notice he had given her of his return.

Driving through the leafy avenues of San Isidro made me think about Andrea, about that wonderful day and night I had spent with her and Claudia at her father's house; and only a few hours previously I had touched her ravishing

207

body. I felt an intense stab of pain at the thought that I might never get to touch it again, not now that David was back in town. I hadn't known then, that afternoon as I kissed her and watched her get into the lift outside the apartment, that it could be the last time I would be with her. There wouldn't be any possibility of her driving me to the airport as she had intended, after having spent the day with me. Not now. It was one consequence of David's return that I hadn't considered until then. It was hard enough to leave Frankie and Stephanie and Anna and Claudia, but the thought of not seeing Andrea again was almost unbearable.

David parked his car outside the famous racetrack at San Isidro and took me to one of the most expensive *parrillas* in town.

Considering that we hadn't seen each other for so long, and both had expressed wholehearted desires to do so, the conversation between us in the car had been lapidary and stilted, David frequently apologising for being tired. That was excusable. I had no excuse. I didn't really know what to say to David any longer.

In the restaurant and a couple of drinks later, both of us had livened up a little.

'So what have you been doing, flying all around the world?' I asked.

'Breaking my balls. Visiting potential clients, sucking up to the rich and powerful, talking to editors, sub-editors, producers, assistant producers, deputy assistant producers, eating lousy hotel food, missing Andrea and generally wondering whether the whole fucking game is worth it.'

'You're tired?'

'I'm fucked, knackered, shagged out and depressed. These bastards are killing me. That's what I want to talk to you about.'

'What?'

'Do you need a job?'

'Pardon?'

'Would you like a job?'

'What type of job?'

'How about my job?'

I started laughing.

'Look, I'm serious. When I was complaining to them about the amount of flying around they've been making me do, I also complained about a lot of other things. I had a right old ding-dong with them, told them I was tired of being their troubleshooter. Well, the long and the short of it is—'

'They fired you?' I joked.

'No. They pushed me upstairs.'

'To do what?'

'Well, as they told me, they haven't exactly defined all my responsibilities. They're negotiable, but I'm more or less going to be head of production. But all I care about is that I don't have to travel around so much. A nice little office in some huge office block, a few minions, a good salary and then home to bed. It's enough for me these days.'

'Is it still current affairs?'

'God, no – that was light years ago. No, now I'm assistant executive manager of the whole kit and caboodle, the next big chief in line, and unfortunately in charge of everything: current affairs, sport, movies, nature, music, adult entertainment, the lot.'

'And now you're going to be the main man?'

'More or less, but from here. Not so much travelling. You wouldn't believe what it's been like, this last six months. They've been making this big push into Europe. I won't bore you with all the technical details, but this cable station wants to be a world player. They probably haven't got a chance but there is big money behind them. Gomez, the owner, wants to be the next media magnate. He's rich, this Gomez – all dodgy money, of course. The whole thing started as a way of laundering his dirty drug dollars. Now he's rich and respectable. He's got the politicians in the pocket. The judges and the establishment all cream their pants every time he bumps into them. It's a shoddy affair, I tell you. But never mind that. I'll tell you where you come in.'

'Where I come in?' I repeated, still incredulous that David was seriously offering me employment.

'Listen. I've thought about it. I know you're smart. A chronic underachiever, but we can sort that out. They want people in Europe. People who can make small talk with the people who matter. They want a little respectable Englishman who knows the ropes and plays legit.'

'But I don't have any experience of—'

'You don't need any experience. I need to have someone I can trust. Somebody on the inside of the operation.'

'A snitch?'

'No, not a snitch. Just somebody who'll be down the line with me, who won't give me bullshit and who talks the same language.'

'And what would my job be, exactly?' I still wasn't totally convinced that David wasn't having a very cruel laugh at my expense.

'You'd be based in Europe. And you'd have more money than you've ever seen in your life. You'd get the opportunity, now that you're a single man, to have as many beautiful women as your heart desires, plus a company car. You get my drift: have a few people to run errands for you, expense account...'

'Yes, but what is the job?'

'Basically to do my travelling for me. To tell whoever it is that you have to tell what I want you to tell.'

'Won't I end up as shagged out as you are?'

'Maybe, but I tell you something: I would love this job if I was a free man, if I didn't love my wife, if I didn't love this city. But you, you have no ties. You have the chance to travel, to make money and to have a different woman every night. Sounds good to me. Look, you could try it for a year. You told me you haven't got another—'

'But—'

'I know what your but is. Your but is your pride. You don't like the prospect of working for me: that's it?'

'That's partly it.'

'Look, I know you. I know you are sound. I trust you. It's not a cushy number. I expect you to work, but the rewards are fantastic. You wouldn't get the chance of a job like this in Europe, I'm telling you. And I'm a damn good boss. No special favours, but I'm fair. Honest.'

'I'll think about it.'

David was, of course, right. Nobody in England would give me the chance that he was presently offering me: not with my CV and my abysmal record of failure. An expense account and more money than I knew how to spend.

I had taken over his long-term girlfriend. I had recently borrowed his wife. Why not step into his career shoes, too?

But something still niggled, didn't feel right, apart from my reservation about having David as my boss. The prospect of working in the stressed world of cable television was daunting. Perhaps I was also a little enamoured or at least snug with my own relentless failure. Maybe I was too old to become a dashing success.

'Think about it, for sure, but I need to know fairly soon. It's a competitive business. It's difficult to expand. Too many people have too much experience in this game, and this cable company doesn't have enough. Argentina is not

211

Europe, it's not the States. I'm just playing it for all it's worth, while I can. I've made myself a reputation. I can work elsewhere if that's what I want. I have no allegiance to these bastards. I've given enough; now I want to take. You understand?'

'Yes, of course.'

'Well, climb aboard. Jump on the bandwagon, because there ain't many passing these days.'

'Like I said, I'll think about it.'

'Maybe I can persuade you. Maybe I can show you at least one or two of the perks. I'll send a car around to you tomorrow about nine. It'll bring you to my office. You'll see that it's not all just about hard work. Look, what I'm offering you is probably the best time you are ever going to have in your life. For God's sake, take the job. I need you and you need it. It's no favour.'

I did think about it. David could be very persuasive. It sounded very impressive. Ten years ago I would have leapt at the opportunity, before I had lost all confidence in my professional self. It did sound like a fantastic opportunity, and whatever qualms I might still have about working for David were diminishing as I considered the advantages of travel, of money, and – as David had said, with an adopted Americanism – international pussy. What had I to lose? Nothing. I have also always had that type of nature that prefers to say yes than no. This has often got me into a lot of trouble, like my agreeing to a heedless devotion to Marie, but a lifetime habit of weak-willed affirmation is difficult to ditch.

There was another distinct advantage that David told me about as he was driving me back to Recolleta. I'd have to visit Buenos Aires three or four times a year to see him in person. Talking on the phone and video conferences were okay, but he liked to see his people face to face. That wasn't the advantage I was thinking about. I was thinking about Anna and Claudia and Beatrice and, of course, Andrea.

David was as good as his word. My buzzer rang at nine. I walked out onto the street into a wall of muggy heat that, even at nine, was oppressive, and saw with amazement a stretch limo and a uniformed chauffeur awaiting me.

I was driven a short distance to a huge glass tower block that overlooked the River Plate. David greeted me as I stepped out on the highest floor. He offered me his hand and casually slapped my back.

'So have you thought about it?' The transformation in David's appearance was dramatic. He was lively, his eyes bright; he moved like a man ten years younger. Maybe this was the rejuvenative power of Andrea. I felt terribly jealous when I thought about David enjoying all the pleasures that Andrea might have brought him while I had slept alone.

'I'm interested – very interested – but I want to know a little more.'

'Okay, a coffee and then we thrash out the details.'

He led me into the outer office of GMP, Gomez Media Productions. Among the filing cabinets, the slimline computers, the coffee machines and the state-of-the-art office desks, sat fifteen or so of the most gorgeous women I had ever seen: which was saying a lot as I had seen so many in Argentina. It was not just that they were attractive, it was the variety of the sexual allure that impressed: women for all moods and seasons and tastes. My God, I thought, as David led me into his inner sanctum, let me just work here, for nothing if necessary. I felt envious of the one or two suited men I could see. Or maybe they were being driven mad, surrounded by such fantastic women every day of their lives, one short shag away from the mental house.

David could see I was impressed. 'Perk number one,' he said as he opened a door in the little reception area into a bright sunny room, that had nothing of the sterility that I imagined existing in the high-powered world of the media business.

His office was huge but cosy: lots of pastel-shaded furnishings; bright modernist prints hung from the sofa lined walls; there was, as you would expect from a media executive, a huge television screen on one side of the wall.

David went automatically to sit at his desk, before getting up, gesturing that the sofa would be better. He rang through for coffees, then pulled out a huge manila folder and passed it to me.

The next three or four hours were spent going through what my job would entail, if I finally decided to take it. A lot of the terms went straight past me, and David often couldn't avoid slipping into the jargon of the industry. From what I understood, GMP was interested in not only making programmes for its own cable network, but also selling them to terrestrial stations and video retailers abroad. This would apparently be my area. David was to be appointed as the executive manager of GMP. I would be working for him, a kind of travelling salesman, flogging GMP's products for all they were worth to whoever, as David disloyally said, was stupid enough to buy them. Europe was to be my patch.

I had never been very good at selling anything. I was beginning to have doubts. David told me that the selling part wasn't so important. He had been flying around the world making as many contacts as he could. There would be somebody underneath me who would have responsibility for making new clients. My job would be to keep the old ones sweet.

'It's a cutthroat business, all right. Jonathan, one of the

reasons I want you is that I can trust you. No double-dealing. You're not greedy. If you have enough you don't need more. That's more important to me than the other bullshit. You work for me and I'll work for you.'

The job was beginning to sound as irresistible as the beautiful women I had seen in the outer office, even if David was going to be my boss.

'Sounds great,' I said enthusiastically.

'Good. You're onboard. But no contracts until after this afternoon. We have some business to attend to; a few interviews.'

I assumed he was going to select some sales people that I would be working with.

David took me out to an expensive French restaurant for lunch. He was really coming up trumps. For all the business spiel, and the Americanisms he had picked up in his travels, he seemed much more like the old friend I remembered. It was a great lunch, great food and wine, and a wonderful conversation. David gave me further insights into GMP with his cynical eye, and occasionally reverted to reminiscing about the past.

'Why did you move from the hotel? I thought you would like it there,' he said, winking at me over dessert.

'You mean Anna?'

He laughed. 'I do... and what about the two blonde girls?'

'Frankie and Stephanie? How do you know about them?'

'I know Stephanie's uncle. He wrote to me asking if I could help them. I met them off the plane when they arrived, as I was leaving. I recommended they should stay in the hotel. I thought you would like them. I could tell what types they were. You know I have the knack. I wouldn't have minded myself. Maybe we can...'

I told him about Albertini and how I had seen David in

action with Anna.

It was my turn to amaze David.

'Don't worry – that'll be taken care of, and I wouldn't let Anna down. That's how I learnt about the hotel in the first place. Gomez has the right connections. Albertini won't get away with it any more.'

'What will happen to him?'

'Oh, nothing too serious or sinister: a burglary, lots of smashed-up TVs and cameras, that's all.'

Whatever antagonisms, confusions or suspicions that had come between us, seemed to dissipate during our frank talk, and in our bright laughter. Frank, you understand, up to a point. I did not mention Andrea, except for eulogising her for her breezy laugh, her hospitality and her great sense of humour.

She was, of course, another complication concerning my taking of the job. Yes, because I could still see her, and no, because she was his wife. If I were honest – and with the terrible sensation that history was about to repeat itself – I could feel myself falling in love with Andrea. Why did I always end up besotted with David's women?

As we passed through the reception area on our way back from lunch, and after my lusty eyes had once again scanned David's outer office, I noticed a stunningly gorgeous woman sitting quietly, apparently waiting for us. She had a fantastic voluptuous figure and beautiful shoulder-length red hair. It almost gave me an erection just to look at her. She was dressed alluringly in a silk blouse and short plain skirt.

'We won't be long, my dear,' David said to her. 'We'll do the introductions then.' He winked at me as we passed through to his main office. 'This is where the fun starts,' he said from the corner of his mouth so no one could hear but me.

Over a post-prandial cognac, David filled me in. 'She's handpicked, of course. She lives in Santiago, a frustrated science graduate after some easy money. As I said, not all of my job is laborious work. This is where we get to play. We have here one of the most beautiful women that South America has to offer. It's a little hobby of mine. I flew her out here yesterday.'

'Why is she here?'

'For our pleasure, Jonathan – purely for our pleasure. Look, I told you before, part of my job is troubleshooting. This means getting into the nitty-gritty of production, looking at procedures and processes: everything from sales to advertising, from checking scripts to examining casting. Well, some things are more interesting than others. I became – because I do have some power here – casting director for one of our in-house adult films. This is a little sideline of mine.'

'Adult films?'

'High class, hard core, big budgets. None of the tacky hand-held stuff, although not all of the girls are totally sure what exactly we expect from them. They're fresh, these girls. They've never done this kind of thing before, so we are going to break them in. Here, pull a chair over.'

David went and opened the door and called out, 'Miss Marta Torres, please.'

Marta walked into the room, looking nervously around her, catching my eye and then gazing down at David's desk.

'Please take a seat, Miss Torres,' David said, motioning to the chair on the other side of his desk. I sat to one side and gazed at Marta's beauty. The creamy silk blouse barely contained her beautiful breasts. The tight maroon skirt gave me a generous view of her shapely stockinged legs. Her eyes were green, maybe hinting at some celtic ancestry.

'Right then, Miss Torres, this is Mr Rose who is helping

217

me to conduct the interview. You do understand?'

'Yes,' Marta replied tentatively.

'It is one of the requisites of the job that you speak English.'

'I speak English, a little.'

'Well, good. During our conversation in Santiago I did inform you that we were making an adult film. Are you aware what this will entail?'

'*Si pienso que si.*'

'Please, Miss Torres, in English.'

'*Lo siento*. I sorry. I think, yes.'

'And you are prepared?'

'Yes.' Marta seemed to become more nervous as the interview progressed, her face blushing red, her hands nervously fidgeting on her lap.

'We are here today to establish whether you would be suitable, particularly since you have no experience of adult entertainment. This means examining your abilities in considerable detail.'

Marta nodded.

'We expect our performers to be perfect in every respect.'

Marta again nodded, even though I was not completely sure that she had understood everything David had said to her.

'You understand that this will involve certain aspects that are not normally involved in an interview.'

'Pardon?'

'Well, I mean it might involve you in situations that are of an intimate nature. We are investing a lot of money in you. We have to be sure we are getting value for that investment.' David was still excellent at sounding authoritative. 'Are you prepared?'

'I think so, yes.'

'Of course, you know you can terminate the interview at

any time if you do not feel comfortable with our procedures.'

'I understand, I think.'

'I think you do, Miss Torres,' David said, staring blatantly at her breasts. 'Let us start by examining your body. Mr Rose, if you would be kind enough to take a look at Miss Torres' breasts?'

Oh, this was going to be a delightful game! I stood up and walked over to the girl. Her body tensed in trepidation.

'Don't worry, Miss Torres. Mr Rose is an expert in his field.'

I stood behind the voluptuous Chilean and looked down on her jutting breasts. Marta kept her eyes straight ahead, staring at David. I ran my hands over her silk blouse, feeling her pliable flesh under my palms. Her fingers lightly clenched the arms of her chair as though she was at the dentist.

'Relax, Miss Torres… you must relax,' David said. The girl eased her grip, only slightly.

I undid the buttons slowly, watching the anxious heave of her bosom. The second button revealed a beautifully decorative dark red lacy bra, its half-cups barely concealing her turgid nipples. Her bra had a catch at the front. I had to delve into the warmth of her deep cleavage to unhook it. I could feel her heart beating against my knuckles. I watched her bulky breasts bounce free, the strawberry-red of her nipples enchantingly extruding from the curvaceous flesh.

'If you would be so kind, Mr Rose, to examine the girl's nipples?'

'Of course, Mr Hutton,' I said, playing along with the game. Marta winced slightly as I pinched her nipples between my fingers and tweaked them. Her delightful breasts were so soft to the touch. I could hear her breathing deeply, and her flesh molded delightfully against my hands

219

as her lungs filled.

'Mm. Very good, Miss Torres. Do you mind if Mr Rose does that again?'

Marta stayed silent for a moment and then hesitantly nodded. I pinched her nipples again, and again she flinched, sighing a surprised little 'oh'.

'Thank you, Mr Rose.' I returned to my seat. 'Now, Miss Torres, we need a little information about your general sexual experience. I am assuming you have had sexual intercourse before.'

'I… yes.'

'Could you tell me of any interesting sexual experiences you have had? I ask this question, as we like our performers to be sexually adventurous.'

Marta looked bewildered.

'Have you had, for example, sex with two men before?'

Marta shook her head, looking mildly indignant.

'No? Well, that is a shame. Would you have anything against having sex with two or more men?'

Marta, having refastened her bra and buttoned her blouse to salvage whatever modesty she could from the situation, considered the prospect. 'I not know.'

While the unusual conversation continued I found it increasingly difficult to tear my eyes from the blouse, stretched over those two luscious breasts that had so recently warmed my palms.

'Until you try, I suppose,' David said.

'*Si.*' Her answer was again tentative, doubtful.

'Have you ever been beaten, Miss Torres? Have you ever had your naked bottom whipped? Have you ever been tied up?'

Marta vigorously shook her head, clearly bemused by the various enticing prospects David had just related.

'Now, could you stand up, please?' Marta did as she

was told. 'Please come round to this side of the desk. Mr Rose, if you would come, too? Miss Torres, would your please lift your skirt?' Marta lifted her skirt a paltry inch. 'No, Miss Torres, higher.' Another inch as her hands gathered the material at her sides. 'Higher, please... much higher.' Marta lifted her skirt higher, exposing a little of her matching lace panties. I was leaning on David's desk, staring at her lace-covered pussy and the decorative edge of her black stocking tops and suspenders. 'Right up to the waist and hold it there.' Marta again did what she was told.

Despite the air conditioning, I was beginning to perspire as my heart beat rapidly with anticipation.

'You are a science graduate, Miss Torres. Is that correct?'

'*Si*, yes.' she replied, her trembling fingers clutching the folds of her skirt.

'Well, adult entertainment is a science of sorts, too. You must relax. This examination is absolutely essential, I can assure you.'

Although Marta looked at both of us suspiciously, she did not move, but kept her skirt held high, over the delicious lace covering her pussy and stretched across her firm buttocks.

'How do you feel with two men staring at you in your panties, Miss Torres?'

She did not answer.

'Do you feel excited?'

Still she did not reply.

'I think it is important that our workers enjoy their duties.'

She nodded.

'Do you feel a little excited, then?'

'*Si*,' she nodded, not looking excited at all.

'Let us see. Mr Rose, if you would be kind enough to explore her bottom—' Marta gasped with shock, staring at me, amazed by what David had just said '—and I will check her pussy. Come closer, Miss Torres.'

Marta moved reluctantly, letting her skirt fall a little over her silky thighs.

'Lift your skirt, Miss Torres,' David instructed firmly. The girl again did as she was told.

'Don't worry, we'll not hurt you.' Miss Torres did not look relieved or convinced. 'When you are ready, Mr Rose.'

As David cupped her quim, I inspected her bottom. She sighed deeply, but then stiffened when I pulled the delicate gusset of her panties aside and prised my index finger between her generous buttocks. She tried to twist and peer over her shoulder at what I was doing.

'Oh, you're nicely wet, Ms Torres,' David said as he explored her.

'*Si*,' she said in a tremulous whisper.

Although I couldn't see exactly what he was doing to her, from the trembling of her buttocks against my hands and the wet sounds coming from between her thighs I had a very good idea.

'How is her bottom, Mr Rose?'

'Perfectly tight,' I said, watching her sigh and close her eyes as I squirmed my finger just into her rear passage.

'Let's remove these panties, Mr Rose.'

I reluctantly withdrew my finger to enable this manoeuvre, and the flimsy garment was soon lying discarded on the plush carpet.

'Right, Miss Torres, on the desk please,' David directed.

Marta placed her naked buttocks on the polished wood of David's long and broad desk.

'Remove your blouse please. Slowly…'

Every little thing Marta did quite simply oozed sex, although she seemed oblivious to this fact. She unbuttoned her blouse and slipped it from her shoulders. I watched her lip trembling as she stared at the two of us and took the clasp which lay in her deep cleavage between her manicured fingers.

'The bra, no. Keep the bra on for the time being.'

She seemed relieved to be able to retain at least some modesty, but the fragile garment which thrust her breasts together and upwards only enhanced the beautiful vision.

'Now kneel, please.'

Marta, looking a little bemused, again did as she was told and knelt up on the desk. Her skirt slithered back into position and swayed around her sculptured thighs as she leant forward on her elbows.

'Could you move a little further over, please, Miss Torres?'

She moved so her bottom perched out over the edge of the desk.

'Now, while Mr Rose continues to examine your rather lovely *culo*, I must remind you of another talent you will require. That is, sucking a penis. Have you ever sucked a penis, Miss Torres?'

She shook her head.

'You may not be a virgin, but your sex-life has not been very experimental,' David said, admonishing the poor girl as he removed his shoes and socks and unbuckled his belt with clear intent.

Again she shook her head, keeping her eyes on David as he pulled down his trousers and then his underpants, revealing his erect cock. Marta gasped at his naked tool, its huge head, its prodigious length. Climbing up on the desk in front of her, he angled his helmet towards her lips.

'Open your mouth, please, Miss Torres.'

His erection prodded her moist lips, and then they peeled apart and he slid inside. I saw him shudder a little with pleasure. 'That's very good, Miss Torres. Very good.'

Marta's head began to bob gently on the stalk that filled her mouth, and I could hear her avid suckling.

I pulled up her skirt to expose her firm, young buttocks, framed by her suspenders and quivering before my eyes. I parted her buttocks and gazed at the little entrance that nestled there. Her bottom clenched lightly as David pulled her further onto his cock.

I pressed the tip of my finger against her anus again, feeling her body spasm a little as I did so. There was a little resistance, and then my straightened digit popped inside. I began to gently frig her bottom, watching the tremulous surge of her buttocks in response to each careful push and withdrawal.

She was sucking David more and more ardently now. I could see the fringe of her copper hair swinging in unison with every jerk of his hand on the back of her head.

With one finger frigging her bottom, I reached for her wet sex-lips. She moaned at my light touch and then moaned again as I found and teased her clitoris, matching the rhythm in her bottom.

'Mr Rose, if you would be so kind as to administer to the girl,' David said, passing his belt over her bobbing head. Marta tried to strain to see what I was about to do, but David held her tight so she could not move.

I lashed her unsuspecting buttocks with the belt. Marta recoiled as the leather stung her skin, and David's grip tightened in her hair. I struck again. She flinched and squealed around the column of flesh that stretched her mouth. Her bottom quickly glowed a delicate shade of red. I hit her again with the loose leather, and her legs slumped slightly with the full weight of the pain. I immediately repositioned them, so her bottom was held high and her pussy-lips were exposed for my delectation.

'Delightful, Mr Rose,' David said after watching me

whip her. I admired his confidence that she would not convulse too much and ruin him for life with her neat white teeth.

My erection was bursting by now, grossly distorting the front of my trousers.

'I'm going to come in your mouth now, Miss Torres,' David said, still bizarrely maintaining the air of an interviewer. Her face was clamped into his groin, his fingers were entwined in her hair, and he had the audacity to wink at me just before his expression contorted and his hips jerked and I heard the kneeling beauty swallowing frantically.

'Now,' David eventually panted as he released Marta from his grip, 'Mr Rose will need to fuck you. We must assess your willingness to comply in every way. You do understand, my dear, don't you?'

Marta looked up at him with doe eyes, then over her shoulder at me, and then nodded.

I swiftly removed my pants, helped the lovely girl down from the desk, and bent her forward over its lustrously polished surface. Without pausing I positioned my cock between her parted thighs, and she braced herself on straightened arms as I entered her. Sheer lust instantly consumed the both of us, and Marta began grinding back against me as fervently as I was plunging into her. She really was a very horny young lady, and her performance was second to none.

'Oh, very good, Miss Torres, very good,' David enthused. He unclasped her bra again and his eyes bulged as I released her hips and her large swinging breasts tumbled into my upturned palms. 'Very good indeed... You're just perfect; a natural…'

Marta began to writhe so lewdly I was barely able to remain mounted. Even the sturdy desk began to creak.

'Oh, *si… si…*' she moaned, her back arching and her hips tilting so my penetration forged even deeper. The timid beauty who had entered the office such a relatively short time before was transformed beyond belief. She really was too much.

I was aware of David watching us closely as I pulled her back onto me, and I joyfully erupted in her pussy.

'You are perfect, Miss Torres. Absolutely perfect,' David said as she relaxed and collapsed on the desk, my slowly wilting erection still buried inside her. 'You may use our facilities to freshen up.'

Marta gathered her blouse and panties from the floor. As she drifted dreamily to the door he had indicated, her sexiness highlighted by her dishevelled clothing, we both watched the alluring sway of her hips. She stopped and turned before disappearing into the hospitality room. 'I very much thank you,' she said in a husky whisper that made my cock twitch afresh, her eyes twinkling mischievously. 'I very much hope I please you both.'

When she slipped from view, David smiled and dressed.

'Bloody hell, old chum,' I enthused. 'After that I think I could do with a little freshen up too!'

'Of course.' He nodded towards the room where Marta had gone. 'Go ahead, and I'll pour us both a drink.' He grinned broadly. 'I think we deserve it.'

In the hospitality room I found Marta, naked apart from her suspenders and stockings, bending her bottom towards a basin and soothing her tender buttocks with a dampened towel. She looked an absolute picture.

The room was surprisingly capacious. There was the obligatory sofa, a large TV, a fridge, the wash-basin where Marta posed attending to her injuries, seemingly unaware of her immense sexual appeal, and next to her a glass shower cubicle. A panoramic window afforded a fantastic view over the river, which shimmered in the afternoon sun.

Marta looked up and smiled at me as I closed the door.

'Oh, Mr Rose, you give me best sex in my life. I never have such pain, such pleasure. You and Mr Hutton make me come. Never I come so well before.'

I pulled Marta to me and kissed her gently, savouring the taste of her rich red lipstick. Her suspenders rasped seductively against my thighs. My cock lurched and prodded against her flat lower belly. She smiled seductively. Without bothering to remove her suspender belt or silk stockings, I guided her back into the shower and turned on the mixer.

There was indeed a large drink awaiting my return.

'You don't suffer from the old brewers droop, I hope.'

'Never. Why?'

'You'll see.'

As we sipped on our whisky, David explained about the soundproofing, how the staff outside the office would know nothing about our fun with Marta.

He also told me she had been accepted for the film and that, if she was willing enough, she could make a lot of money from the business. 'We treat our girls well. Any time they want, they can back out. For most of them, though, it's an education. I don't know one girl who's looked back. They all do well, make a lot of money, and go on to better things. I always do my research: social background, psychological questionnaires and the like. You know how good I am at talent-spotting.' David grinned and winked at me.

'Come on, we have another interviewee arriving soon.'

'What? But I'm knackered.'

'Tough. This is what it's going to be like from now on. We'll get Marta back in here once we're sure of the new girl. We can check out the female female angle.'

'No more,' I said, holding my hand up in mock surrender.

'What are you, man or mouse?'

I squeaked at him.

'You'll cope,' he insisted. 'I'll give you five minutes before your old man's rock-hard again. Besides, I have a few ideas for how the girls can perform for us.'

'Okay, okay,' I relented. 'Let's hear them. Oh, and one more thing. You have a deal.'

'You'll come and work for me?'

'I'd be an idiot not to.'

'Good man. I knew you'd see sense.' He took my hand and shook it, smiling confidently, as though he had always been sure of my decision.

That evening I walked through the cooling streets of Buenos Aires. David had offered me a lift back to the apartment in the limo, but I fancied a little time on my own.

I thought of David, and suddenly realised that as much as I cared for the bloke, he would always be my enemy. The thought of working for him still bothered me. A future scenario appeared in my mind: David lambasting me for some error I had made. David, in short, lauding it over me, reclaiming that superiority which we both knew was his.

But still I knew I would keep my word and take the job.

I considered my enemy. The dawning truth was that I loved his wife. I would take the job for her; to be near her. Ultimately, unlike all the other women that we had enjoyed together, I did not want to share Andrea. A sad pang of melancholia cut through me at the thought of David returning to her, the epiphanic realisation that I wanted Andrea more than I had ever wanted anything in my life; more than success, more than Marie, more than my sexual liberty.

I thought that when I had come to Buenos Aires, what I needed from life was sexual excitement with neither ties nor commitment. I had been wrong. What I needed was somebody like Andrea to share my life, and this desire overrode all others. With Andrea, I could have everything.

A new story was beginning, a new story that was the oldest story in the world; the lamentable eternal triangle. I would have to fight with David for Andrea's love, that much was clear now.

That much was perfectly clear.

The Instruction of Olivia *by* Geoffrey Allen

Victorian England. A voluptuous vagrant, Olivia, is sentenced to hard labour in the notorious House of Correction. Discipline and punishment are freely administered, and Olivia finds no respite from either the birch or the amorous embraces of the sexually frustrated inmates.

When released, she unwittingly embarks upon a journey that takes her into the dark underworld of London. Although determined to remain pure, Olivia gradually discovers her own desires, and finds resistance increasingly difficult.

But who will be the one to gain access to what has always been denied...

Flame of Revenge *by* Josephine Scott

There is a burning reason behind the Master's directive to his slave to use her candle spells to entrap six very different women, and then to arrange for them all, one at a time, to visit the ordinary looking house in Oxford, where extraordinary passions are aroused and dreams are broken under the influence of pain.

The Switch *by* Zak Jane Keir

Stephanie is a dominant woman with two regular partners and a sex life well under control. However, when she meets mischievous submissive Poppy, who persuades her to change places with her temporarily, and hide out with a biker gang, she has to play the submissive's part – and play it convincingly.

Meanwhile, Poppy is set on causing as much trouble as possible, in the hope of getting the punishment she craves.

Captivation *by* Sarah Fisher

When Alex Sanderson is commissioned to paint a mural on a remote Greek island, everyone is expecting the artist to be a man – not a beautiful English girl called Alexandra. Warned to leave by her mysterious employer's housekeeper, Alex finds herself caught up in a complex game of passion and punishment.

Humiliated and passed from hand to hand, Alex embarks on a dark journey of self discovery – a willing participant in her own Captivation.

Sweet Punishment *by* Amber Jameson

Humility was born to be a slave.

Transported from West Africa to Haiti, she is everything Vicomte de Salace could ever wish for. She is obedient and eager to please, which makes it all the more unacceptable when Henri, his body slave, has the temerity to take her for his own. Punishment for Humility is swift at the cruel hands of Baron Samedi, the voodoo god of Death.

When cane fires later destroy two neighbouring plantations, Humility is offered as a sacrifice to appease Papa Zaca, the god of the fields…

Afghan Bound *by* Henry Morgan

Involved in voluntary medical work abroad, David Harper finds himself caught up in the Afghanistan war. His adventures there bring him into close contact with the cruel torture of prisoners.

Escaping death by inches he finds himself in Iran, where he witnesses captured slaves displayed for pleasure in an Arabian night-club and learns that, properly trained, women can find immense pleasure too.

Returning to England he is introduced to some submissive women, and sells his share in a medical practice to create a training centre. All is going well – until a woman turns the tables on him...

Olivia and the Dulcinites *by* Geoffrey Allen

Abandoning her philandering husband, Olivia enters a world rife with superstition and depravity: the convent of Saint Dulcinea, reminiscent of the Middle Ages, when harsh discipline and torture ensured absolute obedience.

Under the constant supervision of the nuns she is subjected to continual punishment and humiliation. Gradually she learns the true and terrible purpose of their intentions, which are not only for her benefit, but to ensure the survival of the convent.

Olivia is driven to desperate measures, but the nuns are always one step ahead. Perhaps there is no escape from the dark terrors of the Dulcinites...

Belinda: Cruel Passage West *by* Bryan Caine

19 year old Belinda Hopeworth has to find her way, alone and penniless, across the America of the 1850's in search of her uncle, her only salvation after her secure and loving home collapses with the ruin and imprisonment of her family.

Beautiful and cultured, but somewhat naive, Belinda finds that America is a harsh land whose colour, character and erotic cruelty cause her much inner conflict as she falls foul of a variety of villains, deviants and fiends, most of whom are extremely eager to help her on her way – in return for certain favours...

Thunder's Slaves *by* Drusilla Leather

Max Cavendish thinks his brother Jonathan's archaeological expeditions are pointless and boring – until he realises the latest one will give him a chance to get his hands on Jonathan's submissive girlfriend, Justine. Together with a beautiful and sexually inventive American doctor, they are heading for a mysterious island, once a Viking settlement but now dead and forgotten.

Only the island isn't dead, and the warriors who live there have their own plans for Justine. Their attempts to free her from slavery and make an escape will cause all the members of the expedition to confront their darkest sexual desires...

Schooling Sylvia *by* Roxane Beaufort

Miss Sylvia Parnell, a beautiful heiress, leaves Bath and the Academy for Young Gentlewomen for Regency London. There she resides under the guardianship of her aunt, Lady Rowena.

Sylvia's innocence and wilfulness present an irresistible challenge to the worldly Rowena. Correction and punishment are routine in this unconventional household, until Sylvia flees, stumbling naïvely from one frightening adventure to another...

Under Orders *by* Lesley Asquith

Innocent Carol, in debt and striving to promote her depressed husband's success as an artist, is recruited into a secret society by the sadistic Max Alexandrou. Submitting to strict discipline as a means of furthering her husband's career, can she eventually savour the sweet pain/pleasure of humiliation?

Bending to the iron will of others – male and female – Carol must undergo punishing tests and ordeals to discover her own true nature.

Twilight in Berlin *by* Axel Deutsch

To a young woman of twenty, Berlin seems the ideal place to pursue her long cherished career as a model. But it is 1930, and the city is a hotbed of vice and corruption, where pleasure-hungry men and women go to any lengths to satisfy their lustful ambitions.

Ingrid is swallowed up in the dark underworld of the vice trade. In a sinister, twilight world where life is cheap she soon learns the price of staying alive.

Net Asset *by* Jennifer Jane Pope

Jobless Lianne Connolly takes in model Ellen Sanderson as a lodger. Ellen talks her into standing in for a colleague who has fallen ill – but this is no ordinary photo shoot. Lianne meets Nadia Muirhead, the driving force behind a team dedicated to creating the world's most erotic comic-strip, with Lianne and Ellen as the rubber clad heroines-in-distress.

But events take a disastrous turn when Lianne is kidnapped, and finds herself having to recreate her role for the mastermind behind a scheme to bring the comic-strip to the Internet.

However, this time there are two essential differences – no salary and no choices. This time it is for real!

Willow Slave *by* Toya Velvet

Seventeenth Century Japan under the Shogun. Life is lived by strict rules.

Beautiful, submissive Ejimo is sold to a brothel by her penurious father, where her sweet ways and demure manner quickly make her a firm favourite with the clients; rich merchants and Samurai alike. Her beauty is such that it even claims the attention of the Shogun himself.

Tasks are set to test her loyalty, bravery, endurance and sexuality. But as her term of slavery draws to an end will she return to her village, train as a samurai, or agree to become an obedient wife?

Sold into Service *by* Madeleine Tanner

1788. Betty, wilful, beautiful and lusty is taken into service at the manor ostensibly to pay off her violent stepfather's debts, in reality to satisfy the Squire's demand for yet another virgin bride.

Here she undergoes a variety of degrading but delicious sexual practices: voluptuous punishment at the hands of the debauched Squire, the intimate attentions and inquisition of the corrupt priest, and the constant humiliations of a collection of bizarre servants. All are part of the Master's nefarious plan for her ultimate defloration.Should she remain a victim of the Squire's outrageous but compelling proclivities or leave?

With conflicting feelings Betty decides she must flee... but can she escape?

Stranger in Venice *by* Roxane Beaufort

When Lady Candice is sent to Venice to further her education she has no idea what lies before her. Education she receives, but in a way her aristocratic parents did not intend.

She becomes involved with a French libertine and his mistress who set about seducing the innocent maiden, introducing her to the paradox of pain/pleasure.

But it is not until Candice meets the mysterious Prince Dimitri that she experiences boundless terror and overwhelming desire.

Who is this darkly sinister prince of lust... this stranger in Venice?

Innocent Corinna *by* Faith Eden

Stolen by a mercenary, just days after her marriage, beautiful Corinna is carried off into the dark forest that surrounds her home, where she is taught the pleasures of submission and the pain of disobedience. Held hostage she learns to succumb to the cruel desires of her new masters and mistresses.

Set in a world of slaves and villains, *Innocent Corinna* is the story of a girl who is forced to choose between her nature and her duty. A princess who dreams of being a slave, she must endure much if she is to save her crown and country.

Out of Control *by* Chelsea Miller

Head of Marketing, Marc Dubois is convinced that his boss, Sarah, is a sexual submissive, behind her sophisticated ice-maiden facade. When they argue about discipline in the office, he hatches a plan to get his own way at work – and to find out the truth about Sarah's nature. He breaks all his personal rules to take her on a journey of sexual enlightenment, over the course of a weekend.

Under Marc's skilful hands, and with the help of his friends, Sarah confronts her deepest and darkest fantasies. Marc discovers what he really feels for her; and their desire spirals out of control...

Exciting titles available now from Chimera:

1-901388-20-4	The Instruction of Olivia *Allen*
1-901388-05-0	Flame of Revenge *Scott*
1-901388-10-7	The Switch *Keir*
1-901388-15-8	Captivation *Fisher*
1-901388-00-X	Sweet Punishment *Jameson*
1-901388-25-5	Afghan Bound *Morgan*
1-901388-01-8	Olivia and the Dulcinites *Allen*
1-901388-02-6	Belinda: Cruel Passage West *Caine*
1-901388-04-2	Thunder's Slaves *Leather*
1-901388-06-9	Schooling Sylvia *Beaufort*
1-901388-07-7	Under Orders *Asquith*
1-901388-03-4	Twilight in Berlin *Deutsch*
1-901388-09-3	Net Asset *Pope*
1-901388-08-5	Willow Slave *Velvet*
1-901388-12-3	Sold into Service *Tanner*
1-901388-13-1	All for Her Master *O'Connor*
1-901388-14-X	Stranger in Venice *Beaufort*
1-901388-16-6	Innocent Corinna *Eden*
1-901388-17-4	Out of Control *Miller*

Coming soon from Chimera:

1-901388-19-0	Destroying Angel *Hastings (Oct '98)*
1-901388-21-2	Dr Casswell's Student *Fisher (Oct '98)*
1-901388-22-0	Annabelle *Aire (Nov '98)*
1-901388-24-7	Total Abandon *Anderssen (Nov '98)*

All the above are/will be available at your local bookshop or newsagent, or by post or telephone from: B.B.C.S., P.O. Box 941, Hull, HU1 3VQ. **(24 hour Telephone Credit Card Line: 01482 224626)**.

To order, send: Title, author, ISBN number and price for each book ordered, your full name and address, cheque or postal order payable to B.B.C.S. for the total amount, and allow the following for postage and packing:
UK and BFPO: £1.00 for the first book, and 50p for each additional book to a maximum of £3.50.
Overseas and Eire: £2.00 for the first book, £1.00 for the second and 50p for each additional book.

All titles £4.99 (US$7.95)